IN THE HELLSCAPE OF EXPLODING BOMBS
AND FIRING HANDGUNS,

of burning oil and flesh, Von Heinen and I both knelt and pulled grenades from our belts. As if from long practice, together we drew back our arms and pitched the grenades into the air.

They went off simultaneously, ripping down a section of fence. We and the rest of the Anglianers rushed through and into the shed. There, next to a skudder, stood one of the Krithian masters, shock and fear on his olive, noseless face. Slowly, carefully, deliberately, I shot him three times.

The Anglianers crowded around the fallen Krith. They'd heard stories of a race of non-humans behind the Timeliners—and behind the war that now erupted across their nation. They could no longer doubt. The creature who lay dead on the floor had never been born on *this* Earth . . .

"A good, swashbuckling adventure tale. Action-packed reading."—*Library Journal*

"Lively action building to a rousing finish."
—*Publishers Weekly*

NO BROTHER, NO FRIEND

RICHARD C. MEREDITH
THE TIMELINER TRILOGY
BOOK TWO

PLAYBOY PRESS
PAPERBACKS

NO BROTHER, NO FRIEND

Copyright © 1976, 1979 by Richard C. Meredith

Cover illustration by Ken Barr: Copyright © 1979 by Playboy

Published simultaneously in the United States and Canada by Playboy Press, Chicago, Illinois. Printed in the United States of America.
Revised edition. Library of Congress Catalog Card Number:
79-53077.

Reprinted by arrangement with Doubleday & Company, Inc.

Books are available at quantity discounts for promotional and in-
dustrial use. For further information, write our sales promotion
agency: Ventura Associates, 40 East 49th Street, New York, New
York 10017.

ISBN: 0-872-16564-7

First Playboy Press printing October 1979.
Second printing December 1979.

This book is dedicated to the memory of Jefferson Conan Meredith, May 1966–July 1975. One couldn't have asked for a better son. . . .

At the narrow passage, there is no brother, no friend.

Arabian proverb

CONTENTS

Prologue: North America,
Line RTBA-79A, Summer — 9

1. The Daleville Diner — 13
2. A Killing — 25
3. A Drive in the Country — 35
4. Skudding — 45
5. "And the Sky Broke" — 53
6. Niew Est Anglia — 65
7. Count Albert von Heinen's Return — 69
8. The Night March — 87
9. The People of Tapferkeitenhaven — 99
10. Dinners, Lessons, and Agents — 111
11. Lessons, Paratimers, and Blessings — 119
12. Trier and the Sign of the Purple Cow — 127
13. "Alarums in the Night" — 143
14. . . . and in Another Place — 159
15. Tar-hortha's Answers — 169
16. To Line KHL-ooo — 173
17. The Tromas — 185
18. Sally Again! — 207
19. The Shadowy Man — 217
20. Vestiges of Time — 231

PROLOGUE
North America, Line RTBA-79A, Summer

There was a touch of early fall across the land that year, a chill to the air that was autumnal, as we fled from nameless, unidentified terrors, dark-uniformed and jack-booted national police, as we sought sanctuary that we knew no place in this universe, perhaps in all the universes, could provide us.

The driver of the pickup truck, a man whose name we never learned, had taken us some two-hundred-odd miles to the east, across states with unfamiliar names, and had finally deposited us, as evening fell, on the crest of a hill overlooking a mining town in the valley below, a dark, sooty, unpleasant-looking place, half-hidden by the rising smoke, the stale air.

The red taillights of the pickup vanished as it turned down a dirt road that led back into the hills and to the nameless man's Appalachian home. Then we stood alone on the road, Sally and I, and wondered how long it would take us to get another ride, and where it would take us, and whether it was really worth it, all the trouble we were going to.

"How do you feel, Eric?" Sally asked me, her green eyes not smiling now. They hadn't smiled in a long time. I couldn't remember how long.

"I'm okay," I said, sitting the battered suitcase on the road's dirt shoulder, easing some of the weight off my left leg. It still hurt me very much then. "How about you?"

"I'm okay too," she said. She'd never complained about her own pain, her own injuries, though I knew they had troubled her. And I knew that she was hungry then, as hungry as I was. We hadn't eaten since the day before. I told myself that I'd find a way to get us food soon, and I too would ignore the pain that throbbed up from my leg. It would pass.

9

We waited on the side of the road for another car or truck to come our way so that we might try to hitch another ride, so that we might be carried farther from the hospital in a place called Jefferson City and from people in places of authority in this world who had begun to ask questions that we couldn't answer. Or if we had answered, they would have thought us insane and locked us away.

The sky above us deepened to a redness streaked with crimson clouds, great bloody stripes across the evening sky, and against the red sky were silhouetted the hills and mountains, purplish and gray, their outlines ragged with uneven tops of trees, forests slashed away here and there to make way for the great open sores of strip mines. In this country coal was king and all else made way for his coming.

Lights had come on in the sooty darkness of the valley town, yellowish, most of them, but brightened here and there with other points of color—reds and blues and greens of neon signs of taverns and restaurants and pool halls and a theater and stores of one sort or another. The headlights of cars and trucks and a bus or two moved along the town's streets, weaving paths like glowing worms.

The river which ran through the center of the valley, a narrow thing with an awkward Indian name, had been a silvery serpent catching the last light from the darkening sky when we climbed from the truck that had carried us out of Ohio. Now it was dark, almost invisible as the valley's shadows deepened, darkened.

And there were lights on the opposite hillside, the stationary and the moving lights, all yellowish, of the incessant mining operations that went on day and night, continually, for this was a nation that couldn't live without a constantly replenished supply of coal, this was a nation on the verge of war with a "yellow-skinned, slant-eyed" neighbor across the sea, and all things had to be in readiness when the day came when the two great rivals for domination of the Pacific Ocean decided it was time to try their cases before the world in combat. Trial by arms had not yet passed from this world.

It was August 1971, and the Second World War, delayed so long, postponed by the European Settlement of 1942, was at hand.

But it wasn't my world, and its problems weren't mine or Sally's.

"Should we stay here?" Sally asked. "We might stand a better chance of catching a ride if we went down into the town."

"I'm not sure I could walk that far," I said, unwilling to admit it, but even more unwilling to try to make that long trip on foot, three or four miles.

"I'm sorry," Sally said quickly. "I didn't think."

"That's okay."

A huge, diesel-powered truck, laden with coal, was making its way up the slow incline of the road from the valley to the mountain's crest, its headlights weak and feeble far below us, smoke rising from its stack to mingle with that which lay so thickly in the valley. It was too far away for us to see the name emblazoned on the side of its cab, but we'd already seen many like it that day, rumbling across the face of the coal-mining land. The lettering would say: UNITED STATES NATIONAL COAL COMPANY. And in smaller lettering: Property of the People and the State, U.S.A. And more likely than not it would have also, upon the door of its cab, a small decal of the American flag, red and white stripes on two thirds of the flag, the upper left section a blue field containing a great eagle bearing a cluster of arrows.

The headlights proceeded slowly up the hill and I wondered what chance we might have of hitching a ride in a coal truck of the national mines. Regulations would forbid it, of course, but the real decision would be the driver's. If he got a good look at Sally, he might pick us up. Sally's looks had gotten us several rides so far. But then if he got a good look at me, he might not. My looks had cost us several rides.

"Which way do you think we should go, Eric?" Sally asked, her eyes also on the approaching truck.

I shrugged. "South or east, I suppose. I am not sure it matters."

There were other questions I'm certain she wanted to ask, but didn't. I was glad she didn't. I didn't have any answers, and I knew the questions as well as she did.

And I was tired. Tired mostly of running, for since slipping from that hospital somewhere in Missouri—as that area of North America is called here—we'd been running and hiding, fleeing from the authorities and their questions, and from something else that this world didn't have a name for, had never imagined.

East we had fled, through cities and towns, past vast military reservations and past equally vast "Black Detention Camps," past convoys of military vehicles and past convoys of trucks with such names on their sides as "National-Standard Oil" and "RCA General," these labeled with inscriptions stating: PRIVATE PROPERTY, PROTECTED BY NATIONAL LAW.

We'd fled east, "from" and not "toward," for we had no real destination, except that we get as far away as possible from those who followed us, who had come to whisper among themselves that we might be "enemies of the people and the state," those white-coated doctors and nurses and interns and orderlies who stood in obvious fear of the national police, of some half-secret organization known as the FBI and its auxiliary arm, quasi-official, the KKK. We had fled and still we fled.

The diesel truck chugged on closer in the falling darkness, now finally making the crest of the hill, roaring as if rejoicing its victory over gravity. Sally and I, our suitcases on the ground beside us, struck the classic pose of hitchhikers, right arm crooked, thumb extended in direction of travel.

The yellow-seeming headlights bore down on us and I thought that the driver was going to ignore us, sweep past us, and throw dust in our faces in his wake. But then as the F-O-R-D emblazoned on its hood was about to go beyond us, air brakes squealed and puffed and the ponderous vehicle began to slow. It came to a stop some two dozen yards beyond where we stood. We grabbed our suitcases and ran, Sally faster than I. My limping slowed me badly.

The door of the truck's cab opened, some feet above the ground, and an ugly, friendly face showed itself. "Where y'headed?" the truck driver asked.

"Where're you going?" Sally asked.

1
The Daleville Diner

I didn't pay any particular attention to the green, four-door 1970 Packard sedan as it pulled into the station, except maybe to note that its left rear tire was a little low and could use some air. And I suppose I thought that I should mention it to the driver, tell him that I'd check all his tires if he liked. Sometimes it was worth a little tip, but not very often.

The Packard, occupied by four men, pulled into the station, up next to the "ethyl" pump and I heard the powerful sound of its twelve cylinders roar more loudly just before the driver switched off the ignition and the engine died. I wiped my hands on a rag only a little less dirty than my hands, hanging out of my hip pocket like a cow's limp tail, and went across the gravel toward the car.

There was nothing special about that morning, but looking back on it I think I felt some apprehension even then, some premonition of what was going to happen. During the past weeks, months, I'd been expecting something to happen, maybe almost hoping that it would. It was like sitting on top of a bomb that might, or might not, be a dud, and wondering whether you'd ever know whether it was, even if it went off. I wanted to know.

I stepped up to the driver's side as the window was being rolled down and asked, "What'll it be, sir? Fill 'er up?" I'd learned to talk like that pretty quickly under Jock's expert tutelage.

Even then the driver of the car was just another customer to me, despite the vague apprehension I felt. I hadn't yet looked at the swarthy face under the shade of the hat's brim; I hadn't yet noticed how terribly tall he was.

13

"No, thank you," the driver said, his voice oddly accented. "We have sufficient gasoline."

Then his right hand came up out of the shadows of the car's interior and I saw the big, black, ugly energy pistol in it, a weapon that had no proper place in this world.

The Kriths had found us after all.

I knew it was the Kriths and not the Paratimers who had found us, for I recognized the man as he tilted his face up and I could see it clearly.

"I thought you were dead, Pall," I said, letting my humble, stupid service-station-attendant role fall from me like last year's fig leaf.

"Please step back," Pall replied slowly, quietly. "Three or four paces should be sufficient." He paused. "And, Mathers, please do nothing foolish that would force me to kill you. As much as I would like to do that, it is desired that you be brought back alive."

With the metal-and-ceramic tip of the energy pistol pointed directly at my chest, there wasn't a thing I could do except exactly what Pall ordered me to do. I stepped back his three or four paces, cursing him silently.

Pall opened the door of the big green Packard, still holding the ugly gun pointed at my chest, unfolded his seven-foot frame from the car. Pall was a *big* man; maybe it wouldn't have been improper to call him a "giant," and every inch of him was lightning-quick muscle.

Still he seemed to be moving more slowly now than he had the last time I'd seen him, and maybe some of his movements were still painful to him. But then the last time I'd seen him I thought that I'd killed him with an energy pistol blast that had hit him right where his pistol was aimed at me now.

He obviously wasn't very dead.

"Keep still now, Mathers," he said once he had gotten out of what must have been cramped confines and stood fully erect. Now, even without his midnight black uniform, high boots and shaven head, Pall was an impressive figure of a man, and I didn't think I wanted him any more angry at me than he already was—at least not until I was armed as well.

The other man in the front seat of the car—I was certain that he was a *man*, though I wasn't quite as certain about the two over-coated figures in the back seat—moved over into the driver's position and turned the key in the ignition. The Packard's big V-12 growled to life. A cloud of exhaust smoke drifted up from behind it, gray in the bright autumn sun.

"To the back," Pall told the new driver after he had looked around, up and down the highway and across the lot of the National-Standard service station and the diner, the only buildings along this stretch of highway. Pall and his buddies had picked a good time; Monday morning just after 10 A.M. The truck drivers wouldn't start pulling in for lunch for nearly two hours. There was nobody there but me and Sally and old Jock Kouzenzas who owned the diner and the service station.

The Packard pulled away, slowly crunching gravel under its sixteen-inch tires, and the driver took it around to the back of the little diner where Jock kept his Hudson parked.

"Let's go inside now, Mathers," Pall said softly, his voice still laden with the accent of a place and a people I knew almost nothing about. He gestured not so gracefully with the energy pistol. "I do hope that the Countess von Heinen is here as well."

I didn't answer. He'd know soon enough that she was.

I'd like to be able to say that my mind was racing, roaring into high gear and developing plans for outwitting Pall and his companions as he marched me across the gravel lot toward the diner's neon sign which read, "Daleville Diner, Jock Kouzenzas, Prop." and the double doors below it which led inside, but I wasn't. My mind was numbed, stunned. Oh, all along I'd had the fear, the premonition that sooner or later the Kriths would find us, but now that they *had* found us, I couldn't figure out how they'd done it. What bit of superscience that I didn't know about had enabled them to track us across the nearly infinite Timelines and find us in this particular and rather obscure one? The power of the Krithian machine frightened me again, and that wasn't the first time, nor would it be the last.

I opened the diner's doors and stepped through. Pall followed me with the energy pistol leveled. My skin felt raw and itching low in my back, waiting for the searing blast that didn't come, afraid that Pall would find his orders a little too much to take and go ahead and do what he really wanted to do to me.

"Eric?" Sally's voice called from the back. "Is that you?"

"Out here, Sally," I called back. There didn't seem to be anything else I could say.

"Is something wrong?" she asked, sensing something out of tune in my voice, and then stepped through the swinging, jalousie half-doors that led from the kitchen. As she came up to the counter her eyes saw beyond me, saw the huge, powerfully built man in the business suit and wide-brimmed hat, and she saw the Outtime energy pistol in his hand. She froze.

A half-dozen mingled expressions went across Sally's lovely features and her hands automatically, involuntarily clutched between her breasts, pushing the white starchiness of her apron into the cavity between them. Her green eyes were open wide with fear.

"Countess von Heinen," Pall said in a low voice, nodding. That was all he said to her and it didn't sound much like a greeting. "Is there anyone else here?" he asked me.

"Where's Jock?" I asked Sally. I knew that Pall and his friends would find him if they tried, and figured it might be better if we admitted from the beginning that he was here. I didn't want anyone to get hurt—at least not until I might be in a position to direct the hurting.

"In the back. Taking a nap," she answered, awkwardly regaining control of her voice.

"He's just an old man," I told Pall. "He's not involved. He doesn't know anything."

Then, through the doorway left of the kitchen, a wooden door marked EMPLOYEES ONLY, came the three others who had been in the car. That door stood at the end of a hallway that ran from the rear of the building. They had come in without passing through either of the apartments that formed the rear half of the building: the one apartment, to the left facing the rear, where Jock lived; the other, to the right, that Sally and I shared. They hadn't yet awakened Jock. I hoped they wouldn't. I knew they would.

The first of the unsavory trio was a man who could have been Pall's brother, except that I was inclined to believe that Pall had never been born from womb, but was spawned by a pool of stagnant water that had mated with dog's excrement. This one was tall, a full seven feet, built like a wrestler, but with no fat, and he carried an energy pistol exactly like Pall's—big, black, and ugly as patricide and incest.

The second man was a human being too, I thought, though I had my doubts. He was as dark as Pall and the other, but not nearly as tall, about my height, I guessed, slender, wiry, yet something about him, his feline movements, his strangely masculine grace, suggested strength that perhaps would be a match for that of Pall or his look-alike.

For an instant I thought this was a second case of return from the dead; I had the fleeting idea that he was a person—a *being*—whom I'd known before in another time, another place, but I *knew* that the one I'd known before was dead. I'd killed him myself.

But like the dead one, worlds away in space and time and paratime, whose brother he could have been, this one's face had a somehow alien, not-quite-human cast to it. It was a face made of sharp angles, craggy planes, lined with tiny white scars that could have been caused by his once having put his head through a plate-glass window.

This one didn't carry a pistol openly, although there was a suspiciously large bulge under his left arm, ample enough to have been a standard-issue Timeliner energy pistol.

He didn't speak, but held the door open for the final member of the party, one about whom there was no question of whether or not to apply the label "human."

This one was a Krith.

Somewhere between the green Packard and the diner's main dining room the Krith had doffed the heavy overcoat and the shadowing hat that he had worn in the automobile and was now naked, without ornaments of any sort, as was customary with Kriths.

And there was something on the alien face that I believed to be the equivalent of a human smile, not one of friendliness, but of triumph.

"Eric Mathers," the Krith said in perfect local English.

I nodded.

"And this I believe is the Countess von Heinen, nee

Sally Beall," he said—gesturing in Sally's direction and then giving her a formal semibow, a courtly gesture wildly in variance with his naked, alien appearance.

Sally now broke from her frozen posture, began to move toward me, her actions jerky like those of an inexpertly handled marionette. Her face wore an expression of shocked fear.

"Stay where you are!" Pall barked.

Sally froze again, though now she gave me a look that appealed for my help. I wished that there were some way that I could give it to her.

"I am known as Tar-hortha," the Krith said, looking at me with eyes that were enormous, brown and liquid. Light coming in through the diner's windows glistened wetly on the moist spheres, the highlight suggesting a pupil in reverse. "I am," he continued, "what you might call, well, a 'special investigator.'"

Why he was speaking local English rather than Shangalis I didn't know, except that it might have been for Sally's benefit.

"It has been my duty," the Krith was saying, "to locate the two of you."

I didn't ask why, I thought I knew some of the reasons.

"Tar-hortha," Pall said in a respectful tone, one that indicated his position inferior to the naked, alien Krith, "there is another person present in this building."

The Krith nodded. "A local?"

"Apparently," Pall ansered.

"Another Outtimer is quite unlikely," Tar-hortha said. "Countess von Heinen, my dear, would you please be so kind as to show Marth the location of this other person?" As he spoke to Sally he gestured toward Pall's look-alike, who then took several steps in Sally's direction. I read them as menacing steps and Sally must have too, for a greater level of fear showed through the shock on her face. "I would prefer that this other person not be harmed," the Krith added, "at least if it is not necessary."

"Go on, Sally," I said at last, feeling the way Benedict Arnold might have felt in conscience-stricken moments. "Get Jock. I don't think they'll hurt him. There's no reason for them to." Who was I lying to?

Sally gave me another look that appealed for my help,

but I was still as helpless as ever, feeling more so all the time.

"Go on," I said again, Judas in my voice.

Reluctantly Sally stepped from behind the counter and led the dark giant, whom Tar-hortha had called Marth, back toward the apartments in the rear, toward the room where Jock slept soundlessly, not dreaming that there were creatures anywhere such as these that were in his diner now.

As they went back, Pall crossed over to the front doors of the dining room, clicked the night latch into position after worrying with it for a moment and then pulled the blinds down over the glass windows, blinds upon which were stenciled in fading red paint the word CLOSED.

"You are acquainted with Pall, I believe," Tar-hortha was saying now. "And this is my companion, Mager." He was now referring to the dark, slender man with the craggy face and the bulging coat. "The other is Marth, a Turothian as well, who is currently serving as what you might call my bodyguard. Pall is with me on special assignment."

"I can suspect why," I said.

The Krith gave me his smile-equivalent. "He does have a special interest in you, Eric."

There was silence for a moment, the four of us now in a rigid tableau: Tar-hortha's tail being the only part of his body that moved, save for the row of tiny openings below his eyes that dilated with heartbeat regularity; the giant Pall stood like a stone tomb guard from some ancient, lost, and fabulous empire; the not-quite-human-looking Mager peered at me as if he were examining the entrails below my clothing and my flesh; and myself, in too great a state of confusion to know what movement to make.

Finally I spoke.

"How did you find us?" I asked the Krith.

And while I waited for his slow-coming answer, I wondered how it was that I'd ever trusted his kind, how I'd ever felt them to be the friends of mankind.

"Finding you was not as difficult as you might expect, Eric," he said slowly, his thick, heavy lips moving across the rows of sharp, almost fanglike teeth. "You see, the late Kar-hinter never did fully trust you, you know, at least not after your encounter with the so-called Paratimers." He nodded his large head, shaped rather like a slightly distorted and somewhat lumpy egg. "He had suspected, even from the time that you were brought from Staunton in RTGB-307, more dead than alive, that upon your recovery you *might* consider turning your coat on us, so to speak. The Paratimers were persuasive with you, I understand, so while you were in the Bakersville hospital he took the liberty of having planted a small transmitter with a very distinctive signal on your body."

I felt as if somebody had just struck me on the back of the head with an oversize baseball bat. Of course! God, how could I have been such a stupid ass? I should have known that he'd have done something like that! Dammit, I should have known *that* when he found Sally and me in the Albigensian Lines after our flight from Eden—how else could he have followed us there as easily as he had, across that many Timelines, even though he must have suspected our destination from the beginning? I was more glad than ever that I'd killed Kar-hinter, but that small satisfaction would do nothing to help us now.

"Oh, it was tedious, I will admit that, Eric," Tar-hortha said, the rows of feathery membranes that ran from about where a man would have temples to the middle point of his jaws twitching in the air like the nose of a curious rabbit, "checking individually Line by Line until we found the only one where the telltale signal was being transmitted, a long way from your last known *geographical* location. You know how long it has taken us, but I doubt that you appreciate the Krith-, man- and computer-hours that have been packed into that time. But . . ." He paused as if ruminating thoughtfully, the short, prehensile tail that grew from the twin mounds of his humanlike buttocks twitching aimlessly in the air as if swatting flies. "But now I have you and I suppose that it has been worth the effort." I don't think he was certain of it. He had his own orders from his own superiors, I suppose.

I'd known that the Kriths considered me to be dangerous, but up until then I hadn't suspected just how dangerous they considered me. To have spent all the time and manpower it must have taken to check *all* the Lines that

Sally and I had crossed in fleeing from the Albigensian Lines . . . Somebody wanted me pretty badly.

"The Tromas do consider you important, Eric," Tar-hortha was saying, "even if I am personally uncertain of the value they place on you. Surely they know better than I." That was as near to heresy as I'd ever heard a Krith speak, suggesting that it might be possible to doubt the mysterious and sacrosanct Tromas of the Krithian Homeline.

"Thanks for the compliment, I guess," I said. "At least the one from the Tromas."

Before more could be said the EMPLOYEES ONLY door opened and Sally and Jock Kouzenzas, followed by the giant Marth and his energy pistol, came into the dining room. Poor old Jock, his thin white hair amuss, his slender, lined face still slack from sleep, was confused, dazed, frightened as he tried to rub the sleep from his eyes. I'd never planned on getting the old man involved in this mess, but I should have known better from the beginning, when I let him take us under his wing.

"Eric," Jock said, seeming to see me before he had taken in the others who were in the room, his voice not quite his own, "what the hell's goin'—"

Then he saw Tar-hortha, came to a stop in midstride. His mouth dropped opened and his eyes seemed to bug from his head like a comic-strip character as he looked at the sable-brown, satin-skinned, prehensile-tailed, and totally naked alien.

"My God!" he gasped.

"Easy, Jock," I said, my voice sounding foolish even in my own ears.

"Holy God in heaven," Jock said, making the sign of the cross in the air before him. The blood drained from his face. A pallor like death came over him and for a moment I was afraid that he was going to have another heart attack. It's a wonder he didn't. Sally grabbed his arm and helped to steady him.

"It's not really the Devil, Jock," I said, though now as I looked at the Krith through Jock's eyes, I could see how he might mistake Tar-hortha for Satan. "But as close as we're ever likely to see on this earth," I added, looking into the Krith's deep, brown, pupilless eyes.

Sally helped Jock to a chair at one of the dining tables. The old man, seeming to have added another decade to his years in seconds, looked up at Sally beseechingly, and said in a faint voice, "What is all this, Sally? Can you tell me what this is?"

"There's no need to bring him into this," I told the Krith angrily, angry at myself for not having said so before. "He didn't know anything about this before now."

Tar-hortha looked at him for a moment, but didn't speak, one of his hands casually resting on his flat, well-muscled stomach. After a while he turned to face the one he called Marth, still not speaking, but asking questions with his eyes, the lines around his huge, wide mouth.

"He is probably telling the truth," Marth said, his voice accented much like Pall's, in the fashion of the Turothian people. "I do not think that they have told the old man anything about Outtime worlds."

"How unfortunate is his innocence," was all that Tar-hortha said, but those sinister words were enough, coming slowly from the alien's mouth as he stood casually scratching himself.

Standing there in that room, the dining tables, the chairs, the jukebox filled with country and western records against one wall, the red-topped counter with its cash register and a transparent case displaying slices of cake and pie and doughnuts, the soft drink and coffee and milk dispensers behind the counter, frosty with cold, the checkered red-and-white curtains across the windows, the yellow, fading walls on which hung reproductions of paintings of pastoral scenes, and a large picture calendar from one of Jock's suppliers which showed a litter of three- or four-week-old kittens and which said September 1971, but which should have been changed several days before, all so commonplace and prosaic in the world of Jock Kouzenzas, yet all in its own way exotic to one from some other Line, some other world—standing in that room, the air filled with a tension that I could almost reach out and touch with the tips of my fingers, I wondered why the Krith and his human and maybe not-so-human companions didn't get on with their business. They'd put a lot of effort and expense into it and the thing was about ready to culminate and although I didn't know exactly what that business might be, I was certain that I wasn't going to find it pleasant.

Better to get it over with, maybe. . . .

Tar-hortha's double-lidded eyes had surveyed his surroundings, the people in the room. "It all seems satisfactory," he said precisely after a few moments of silence. "Please be good enough to hold them here for a while, Pall. I will consider you the responsible agent here."

A strange expression flickered across the thin, craggy face of the one called Mager, though whether that expression was wry amusement or annoyance or something else entirely I couldn't tell.

"I will be back shortly," Tar-hortha said.

Pall nodded, but didn't speak.

An expression that might have been that of intense concentration came over Tar-hortha's sable-brown face; his double eyelids blinked in rapid succession several times; the nipples of his mammalian, almost feminine breasts hardened; his tail twitched, as did the feathery membranes along the sides of his face; his hands tightened into fists; and his hairless body tensed as if it were in expectation of *something.. . . .*

Then, like the Cheshire Cat from *Alice in Wonderland,* Tar-hortha began to fade from our view, to vanish, as they say, into thin air.

In less time than it takes to tell it, he was gone, and there was only a small clap of air left behind to tell us that he had ever really been in our presence.

Jock Kouzenzas crossed himself again and groaned and whispered something that might have been *Ave Maria* in a strained and guttural Latin.

He was now convinced, if he hadn't been before, that Tar-hortha was the true and living Prince of the Power of the Air, Beelzebub, the Devil himself.

But then maybe old Jock was right.

2
A Killing

The six of us left in the diner didn't speak for some time. There seemed to be little to say, and I doubted that Pall or Marth or Mager would be very willing to answer the questions I had to ask them. And I hardly need to observe that the energy pistols in the hands of the two large men put something of a damper on the festivities.

Pall hardly moved at all, and Marth, standing near the table at which Jock and Sally sat, was no more active, although the wiry, craggy-faced Mager now seemed nervous, filled with a pent-up energy he had not shown in Tar-hortha's presence, and began pacing the floor in silence.

While I dared not approach Jock and Sally, I did take the liberty of pulling a chair out from a table and sat down. The solidness of the chair under my buttocks felt good and I realized how suddenly tired I felt, how drained of energy, and how weak my legs had become. It was almost as if I had just gone through a period of great physical exertion—although I felt certain that such exertion was yet to come. I would *have* to do something sooner or later, but right then I didn't have the slightest idea what.

I'd been sitting in the chair for less than a minute when I found myself speaking almost without realizing it, almost without wanting to. "I never expected to see you again, Pall," is what I was saying.

The giant of a man looked at me for a few moments, an amused expression on his ugly face, a face usually so devoid of emotion, usually as cold and expressionless as that of a corpse. Then the amusement turned to bitterness to remembered anger. "Yes, I suppose it was something of a surprise to you, was it not, Mathers? You assumed me dead, no?"

"I did."

25

"That is obviously not the case, you see," he said, some portion of his amusement returning. "I was fortunate. When you so treacherously shot us down in that so-called Albigensian Line, the survival suit I was wearing deflected most of the energy of your weapon, as you should have suspected that it would. And furthermore, your aim may not have been as good as you thought—those were awkward circumstances, no? I was able to get myself back into my skudder once you and the woman"—there was something nasty about the way he said that last word—"you and the woman had fled from those who *attacked you*. Alone, I crossed-Lines to a place where I could receive medical aid from fellow Timeliners. Then, of course, I set out to locate you." There was finality, bitterness in those last words.

"Of course," I said.

"And now I have found you," he added, the amusement fully back now and something more—triumph, probably.

"Now that you have, Pall, what are you going to do about it?"

"Unfortunately that decision is not mine to make," Pall said slowly, the bitterness returning; maybe that's where a lot of it had come from in the first place, the realization that, captive though I was, I wasn't mouse to his cat. "Tar-hortha and *his* superiors will determine your final disposition."

"I see," I said.

"Whatever it is," Pall said, half-turning as if gazing out through the curtained windows, "I am rather certain that your murder of Kar-hinter will not go unavenged."

"Will you tell me where you're going to take us?"

And as I expected, Pall's only answer was, "You will see, Mathers. In time you will see."

All this time Sally had been watching the two of us, her face a mask of consternation and fear, her wide green eyes asking me to do something, anything.

I wished I knew what to do, but still I didn't.

Jock mumbled to himself old, childhood prayers and seemed fearful of looking directly at our captors.

There was silence again in the room while we waited for Tar-hortha's return. I didn't expect the Krith to be gone long. I suspected that he had done no more than self-skud across to an adjacent Line, uninhabited and/or controlled by Kriths, where a skudder stood ready to come pick us up once he and his companions had captured us, as now they had.

My guess, it turned out, wasn't far wrong.

Very little time had gone by when suddenly, in the air before us, coming first as a vague smear of haziness, the ugly, naked figure of Tar-hortha rematerialized, seemingly more quickly than he had gone. There was something that I read as satisfaction on his flat, noseless face.

"It is set," he said without preamble. "Marth, go start the car at once."

The swarthy giant, Tar-hortha's bodyguard, nodded, turned, and went out through the doorway and down the hallway to the big Packard parked in the rear.

"We have a short trip to make," the Krith said, directing his words at me and Sally. "I hope that it will not be too inconvenient for the two of you to leave this world now."

"As if we had any choice," I said.

Tar-hortha smiled as the V-12 engine of the Packard out back roared to life. He said nothing more.

"What about this one, Tar-hortha?" the craggy-faced Mager asked, gesturing toward Jock who still sat at the table, dazed and in fear.

"Actually he is of no use to us," the Krith said. "If we were to take him with us, he would be, what you might call, so much excess baggage. We had best leave him here."

"Alive, Tar-hortha?" Mager asked coldly.

Kriths are not really very much like us. You can never tell what might be going on inside those large, lumpy heads of theirs, but I'd never known a Krith to be unnecessarily cruel, nor particularly kind either. That wasn't their way. So I hadn't expected Tar-hortha to go out of his way to treat Jock gently, but neither had I expected him to be totally uncaring of him. Kriths can be aware of the existence of other creatures, if not particularly concerned.

"We have not the time to wash his memory of these

events," Tar-hortha said without emotion, human or Krithian, in his voice.

"He can't possibly harm you," I said.

"Nobody would believe his story even if he told it," Sally said urgently. "And even if anybody did believe him, what could that—"

"The Tromas have been explicit on that point, my dear," Tar-hortha interrupted. "Some things must never be revealed to those who are not, shall we say, 'initiates.'"

"But—" I protested.

"Enough!" Tar-hortha snapped, silencing me with a wave of his very manlike hand, a snap of his simian tail. "Do take them out, Pall," he went on, pointing to me and Sally.

Pall gestured with his energy pistol.

I stood there for a moment without moving. Old Jock was a nice fellow. He'd been good to Sally and me. After we'd fled from the hospital where we were on the verge of becoming prisoners of the national police after we'd hitchhiked a third of the way across the North American continent, after we'd been treated as hobos and criminals, Jock had taken us in. He hadn't known a damned thing about us except what we told him, and even though what we'd said was a pack of lies, he believed us or at least pretended to believe us. He'd given us work and a place to stay and three meals a day and he didn't ask us any questions that we didn't want to answer.

I don't know what Jock had really believed us to be, and I really don't know why he'd been so kind to us. Maybe he realized that we weren't actually criminals, Sally and myself, though we'd committed our share of petty thefts to stay alive until we found Jock and he took us in. We'd been strangers in a strange land if ever there were, and maybe he dimly realized that, maybe he was vaguely aware that we were fugitives from something far more evil than our petty crimes had made us. He never said so, but maybe he believed that we were really fugitives from the Fourth Reich of Chancellor Heinrich Goertz: we didn't speak exactly the same dialects of English as did Jock and the people of this part of the United States of America, and we were obviously ignorant of native customs. We must have seemed an odd pair to old Jock.

I don't know why he took us in.

But I do know that Jock had been good to us, had given us a chance to catch our breath and look around ourselves and think about what we were going to do next while we hid behind the disguises of waitress in a second-class hash house and a rather inexperienced grease monkey.

And I liked the old man.

I wasn't about to let them . . .

"Go out to the automobile," Pall said in a soft tone that was filled with all the ice of a Pleistocene glacier.

At that moment I had risen from my chair and was standing somewhere between Pall and Mager, both of whom were about the same distance from me, Mager nearer to the table where Sally and Jock still sat. Tar-hortha was a little farther from me.

"Okay," I grunted to Pall and started slowly toward the rear door. Sally and Jock were still seated at the table, Sally trying to comfort the old man; they and Mager were between me and the door.

"Let's go, Sally," I said.

She looked up at me, her face incredulous.

My back was now to Pall and the Krith; I could see neither of them. I could see Mager and the expression on his face, the energy pistol that he'd now decided to draw from the shoulder holster inside his coat. As I walked toward him I gauged my distance, the force I would need, what actions I would have to make, and how I would have to make them. I had little room for error.

And, gingerly with certain sensory channels, I checked out my long unused combat augmentation. The "augie" circuitry and components were all in working order, so I was told by returning sensory impressions from inside my body. I hoped it was so. I put them on standby, ready for activation at an instant's notice.

Tar-hortha knew I was an Augie, of course, but was he really taking that into consideration now . . .?

I moved forward as if I were obeying Pall's command and . . .

Good old Sally! I said to myself. Now the incredulity

was gone from her face, replaced by hints of understanding. She must have realized what I had in mind, what I was about to do. She rose to her feet as if obeying *me*.

"Stay where you are, old man!" It was Pall's voice. He was speaking to Jock who seemed to think that he should rise and go with Sally. He was still too shocked, too stunned to fully take in what was happening, to realize what they intended for him. *That's okay*, I told myself, *better for him now*.

"W-what are you—" Jock started to ask in a broken and stammering voice.

"Get down, Jock!" I yelled, willed my combat augmentation to click all its components into operation, leaped.

The world around me started to run down, to become slower and slower, until everything but myself was moving at only one fifth of its normal pace. Lights seemed to shift to the red—although this may have been more imagination than fact—and sounds dopplered toward the bass.

Sally, in seeming slow motion, shoved Jock aside, grabbed the back of the chair she'd risen from, lifted it off the floor, swung it toward Mager's midsection as I moved across the last paces toward him, my augmentation coming up to full speed. The chair connected with the craggy-faced man's abdomen before he could react, before he could switch on his own augie circuits—human or something else; he was a Timeliner too and was certain to be augmented. He stumbled backward, cursing, gasping for breath.

Pall too yelled and cursed, his voice sounding slow and hollow, meaningless rumblings, and as my hands grabbed Mager, snatching him upward and grabbing at the energy pistol in her nearly lax hand, I heard from behind me the rasp of an energy pistol, distinctive, even slowed as it was, and felt the heat of its beam pass near me—the speed of light doesn't seem to slow up a bit, even at X5. I don't suppose it does.

Sally was screaming now and Tar-hortha yelled, his words dragged out in so long a rumble that I thought he might never finish what he was saying, and though I couldn't understand a word of it, I felt that he was yelling to Pall: "Don't kill him, you fool! The Tromas ordered that we bring him back alive."

The chair in the gut had only stunned Mager for a moment. His eyes began to clear and he switched in his own combat augmentation even before I could get the pistol from him. He was quick! And he was even quicker as his actions and reactions came up to five times as fast as they had been before. He straightened, his arm flung out to knock me aside.

The barrel of his pistol came across my right cheek, slashing skin to the bone and spraying the air with lazy droplets of my blood. My head was knocked back so rapidly that had my vertebrae not been suitably strengthened, I'm sure my neck would have been broken. My body was carried along with the blow, staggering backward, fighting to hold my balance. Inside my head lightning flashed and stars novaed.

I caught myself in my backward stagger, lurched forward again, and then leaped toward Mager before he could bring the pistol back into firing position.

· This one called Mager was really no bigger than I am, but there was a fierce, wiry strength about him that would have made him a good match for Pall or Merth, and he was augmented and as well trained in hand-to-hand combat as I was. Still I'd like to think that maybe I could have handled him if it had been a fair fight, dazed as I was.

But it wasn't a fair fight.

I'd never expected it to be.

I'm not that big of a fool.

Pall must have gone into augmentation about the same time as Mager, for suddenly there he was with us, coming up behind me with his energy pistol reversed in his hand, grasping it by its hot barrel, maybe even crisping the tough skin of his palm. I hope so.

I didn't see any of this at the time, of course. I just figured out later that this is what must have happened.

As Mager and I struggled in a reddened world filled with bass booming sounds, other noises that maybe only dogs normally hear, Pall reached us, swung the pistol, connected with the side of my head just under and behind my right ear.

Now whole galaxies, not just single stars exploded inside my head and I felt my legs going out from under me. The floor came up toward me slowly at first, and then more quickly as my augmentation automatically cut itself out.

I slipped into grayness, once, then several times, the world coming into ragged focus and then going out again, and I lay there on the floor, unable and unwilling to move. The blow had been an awkward one and hadn't connected as squarely with my skull as Pall might have liked. That is, he hadn't broken my head. But it did rather incapacitate me for a while.

Pall and Mager took their time in switching off their augmentation. I suppose they wanted to make certain that I wasn't coming up for another round, but at least when they spoke again their voices were normal.

"It is time we left this place," the accentless voice of the Krith said from somewhere a long way off.

Sally sobbed, said something I couldn't understand.

"He is not badly hurt," Tar-hortha said, "though I must say that his being injured has not been unpleasant for me to witness."

"*You* go on," I heard Mager say, his voice coming with a ragged breath; he must have been talking to Sally.

"Let's get *him* out of here," Pall's voice said from somewhere above me during a gray spell.

Then rough hands grabbed me under the armpits, hoisted me up as if I were a rather large sack of corn meal. My legs were rubbery under me, but I thought they would hold me up if I wanted them to badly enough. Did I?

"It will be easier for you if you make an effort at walking, Mathers," Mager's rough voice said in my ear. "I hope you follow my thoughts."

"Yeah," I groaned. I tested my legs, half stumbled against a table, supported myself with it while my head swam a long distance up the river and then floated back down it with the current. Maybe I could walk.

Dimly, through eyes that I found hard to focus, I saw Marth come back into the diner. He came up to Mager, they exchanged words, and between the two of them, with what little assistance I was able and willing to give them, they hauled me down the hallway toward the green Packard sedan sitting in the rear, its motor still going with a loud kitty-cat *purrr*.

Dammit! I still wanted to struggle, to fight them, to kick in their ribs and gouge out their eyes, to kill them before they could kill old Jock, but . . . Dammit!

I stumbled down the three steps at the rear of the building, leaned for a moment against the fender of Jock's red 1968 Hudson Hornet and then, after Mager had opened one of the Packard's rear doors, Marth dumped me inside the vehicle. I think that I went under again for a moment or two. I'm not certain. Everything was one shade of gray or another anyway.

Then Sally was starting to get into the car with me, but Marth said, "No, you are going to ride in the front seat, Countess." His voice was not as polite as the words might sound.

"He needs help," she said in protest. I thought that she was probably talking about me. I wasn't sure. I couldn't get my eyes open to see.

"Do not worry about him, Countess," the Outtime giant said. "He is not badly hurt."

I wanted to tell him differently, but I couldn't.

"But . . ." Sally protested. It didn't do any good. Marth wasn't a man to listen to a lady's plea. He probably tied tin cans to stray cats' tails too.

Marth had opened one of the car's front doors and was gesturing for Sally to get in when I was able to pry my eyelids open. She quit protesting and did as he said. Maybe the energy pistol he jabbed in her ribs had something to do with it.

Both Pall and Marth got into the car then, but Tarhortha and Mager weren't there. They were back inside the diner.

I thought I knew why.

Then, through the fog and pain that were inside my head, I heard an energy pistol rasping again from inside the building.

I did know why.

And I hated the Kriths and their Timeliners and everything they stood for even more than I had before, more than I thought I could have ever come to hate anything in all the universes, and it was a hate compounded out of fourteen years of experience as a Timeliner, a mercenary soldier fighting the Kriths' wars for them, out of times and places and experiences far away in space and time and paratime; it was a hate built on their lies and their deceptions and their broken trust, a hate built on the blood and pain and terror and death of uncounted millions; it was a hate that came up out of the bowels of the earth like molten stone and down out of the heavens like a vile and seething rain. . . .

One day I'd get even with them for killing that old man, for that and for so damned much else.

One day . . .

But right then all I did was pass out again.

3
A Drive in the Country

The automobile trip wasn't the most pleasant experience that I can recall, but then it could have been a lot worse. I wasn't conscious through a lot of it.

How far we traveled I'm not certain, but it was probably about twenty or twenty-five miles up U.S. Highway 441 out of Daleville. When I finally did get my eyes fully open I vaguely recognized the country. I'd been that way a couple of times before with Jock on errands connected with the service station and the diner.

Once we passed a tavern called The Snake Pit, gaudily decorated with a great red and green cobra with hood expanded, covering half of the front of the building. From its half-open doors, as early in the day as it was, came a loud, whining voice singing of an unfaithful woman and nights spent drinking to forget her, the voice accompanied by a twanging, off-key guitar. Though I'd never been inside the place, I knew where it was located: ten or twelve miles south of Milledgeville. I had my position in space fixed in my mind, though what good that knowledge might do me I didn't know.

After a while I was able to sit up straight in the seat, cramped as it was with Mager close on one side of me and sable-skinned Tar-hortha on the other. In the front seat Sally sat between Marth, who was driving now, and Pall. Every now and then Sally looked back at me, trying not very successfully to smile.

"Eric," Tar-hortha said as I moved against the pain, felt the gash on my right cheek which was almost closed now, covered with caked blood and dirt, as I gingerly rubbed the side of my head where there was a great lump and more dried blood, "are you feeling any better now?"

"Go to hell," I told him in as friendly a manner as I could muster, which brought no response from Tar-hortha but an immediate one from Mager. He poked me

35

in my left ribs with the barrel of his energy pistol and said in guttural tones, "It would be wise for you to watch your language, Mathers." He was speaking in Shangalis now, not in English. "*He* is not someone to whom you speak in that manner."

I looked into those strange brown eyes set into an ugly, scarred face and wondered if Mager were a human being or something that was just made up to look like one. "Yeah," I muttered and started to add some additional wisecrack, but thought better of it and kept my mouth shut.

"Forgive me, Eric," the Krith said in his usually emotionless voice. "My intentions for you do not require either pain or humiliation. At least, not for the moment. These you have brought upon yourself."

"Just what are your plans for me, Tar-hortha?" I asked, still trying to get my eyes to focus. Right at the moment they'd slipped totally out of control and I was seeing two Tar-horthas, one situated to the left of and just above the other; the world behind him had the same disturbing quality.

"As you have been told before, Eric," Tar-hortha said in the tone you'd use to scold a small child for raiding the refrigerator for the last slice of cake you'd been saving for yourself, "you will be made aware of them in due time. As for the present, your best course of action is to give us as little difficulty as possible."

"I think I understand." I wondered how it was possible for me to be sitting there so calmly between Tar-hortha and Mager when back at the diner Jock's body lay on the floor, cut down by an energy blast that the Krith had ordered and that Mager had executed. I should have been in a blind, killing rage and trying to take them both with my bare hands.

But then maybe I wasn't that stupid. I wasn't going to avenge Jock and protect Sally by getting myself killed out of hand; and I still suspected, orders or no, that Tar-hortha and/or Pall would gladly kill me if I were to force the issue.

And, well, a throbbing head, a nauseated gut, and knees made of half-set gelatin aren't exactly conducive to sudden and violent action.

I sat in the rear seat of the automobile as it bounded down the highway, sixty or seventy miles an hour, and tried to get both my eyes to look in the same direction at once.

On the road a cream and black car of the national police, red light mounted atop its roof, machine gun hidden under its hood, roared up behind us, honked twice, and then gunned its motor and sped around us. Two hard-faced nat-cops sat in the front seat, black uniformed and (I suppose) jackbooted. One was driving, the other gazing off into space, a huge, black cigar between his teeth. Then the Plymouth was dwindling out of sight, turning a curve and vanishing.

I wondered what the two nat-cops, so despised by Jock and his neighbors, would have thought if they'd known that Sally and I, people they'd seemed suspicious of anyway, were being kidnaped by two giants, a craggy-faced non-man and a monster who, literally, looked like the Devil.

Had the circumstances been a little different, I might have laughed out loud.

"I do hope that you understand *now*," the Krith said just after I lost sight of the national police car.

"Eric," Sally said cautiously from the front seat, "are you really okay?"

"I'm okay," I said, hoping it was true. "They didn't hurt me."

It appeared that she wanted to say a great deal more, but decided that she shouldn't. Not now at least.

I turned back to Tar-hortha. "You really didn't need to kill him, you know." I don't think any emotion showed in my voice. I hope not.

"Perhaps, perhaps not," the Krith said, only barely looking in my direction. "Yet what is done is done, is it not, Eric?"

"You're very philosophical."

"Hardly," he replied sarcastically. "But what happens on this Timeline is of little concern to you now."

"Then you are taking us Outtime?"

"Of course."

Then, as if to reinforce what he'd just said, Tar-hortha

told Pall and Marth to be on the alert for the turnoff, it should be coming up soon. Pall grunted an affirmative; Marth nodded.

If I hadn't spent so much of my time during the past fourteen years skipping from one Timeline to another, I might have found the situation odd. It was a warm day in early October. The sun was shining brightly through a nearly cloudless sky; only near the horizon was there a cluster of white, puffy, cauliflowerlike cumulus clouds, and they certainly weren't indicative of bad weather. Birds were singing in the brush and the trees that lined the highway in this isolated section of central Georgia, trees beginning to show autumnal colors. The chill of fall was still a long way off, it seemed, despite earlier indications to the contrary, and the grass and the shrubs and brush seemed mostly to be as bright and green as they had in early summer when Sally and I had first arrived in this world, quite by accident in this particular one.

It was, all in all, a lovely, rather pleasant place, this world in which we'd found ourselves, or rather this portion of this world, for outside, away from the seclusion of Jock's diner, this world had its full measure of trouble: the "Black Detention Camps" recently formed by the Washington government; the summary executions of "security risks" and "communist sympathizers" and anyone else too vocally opposing the Wallis administration; the specter of war that loomed on the horizon, a war that would surely engulf the whole of the civilized planet and include the use of nuclear weapons; so much else I didn't have time to catalog.

Yet still, somehow, I thought it was a nice world, or could have been a nice world if more people in it were like Jock Kouzenzas and were certain changes made in the manner of men who governed it. . . .

I said that the situation would have seemed odd had I not experienced so many different paraworlds in my life, and maybe it did despite that, for there had been moments during the past few weeks, since Sally and I had come to work for Jock and live with him, that I'd begun to believe that this world, with all its faults and shortcomings, was really mine, the one in which I would spend the rest of my life, the one in which the children that Sally and I would have would be born and raised.

Oh, maybe I'd never really believed that. Maybe it was just fantasy, wishful thinking, for often there were times when I wished that I'd never heard of the multitude of worlds that exist side by side in time.

But I did know of them, that there were many universes beyond this one, universes I'd seen, experienced, and beyond that was our knowledge, mine and Sally's, that there were forces active across those universes that were not working for the benefit of human kind, two great alien forces moving from both ends of the transtemporal spectrum that would one day meet, strike head on, and what came out of that would probably be war, perhaps was already war that would soon sweep across all the Timelines, blasting, burning, destroying world after world after world . . . until, maybe, at last there wouldn't be anything left at all. Nothing. Nobody.

I know, Sally knows, and maybe no one else does, I thought. Maybe no one else knows in all the damned universes that lie side by side like the pages of a book with more pages than a human being could hope to count in a lifetime, and each of these pages is a whole world, a complete human world with men and women and children and hopes and loves and fears and desires and ideals, with plans for making the world a better place, with schemes of enslavement and destruction, with glory and suffering and . . .

Dammit! Dammit! Dammit!

What could I do?

How was I going to save the world?

Hell, how was I going to save Sally and myself?

The big autombile slowed as Marth applied his foot to the brake pedal. At first I couldn't tell why. The highway before us seemed to stretch almost to the horizon and there wasn't the first sign of an intersection. I figured that we were still at least three or four miles from Milledgeville, maybe farther.

Then I saw the dirt road off to the left, just beyond the shield-shaped sign that read "U.S. 441 North," a dirt road that cut through the pines and brush, it unmarked, undistingushed in any way. But then that figured.

Marth braked the car almost to a complete halt on the deserted highway and cut the wheels so sharply that the power-assisted steering mechanism let out a great, unhappy whine. Then he hit the accelerator again and the car bolted forward down the bumpy dirt road, my teeth chattering against one another and my head hurting worse than it had before.

Marth's driving was apparently too much even for Tar-hortha, who said, in a tone of great but restrained annoyance, "Please do slow down a bit, Marth. Actually we are not in that great a rush, you know." This in Shangalis, not English.

The swarthy giant behind the steering wheel didn't reply in so many words, though he let his foot slide back from the accelerator and the car slowed.

I started to say something, to pose a speculation to the Krith who was my captor, but suddenly words became superfluous. We rounded a bend in the dirt road and I saw what our destination was.

From its appearance the clearing in the woods hadn't been there long, days at the most, perhaps only hours. Trees and brush had been hastily chopped away and pulled to one side, portions of the piles still green and fresh. In places it looked as if the vegetation had been bulldozed to the bare earth. It was a scene of quick and merciless rape of the forest, but that wasn't what really caught my eyes.

What I did see were the two huge, squashed spheres that sat in the middle of the clearing, two very familiar glasslike bubbles mounted on small, dark bases, vehicles never designed to move in space, only across the Lines of Time. Two skudders.

Neither Tar-hortha nor the others offered explanation then. They merely waited until the automobile came to a full stop, opened doors, and told Sally and me to stay put until we were ordered to move.

And they didn't tell us to move until the two humans, Pall and Marth, Mager (human or not) and Tar-hortha had climbed out, the men drawing their pistols and aiming them at us. During this time the two men who had been in each skudder climbed from their vehicles, bringing their own energy pistols with them. Seven guns faced us.

"Now you may get out," Tar-hortha said in local English.

"I don't believe we're trusted," I said lamely, trying to keep up a good front, more for Sally than anything else. Nothing I could say or do now could conceivably intimidate the Krith or his companions.

Tar-hortha Krith-smiled again, saying, "I would advise you not to use your augmentation *here*, Eric. Human reflexes, even without augmentation, are sufficient to cut you down. And all these men *are* augmented, by the way."

"I'm sure," I said.

"Now I will tell you this much," the Krith said, standing quietly in the early October sun near the edge of the clearing torn from the forest, the ring of armed men around me and Sally, all their energy pistols ready to burn us to smoldering, unrecognizable crisps should their alien superior deem it necessary. "We are going to board those skudders and we are going to take a very long trip across the Lines. We are going to a place that even you, Eric Mathers, have never visited. I hope that will satisfy your curiosity for the time being."

All this in English for Sally's benefit.

And that was all he would say on the matter, though I wondered if our destination were the legendary Krithian Homeline or somewhere near it. Maybe so. There had once been a time when I had wanted very much to visit there. Now I didn't exactly feel that way about it.

"Pall," he said, turning his attention away from us," "would you please take the Countess into that skudder." He gestured to the one on the left. "Tomaz and Robart will accompany you. You have your orders and you know our destination."

Pall, his face of carven stone, yet looking as if he would prefer to stay where he could better guard *me,* nodded without speaking.

"You, Eric," the Krith said, facing me again, his face now even more unreadable than a Krith's usually is, "will accompany Marth, Mager, and myself in the other skudder."

So they were separating us, I thought. Did they consider us so dangerous that they were afraid to have us together in the same skudder? Maybe that was a compliment. Wasn't it?

"Proceed, Pall," Tar-hortha.

With a caustic look in my direction, the big, swarthy man reached out to grab Sally by the waist. She tried to pull away from him, fear and anger on her face, but he was too quick for her. She said nothing as his huge hand closed viselike around her wrist, but from the look that now suddenly came to her face, I could tell that he was hurting her. But then maybe just being touched by him would have been painful to her. I could understand why.

"Sally," I cried, now unable to hold the words back, "I'm sorry."

"No, Eric," she cried.

I made a tensed motion toward her, but the barrels of the six remaining energy pistols leveled at us both held me back.

Oh, dammit! Again. My head was still throbbing from my last attempt to do something about the situation, and now and again blood still came from the gash on my cheek. And what had I accomplished the last time? Jock was dead. That's all.

I felt gorge and fury rising inside me. I wanted to strike out again, to do something, *anything,* just to show them that I wasn't going to be led quietly like a steer to the slaughter. I wouldn't let them hit me in the head with a hammer and then cut my throat . . . but I knew how hopeless it was, my trying to do anything now.

And—maybe this was the only thing that kept me from doing something stupid then—I knew that they had no intention of killing Sally. If they had, they would have already done it. Sally was valuable to them, just as I was. She'd been with me into the desolated Albigensian Lines. She'd seen what was there. And, furthermore, Sally knew the so-called Albigensians, the Paratimers, far better than I did. Hadn't she been the mistress of one of *them?*

Still, knowing, believing that they really wouldn't harm her, not yet at least, I didn't want her parted from me. I wanted . . .

What difference did it make what *I* wanted? I couldn't do a damned thing about it. Not yet.

"I believe they're taking us to the same place, Sally," I said, weakly, maybe foolishly. "They won't keep us apart for long." I wanted to look at Tar-hortha, to ask him to confirm what I was saying. I didn't. I was afraid to.

For a moment she seemed weak and frail, like a frightened child, but then the Sally I knew reasserted herself. She drew herself erect, threw back her shoulders, and even managed to give me a smile as Pall led her away toward the skudder.

If I'd known then how long it was to be before I saw her again, I might have fought despite the guns and the odds against me.

"Now you, Eric," Tar-hortha said, switching back to Shangalis again.

"Do I have a choice?" I spoke the same language as the Krith.

"No more than did the Countess," he said. "This way, please."

The two men who had originally been in the second skudder preceded us. Tar-hortha walked at my side, unarmed in the Krithian fashion, and Marth and Mager followed, their energy pistols pointed at the back of my head and the small of my back respectively. It may not have been a guard of honor, but it was nonetheless a guard.

The first two climbed into the craft, stooped within the hatch and waited until the Krith gestured for me to climb in ahead of him.

There seemed little point in argument. I did as I was told.

And as I climbed into the skudder I felt a jet of wetness enter my skin from a strange-looking gunlike thing that had seemingly materialized in the hand of one of the men inside the craft, a jet that cut through the cloth of my shirt as if it weren't there, but which caused me no pain.

"I regret that this is necessary, Eric," Tar-hortha said from behind me as I stared in a mixture of anger and humilation, becoming aware of what they were doing to me. "A simple precaution, you know."

"Drugs?" I asked, holding my voice and my fists under tight rein.

"I am afraid so. Nothing dangerous, mind you. You may even find the effect pleasant. Some people use this drug for the simple pleasure of it."

"Thanks."

I continued my movements into the skudder, even as I did beginning to feel something of the drug coming over me, dizziness, disorientation, perhaps even hints of hallucination.

At least it made my head stop hurting.

For a while.

4
Skudding

Kriths aren't stupid, are rarely careless, so what happened was mostly dumb luck.

Or maybe I did have fate on my side, as I sometimes felt that Tar-hortha believed.

Anyway . . .

The drug they'd given me was some sort of hallucinogenic, I believe, though maybe it did some other things too, and was slow to reach its full effect, though I did begin to feel it almost at once after the injection. As I settled myself into the seat as directed by Tar-hortha, Marth beside me, the Krith, Mager, and a young guard named Sulla across from me, the skudder pilot cramped into his own seat, I felt dizziness, the disorientation, the beginnings of something like hallucination, at least some distortions of time and space—but I don't believe that yet my mind was very dulled. I thought I was thinking clearly, as one does after two or three drinks, not yet in a state that could be called drunken.

The skudder pilot, a man with the reddish skin and the aquiline nose of an American Indian, flipped switches across the control panel. A buzzing began as the craft's probability generator came to life, an electrical sound that was accompanied by the smell of ozone, less real than imagined. "Everybody ready?" the pilot asked in Shangalis.

"Ready," Tar-hortha replied with unusual terseness. He may have been nervous, if a Krith is ever in such a state.

The pilot waited until the generator rose to full potential. From where I was sitting I could see across his shoulder, saw the familiar indicator lights come on as circuits reached operative levels.

"The Paratimers are one up on this, you know," I said, waiting for the final signal lights to come on, my tongue becoming thick and fuzzy in my mouth, yet still able to function without impairment.

"What do you mean?" Tar-hortha asked.

"Their sautierboats," I said, glad to have some needle to prick him with, small as it might be, "their version of the skudder. It doesn't have to be wheeled around from place to place, you know. It can move through space just like an aircraft."

"Yes, we are aware of that," Tar-hortha said coldly. My needle had pricked him! "It may be of interest to you," he went on defensively, "that we have captured several of these so-called sautierboats. They have been taken to Indus 29 Prime where they have been studied thoroughly for some time." A few months at best, I told myself. "We are already adding modifications to our skudders to give them the same capabilities."

"Good for you," I said.

Marth gave me a dirty look, but at least he had put his energy pistol away. So had Mager. But the guard whose name was Sulla, the one who had given me the drug injection, hadn't. It was in his lap, sitting across from me. Almost within my reach if I were to move fast enough . . .

"Potential achieved," the red-skinned skudder pilot said, the final green light flickering on. "Stand by."

That was all the warning we got. He hit the single activating switch.

Flicker!

The world outside the skudder ceased to be for a moment, and then was there again, but different. The raped area was gone. Trees and brush, loblolly pines and magnolias, mimosa with feathery autumnal leaves under a cloudless sun grew right up to where the skudder sat, seemed almost to be growing right inside it. A jay was frozen in flight by the stroboscopic effect of our quickness and I caught a glimpse of a big diamondback rattler sunning himself on the ground below the skudder, not yet ready for winter's hibernation.

The other skudder, the one Sally was in, was no longer visible. We had moved Outtime first. It was "following," maybe at this instant in the meaningless limbo between worlds. I didn't expect us to be sufficiently in phase to see it again until we reached our destination, if then. . . .

Flicker! Flicker! Flicker!

We were moving across the Timelines, accelerating until the passage of universe after universe was no more than a flash of light and then a flash of grayness that represented Nothing with a capital "N."

My stomach jerked each time a world flickered by us and I wanted to vomit, but didn't. It was as though a huge, savage hand had gotten inside my guts and was trying to pull me apart from the inside. Skudding had always affected me that way. It does most *people*.

Of the occupants of the skudder only Tar-hortha now seemed at ease. It wasn't bothering him. But then he was built for skudding. He had evolved that way. Or so I believed at the time.

Mager was grimacing with each flicker, but I somehow had the feeling that his discomfort was phony, that he was just putting on a show for ignorant slobs like me. Why? What *was* he, anyway?

"Relax, Eric," Tar-hortha said in a soothing voice, perhaps to annoy me, to demonstrate his own lack of a discomfort that must have been obvious on my face. "The drug you were given *can* be pleasant to experience, I am told, even within a moving skudder. Allow it to give you that pleasure."

And I began to realize what he meant. As I started to adjust to the flickering of the skudder, I found myself beginning to lose all sensations of discomfort. A pleasant sort of euphoria came over me, and I found the sights and sounds and even the odors around me growing more intense, more interesting, more pleasant. I found myself noticing subtleties of the skin color of the Krith that I had never noticed before, slight variations here and there across his flesh, spots of olive and green amid the brown, a greenness that grew like living plants in the springtime of the world, lush and lovely and clustered with bright flowers and singing birds, and gurgling fountains around which beautiful, naked nymphs played as they . . .

Stop it! I yelled at myself inside my head. The drug was beginning to do to me exactly what the Krith wanted to do, to make me docile, quiet, co-operative, tied up in a subjective existence that I found more agreeable than the world outside—and damned if I was going to let him get away with it!

I fought against the pleasurable sensations of the drug and called up half-forgotten rigors of my early Timeliner training and did battle with the pleasure of the drug, and as I fought I asked myself what I was going to do about all this. Sally was in that other skudder and there was no way for the two of us to get together again before we reached our destination, whatever that might be, and I didn't want to be separated from Sally any longer than necessary. I didn't want to admit to myself, even then, that what I felt for her was something frequently called "love," but I suppose it was, or something so like it that I couldn't distinguish between them.

Yet, I thought, if I waited to try to do anything until we did get to wherever we were going, then it would probably be too late to do anything at all, and Sally and I would be at the mercy of whatever it was that Tarhortha's superiors intended for us. But if I were to get away somehow, maybe I could later get to Sally, unencumbered with gun-carrying guards and a not-so-friendly Krithian "special investigator." Maybe my only hope of ever finding her again was to let her go now.

Did any of this make sense?

Maybe I was already too far gone under the drug.

Flicker! Flicker! Flicker!

An hour or so may have gone by—time distortion seemed to be one of the drug's first effects—while I sat in the skudder's seat, pretending to be under the influence of the drug. Sometimes I wasn't pretending.

All this time the guard named Sulla had been sitting quietly across from me, his head nodding every now and then as if he were about to go to sleep despite the stomach-wrenching sensations of the skudder's movement across the Lines. The energy pistol still lay in his lap, and his right hand rested on it, but lightly.

Finally, when I believed them all to have been lulled into a sense of security by the steady, now almost hypnotic flickering of the skudder, I decided to act. I hoped that the drug had had no effect on my augmentation circuitry, though I feared that it might have. I'd just have to try it and see.

And what I was going to do after that no sane man would have, except me, I guess, assuming that I'm sane. But then I'd been through it once before and I knew it *could* be done, though it wasn't a pleasant thing to consider. Yet, what else could I do? I couldn't hope to take command of the skudder—so my only choice was to get out.

Carefully, hoping that the slight tensing of my body wouldn't be noticed, I willed certain little-used muscles to move, and in their movement did the equivalent of flipping switches in a tiny control until buried between my shoulder blades.

For a moment I thought that something was wrong, that it wasn't going to work after all, that the drug had had a direct effect on my electrobiological augmentation systems.

Then the world slowed. The "flicker" became a "fliiickeer" and the buzzing of the probability generator became a rumble. I was ready.

Something swept across me; a rapid succession of images confused me. The hallucinations came on quickly, struck me hard, then departed, leaving behind a tangled, faded web of colors and sounds, odors and tactile sensations that hardly related to any world I knew. A fraction of a second and my mind was as clear as ever, I thought. I hoped.

There may have been the dawning of comprehension in Tar-hortha's large, brown eyes. He may have noticed the increased rate of my breathing, the batting of my eyelids, something. But it was only a dawning when I moved.

My hand was darting across the space between me and Sulla, brushing away his limp hand. My fingers curled around the butt of the energy pistol, snatched it away.

As I stood up, the weapon in my hand, both Marth and Mager seemed to show awareness too, perhaps began to prepare to activate their own circuitry. They couldn't do it before I pulled back on the energy pistol's trigger and sent a beam of pure hell down between my feet, a tight, narrow beam into and through the floor-board and into the delicate maze below that was the heart and brain of the skudder.

Marth came into augmentation amid a blaze of red-dish light and slowly billowing smoke. His scream of pure anger started slowly, but came on more quickly as he moved toward the full speed of his augmentation.

I leaped back, swinging the energy pistol in a wide swath that did little real damage, ionizing air and singe-ing surfaces, hair, clothing. Marth fumbled for his weapon in the awkward clothing he wore, and so did Mager, also coming into augmentation. They were both too slow, too late.

Mager, who was more nearly behind me than across from me now, managed to free his pistol from his shoul-der holster—but I shot him in the face while I straight-armed Marth out of the way.

In the blaze of light and coherent energy from the pistol in my hand, Mager's head became a ghastly, cauterized lump of burned meat and blackened bone, but he kept on moving, kept on struggling to aim his pistol —as I'd been afraid he'd do. I shot him again, in the chest where I suspected his secondary brain to be, and then turned to burn away Marth's right hand, which then held his energy pistol.

The pistol in what was left of the giant's hand did exactly what I feared it would do—and wanted it to do.

Covering my face with my left arm, I threw myself toward the seared and smoldering plates of the skud-der's floorboard, while the energy pistol in my right hand continued to fire.

I hadn't quite reached the floorboard when the cramped interior of the skudder filled with light and bass-dopplered sounds and slowly flying bits of metal. Marth was screaming and so was Tar-hortha, and maybe I was too. I don't know. I don't really remember.

For only a moment did I attempt to lie still, feeling, more than hearing, the Flicker! Flicker! Flicker! of the skudder slipping from one universe to another, though now it seemed to do so less smoothly, more erratically.

Then I rose again, partly blinded, burned and cut in more places than I wanted to become aware of.

Mager was quiet now, maybe dead at last, two of his brains burned away in the energy blasts—did he have still another? Marth was writhing in pain, screaming in incoherent agony. Tar-hortha was bleeding from at least a dozen minor wounds and seemed too concerned over his own injuries to care what I did. And the guard named Sulla had taken a piece of gun fragment in his right eye; he wasn't ever going to move again. Only the skudder pilot seemed unhurt, and he was too busy fighting the dying controls of the damaged vehicle to try to stop me— and what I was going to do was suicide anyway, according to all the rules.

Stumbling over broken flesh and writhing bodies, I reached the skudder's hatch, undogged it and jerked it open, and was hit by something like a wind that was blowing out of the inner regions of a frozen hell.

"You did it before," I said to myself aloud, "and it didn't kill you. Dammit, man, you can do it again."

But another part of me, the one that once in a while makes very good sense, said, "The hell you can! One time you were lucky. Now you're pushing it too far."

And behind me Tar-hortha was coming out of his initial shock, growing angry as only Kriths can grow angry, for the race of Kriths is very, very sensitive about personal injury. Indeed!

I tried to steel myself for the jump, but felt a cold fear wash over me and that voice was telling me again that what I was about to do was almost certain death, when a sable-brown hand closed around my left ankle and tried to jerk me back. The sounds that were coming from Tar-hortha's full-lipped mouth were not English, weren't Shangalis, weren't even coherent, and one glance back at him showed me his mouth, opened in savage rage, rows of sharp teeth like a great cat's coming to tear at my flesh.

And behind Tar-hortha, amid the smoke and carnage that filled the skudder, stood a shadowy, almost formless figure with the vague outlines of a standing man, an alien presence that I might have somehow found comforting if there'd been time to think.

Then I jerked my ankle out of Tar-hortha's grasp, and

in the process threw myself out of the skudder and into nothingness right in the middle of a Flicker!

There's no point in trying to describe the sensations I felt before I lost consciousness. But unconsciousness was a welcome, blessed thing when it did come.

5
"And the Sky Broke"

The universe moved aside, shattered by strokes of violent violet lightning that walked across the sky like God and yelled a meaningless thunder in His voice.

Sky grew up from craggy plains, umber and ocher and sienna, the plains, boulders, and weathered fragments of rock, fractured and shattered; sedimentary rocks like sandstone and shale and limestone were absent, but in ample quantity were broken slabs of slate and marble, hornfels, and quartzites, glistening phyllites and crystalline shists, of quartz and mica and chlorite, gneisses of moscovite and hornblende, and too were fragments of obsidian and black basalt, pumice and andesite and rhyolite as if the earth had fractured again and spilled extrusive stone, hot volcanic lava across the ancient and broken slates and marbles. Here were ragged crests and harsh shadows in the flickering light of thunderbolts that came from somewhere above, sky abuilding.

And all the while the sky grew up, piece by piece like a mosaic, building itself into a faceted dome of variegated colors and textures, though blue was the dominant color and smooth the dominant texture.

At last the sky was complete, a dome over the plain that was the world and for a few eternal moments held itself in place by the power of its will, fast and rigid, unyielding to the spheres passing through it, singing their songs as they would.

And then, from the invisible edge of the world, beyond the crags and peaks and strewn boulders and fragmented slabs, across the broken and littered earth, came the voices as if out of the wind, as if they were the wind in and of themselves, these voices unearthly in beauty, and terrible.

And with the voices, as the voices sang and their sounds echoed from the dome that was the sky, faceted

dome of blue, dome of glass and gems and minerals dome
of azurite and galena, of calsite and gypsum, of talc
and blue quartz, of amethyst and onyx, of aquamarine
and dematoid, of tourmaline and emerald, of blood-
stone and jade, of lapis lazuli and hematite, of zircon
and sapphire . . .

And the universe quaked, shuddered as if in mortal
fear.

The sky broke, came tumbling down in a thousand
bright fragments, pieces sharp as ice, cold as glass, and
below them on the ragged plain was I, and the pieces of
falling sky struck me, cut me, killed me, and as I died I
saw that which was beyond the sky.

It was nothing.

Nothing at all . . .

When an Augie loses consciousness, his circuitry automatically cuts off. That's a characteristic that can save
him. Augmentation running too long can easily burn the
life out of a man. That would have happened to me when
I fell out of probability, had it not been for that built-in
safety factor. I can thank the Kriths for something.

Even as it was, I don't suppose I missed death by
much, and it still frightenens me to think about it. But
what was worse at the time was what the drug Tar-
hortha's men had given me did to me while under augmentation and what followed.

With my metabolism running at its normal pace the
effects of the drug had been rather mild, sufficiently
mild for me to have planned and executed my escape.
But when augmented . . .

Well, while under augmentation I hadn't really noticed;
the time had been so brief and so much had happened
so quickly; but when I came out of it, stunned and battered by leaping out of the skudder's probability field
and coming harshly to earth in some unknown Timeline,
well, the effects were multiplied by five, maybe more.

For a while it was hell. . . .

There were moments of rationality, moments when I
opened my eyes and realized that wherever I was it was
night and it was raining. I was lying on the sodden ground,

rain pelting across my tattered clothing and my battered body. I was cold and shivering and aching in my head and in other places and I was afraid that maybe my left leg, in which I'd taken a bullet not too many months before, was broken again.

But then the hallucinations and the dreams and the fantasies and mingled memories would come over me again and for a while, maybe seconds, maybe minutes, maybe hours, I would be lost in them again.

The rain came down harder, and off in the distance there was true, not illusionary, lightning breaking from the sky and for a few moments illuminating the sodden earth.

I rose to my hands and knees and tried to focus my eyes and see what was around me, but all I could see was trees, pines and oaks I thought they were, and brush and brambles and tangles.

When I tried to get to my feet there was another great flash of lightning as if the whole sky were breaking apart as in my fantasies. Then my legs gave away and I fell. I remember my face splashing into mud and water, but that's all I remember for a while.

Now I was in the motionless sautierboat with the technician and was trying radio frequency after frequency, but didn't know whether I'd make contact with Kar-hinter's base in the Outer Hebrides. Then there was a banging on the hatch.

"Who's in there?" a muffled voice called. "What's going on?"

The captured technician looked at me for an instant, then back at the hatch.

"Stay still," I told him, but that didn't do any good. Still looking directly into my pistol's barrel, he jumped at me, a yell of pure hatred on his lips. I fired, and then his face wasn't much of a face.

The technician lay at my feet and I hated very much that I'd had to kill him.

The banging on the hatch had stopped, but a voice called, that of one of the Paratimer leaders, Scoti, and was saying, "Mathers, we know you're in there. Come out and . . ."

"Come get me," I yelled back and delivered one last, frantic message into the microphone.

Through the transparent dome I could see men cluster in the hangar's open door. Scoti came out from under the craft, running and gesturing for the others to clear out. I caught a brief glimpse of the weapon he held. But that was enough. An R-4 power pistol.

Now the space in front of the hangar was vacant except for Scoti who knelt with his left elbow on right knee, left hand around right wrist, sighting across the weapon's barrel. I saw the flash. . . .

And I saw the universe explode. And I felt heat and flame and blinding light so bright I couldn't see it. And that was all. . . .

The rain let up and I thought I saw a glimmering of dawn along the horizon, but I may have been mistaken. Or perhaps I saw the flashes of artillery, though I never did hear that there'd been any sizable cannon used in the area where I lay for so long. Perhaps it was only hallucination.

I wanted to stand up and try to walk away to a drier place, but I was too weak and too scared to make the effort. It was easier to lie there and let the rain fall on me.

And maybe it didn't matter anyway. I wasn't going to be alive much longer and then it wouldn't matter whether I was wet or dry.

Then there was a strange chill in the air, something out of my memories from just after the explosion of Staunton, an alienness, an unknown quality that I couldn't identify but knew was more than shock and pain, and around me was the stillness you find only in nightmares.

A voice was speaking, a voice out of a nightmare, yet with a familiar ring to it, though I couldn't place it. It was saying: "Stay alive, Eric. For God's sake, man hang on just a little while longer. They're coming to help you. The pain won't last long. You can stand it, Eric. *I did.*"

And then the voice was gone and I was lying on the rain-sodden ground and wondered if it had been a memory of something that may have happened—or had someone, something just been there with me.

I didn't know.

I began to float away into illusion again, but I knew I'd try to hang on. The voice had said help was coming, hadn't it?

And I remembered that message that was supposed to have been projected backward in time to a receiver on the desolate surface of the Moon:

FROM THE YEAR 7093 (which is about 4000 A.D.), GREETINGS. WE HAVE WAITED UNTIL THE LAST POSSIBLE MOMENT TO SEND THIS BACK TO YOU. BUT WE KNOW THAT WE CAN WAIT NO LONGER. WE ARE ALL DOOMED. WHILE THERE IS STILL TIME LET US TELL YOU WHAT HAS HAPPENED TO US ALL.

THERE IS A CIVILIZATION OF BEINGS ON THE FAR SIDE OF THE GALAXY. THEY ARE TOTALLY ALIEN, INIMICAL TO ALL THAT IS HUMAN AND KRITH. THEY HAVE BEEN BIDING THEIR TIME, AWARE OF US, BUILDING A GREAT ARMADA OF INTERSTELLAR WARSHIPS TO COME AND DESTROY US ALL.

WHY THEY HATE US SO WE DO NOT KNOW. NOR DO WE KNOW HOW TO FIGHT THEM.

HUMANITY AND KRITH STAND ALONE AGAINST THE ALIEN HORDES COMING TO DESTROY US. AND WE ARE ALL BUT DEFENSELESS AGAINST THEIR WEAPONS.

ALL THE WORKS OF OUR GREAT MUTUAL CIVILIZATION SHALL PERISH UNLESS . . .

It was cold and dark and raining and around me were the dark silhouettes of loblolly pines and live oaks and the call of a night bird off in the distance, but as I struggled to my knees and tried to focus my eyes the scene changed. The pines and oaks soared, towered into the sky and then were not trees, but buildings. The grass and vines and brush gave way to streets and parks and the darkness gave way to globes of light that floated in the air.

I could see the city but dimly and with double vision, poorly and out of focus and half-hidden by rain and mist, but what I saw told me that it was no city I'd ever seen before. Something about it told me that it was no city ever built by humankind.

Despite the floating light globes much of the alien city

lay in darkness and shadow, and after a while I saw movement in those shadows, furtive movement, stealthy and quiet, a figure here, another there, wrapped in dark clothing, but now and again betrayed by a glint of light from metal. All the moving figures in the quiet city carried weapons.

One of the dark-clad figures stepped briefly into light and for a moment I saw him clearly: a man in his thirties, tall, scarred from battle, tanned, blond with a short beard; he carried a Paratimer R-4 power pistol in his right hand, a knife in his left. This man whom I shockingly recognized instantly turned as if facing me, as if peering into *my* eyes, and on his lips was a twisted, bitter smile of anger and hatred, of satisfaction and revenge. Then he turned away and vanished into shadows.

In another place another figure revealed itself momentarily and it was a tall, scarred, blond and bearded man in his thirties, though he carried a large, heavy energy rifle in both hands.

And in still another place, stepping out of the shadows for a moment to make his way forward, was the same man.

An army of men in the night, all identical, all perhaps cloned from a single person.

The army of raiders slipped silently through the night, all headed for a single destination wherein lay something they/he wished to destroy.

There was a chill in me such as I'd never felt before.

Time had gone by now, how much of it I don't know, and they had almost reached their goal when, in the sky above the non-human city, a great light burst, white and brilliant, destroying the shadows and revealing those who had been hidden in them.

For a moment the raiders stopped in their tracks, startled by the light, then, as if guided by a single mind, darted forward, running through the streets, across the parklike areas toward the largest building of the city.

From that building gunfire opened, sending shot and flame down into the streets and parks, and from the portals of the building issued an army of men, they too all identical or nearly so, and all of them looked very much like a man—a being—whom I'd known as Mager.

The Mager force rushed into the streets, automatic slug-throwers in their hands, spitting leaden death into the attackers.

The leading element of the raiding force was within range and one of the blond men took a bullet in the chest. . . .

I staggered back from the impact of the slug as it ripped through my right chest, just below the nipple, I thought, shattering ribs, puncturing a lung, exiting through my back, tearing away great globs of flesh. I staggered backward more shocked than pained, stunned, dazed, knowing as the pain began that the wound was mortal and I was going to die.

I tried to raise the captured R-4 power pistol, to take at least one of the Magers with me, but I didn't have the strength; the pistol was too heavy, slipped from my weakened grip, fell to the earth, and in moments I followed it, darkness, pain, and death coming over me as I fell.

The first of *me* died, but more of *me* came on, a dozen, two dozen, and here and there, as the collective-I rushed forward, the individual-I took more wounds. One of me was hit in the head, my skull shattered. I died instantly.

But I'd also taken a gut wound, a *me* some yards away, and lay in agony as blood seeped onto the ground.

And I ran forward, a different *me*, a stream of bullets ripping away my left arm, but somehow I still fired with my right until I collapsed in agony.

Yet still, dying here and there, others of *me* wounded terribly, *I* came on against the Magers and still they killed me, though I wouldn't stop until they'd killed *me* all. . . .

And maybe they never would.

The hands that touched me were probably very gentle, but at the moment they seemed rough and savage, like angry men pawing over my corpse to see if there were anything of value on it.

Dimly I could see their dark faces in the early light and vaguely I could hear their voices, but I couldn't understand a word they were saying. They seemed to be speaking a language I'd never heard.

I had the impression that the rough hands and gruff voices were trying to help me, that they were those whom a vision had promised, but right then I was unable to respond to them. I let them do as they wanted with me, confident only in the feeling that they knew I was alive, if barely.

Then my mind drifted off again. . . .

Sally and I were in a stolen skudder, flickering across the Lines of Time. I held an energy pistol in my hand, safety off, held my breath and . . .

We came out of probability.

I don't know exactly what we expected to find, but what we did find wasn't it, was like nothing we'd hoped to see here in a part of the Lines where we'd expected to encounter a high and complex civilization of cross-Line travelers.

Oh, there'd been a high degree of technology here once, but now . . .

The transparent dome of the skudder gave us a 360° view of the countryside. The sky was blue-black, sprinkled with a smattering of the brighter stars, and in that sky hung an enormous, bloated sun whose corona beamed brightly around it. It was broad daylight, yet the sky was halfway dark and I knew that this earth had little left of its atmosphere, more than the moon, but not enough to support human life.

Before us a rocky, gray-brown plain stretched toward the horizon, then abruptly ended two or three miles away in a huge pile of rocks, a chunk of earth lifted up and tilted skyward, revealing centuries of geological evolution, now all but ended.

In the other directions it was the same: gray-brown stone and earth, waterless, airless, lifeless rock, a world totally dead, that might have always been dead, that might have never known life and man. I'd never seen a world so totally devastated.

A skudder's hull is impervious to most forms of radiation, so I wasn't too worried when the counters on the hull went wild, measuring a nuclear radiation level a thousand times higher than it should have been.

"What is this place, Eric?" Sally gasped, her voice filled with fear.

"The *where* is exactly the place where we started," I

said slowly. "It's the parawhen that matters." I paused. "There's been a war here, Sally, one hell of a war. This planet's good and dead. We've still got a long way to go."

The probability generator was standing by. All I had to do was spin the destination dial for a few Lines ahead, hit the actuating switch and Flicker! Flicker! Flicker!

We came out in a world that wasn't very different, just a bit less totally destroyed.

"Not again," Sally gasped.

"Parallel war. Maybe not as bad as the other, but just as total as far as human life is concerned."

"Could we possibly be near Mica's Line? He never told me about anything like this."

"Maybe he was ashamed of what his relatives had done," I said, feeling a growing apprehension. "We'll go on."

But as I glanced at the controls and computer readouts I saw that we were nearly on top of where I thought Mica's Homeline to be. Maybe his Line's an island in all this destruction.

Flicker!

The next Line was almost identical, except that the nearest crater was a mile away and the radiation was a few roentgens lower.

Flicker!

It was as if we were back in the first Line. The atmosphere, what of it mattered, was blasted away and a naked sun blistered the naked rock of a dead, naked Earth.

Flicker!

The sky was almost blue. The earth was brown and barren, though here and there were stark skeletons of what had once been trees and a brown ash that might have been grass long ago covered the earth. The radiation level was still far too high.

Flicker!

Blue sky, brown earth, radiation levels that perhaps men could survive if buried deep under ground.

"There could be someone alive here," I said. "Mica's people could have an outpost."

I tried the radio, but there were no transmissions.

"We'll go on."

Flicker!

Things were about the same on the next Line. The radio was dead. The air silent. No one answered the signals I sent.

We went on.

Flicker!

The next Line had a blue sky that looked normal enough, though no clouds were visible. The earth, as far as we could see, was brown and gray, scorched grasses and burned trees and nothing much else. The radiation was lower here, but still high enough to kill an unprotected person almost instantly.

Out of a hope I now knew to be foolish I cut in the radio's receiver, slowly scanned the frequencies—and picked up a carrier on 104 Mhz.

"What is it?" Sally gasped.

"There's somebody here," I said.

"Paratimers?"

"I don't know. It could be locals who survived the war or it could be Paratimers."

"Talk to them."

"I'll try," I began to say, "but . . ."

Ahead of us and to the right, maybe a hundred and fifty feet, the air shimmered for a moment, then a solid object materialized out of the nothingness, a squashed sphere that was unmistakable.

"Eric!" Sally cried.

"Easy."

"Who is it?"

"I can make a guess," I said and told her that I believed it to be my former Krithian boss, Kar-hinter.

"What are you going to do?"

I weighed the possibilities in my mind, said, "We can talk to Kar-hinter and see what he wants."

"What good will *that* do?"

"Damned if I know, but it can't hurt."

My hands fell to the radio controls and I switched to the Krithian/Timeliner emergency frequency.

". . . Eric. Please respond if you are receiving me."

"I hear you," I said into the microphone, satisfied

that the voice on the other end was that of Kar-hinter.

"Eric," the Krith answered at once, "please do not be foolish. You do not know what you are getting into."

"I have a fair idea," I said. "Listen, Kar-hinter, you know that what you've been giving us is nothing but a pack of lies."

"You listen to me, Eric," Kar-hinter snapped back, a very human sounding anger in his voice. "We have already sent patrols into the world where the Paratimers claim to live, their world of origin and all."

"And where's that?" I demanded.

"Here, Eric, here and there is no human life for a hundred Lines in either direction."

"Another lie," I said flatly. "There's someone on this Line using radio, Kar-hinter. I just picked up their carrier."

"I said *human* life, Eric. The Paratimers aren't human."

I tossed and turned upon what I later perceived to be a small army-type cot, fought with delusion and hallucination and madness and fought with a fever that came from some illness I'd caught lying on the wet earth in a chill October rain while my mind wandered across the universes.

Someone fed me warm soup and cleaned me up when I fouled my bed and shaved the stubble from my face.

For four days I was totally out of touch with the world except for the briefest flashes of rationality, and I wasn't certain that *they* were anything but more illusion.

One of those brief flashes, though, seemed harder, more real than the others, as if it were fact and not something conjured up by fever and drugs, and it was one in which I opened my eyes and saw a dark-haired, hard-eyed man standing above me who was very familar, a man whom I'd once shot and kidnaped while in the service of the Kriths, a man who had once come very close to death because of me, a man whose wife had gone running across the Timelines with me in search of answers we never found. . . .

This man, if he were real and not some fantasy, stood

above my cot dressed in clothing that might have been called combat fatigues, olive drab and loose fitting, an ammunition belt across his chest and a big pistol on his hip. He wore no emblems of rank on his uniform, yet there was about him an air of command. He looked down at me with a strange expression on his face.

I tried to speak, but my tongue was still too thick in my mouth and nothing came out but a gagged mumble.

"Mathers," he said slowly, speaking the brand of English used in the Line where his wife, Sally, had come from, the Line where I'd first met him and her, "I don't know whether to kill you and feed your corpse to the Skralangs' dogs, or whether to welcome you as a comrade." He paused, his face twisting into an odd grimace. "I don't suppose I need to decide just what to do with you yet. I can let you live for a few more days and then decide."

He was still standing there looking down at me when I slipped back into unconsciousness.

My last thought was to wonder whether I'd ever wake up again. A shooting, a kidnaping, the stealing of his wife—though she'd been wife in name only, not in point of fact. Graf Albert von Heinen had reason to hate me.

6
Niew Est Anglia

Freya Athelson could have been the daughter of a Viking
chieftain, blond, statuesque, in her twenties, her hair
fixed in two long pigtails. Her eyes were blue, her nose
straight, her lips full and red against her fair skin. The
Viking illusion, though, was broken by the fact that she
was clad neither in the linens and silks of the hearth and
boudoir, nor in the leather and chain mail of the battlefield. No Valkyrie she, though soldierlike she dressed
in a blouse and slacks of olive drab, heavy leather boots,
a web pistol belt from which depended a holster loaded
with a big, military-issue revolver, and simple gold
squares on the lapels of her blouse. There was a silver
ring through the lobe of her left ear and on the middle
finger of her right hand a silver ring in the likeness of a
serpent eating its own tail.

Freya was my nurse and jailer. She was the one who'd
been feeding me and bathing me and washing away
from my body the excrement I hadn't been able to control during my delirium.

Of course I didn't know about all this until I was able
to sit up by myself and hobble to the toilet and back to
bed, when I could hold a spoon in still-quivering fingers
and transfer the meat-and-potato soup from a bowl to
the vicinity of my mouth without spilling more than half
of it.

Then I was given clothing not unlike that worn by
Freya and the others of this place, but for a while I
was told nothing about where I was or who they were
or why they'd saved my life, these bearded soldiers and
fair-skinned women. They might have wanted to tell me,
but they couldn't. The language they spoke was unknown
to me, and I could offer them none they could understand.

And it wasn't for several days that I found out whether

I'd actually seen Albert von Heinen or whether it had just been another feverish fantasy.

By observing, though, I was able to learn a few things about the world into which I'd been plunged when I'd leaped out of Tar-hortha's moving skudder.

Obviously the people who'd rescued me were soldiers. There was no doubt that theirs were military uniforms, nor that their weapons had been issued from a single armory, nor any doubt that the one whom I believe to be called "Ufan" Aelfric Dagrefson was an officer, the one in charge, nor that "Leufan" Wexstan Wilhelmson and "Leufan" Halga Hrothgrason were his junior officers and part of his staff; Freya also carried the title "Leufan," I learned later.

Each of them wore in his or her left earlobe a silver ring, as did a sizable percentage of the enlisted personnel. A badge of some kind of distinction.

The stone and timber building in which they lived might have once been a farmhouse, I thought, for it consisted of:

A large, old-fashioned kitchen dominated by two huge, intricately decorated wood-burning stoves which still served their original purposes, tables and chairs, cabinets and cupboards;

What might have once been a living room or parlor now converted into an office containing Aelfric's large, oaken desk, strewn with papers and maps, and including the equally paper-strewn desks of the three eufans of the company;

Bedrooms which had been converted into barracklike sleeping quarters by the addition of an odd assortment of bunk beds and cots and partitions;

And the room in which I was finally kept, one not much larger than a healthy broom closet where I was continually under the watchful eyes of Freya or one of the enlisted men.

The house lacked indoor plumbing and at first I wasn't allowed to go to the outhouses in the rear yard. I had a chamber pot.

When I was strong enough I was allowed to walk around a bit, to peek into the other rooms, to even eat at the officers' table in the large kitchen where the officers were served separately, but I was allowed this privilege only as long as Freya was at my side and I didn't get in anyone's way.

Outside the farmhouse was a wide, grassless area of clay and sand in which were parked several vehicles developed by a technology I would have guessed to be slightly prenuclear, powered by internal combustion engines, heavily armored with thick steel plates, painted a motley green and brown and ocher, sporting deadly-looking cannon and large caliber machine guns, equipped with tanklike treads in the rear, wheels in the front— in another world they might have been called "half-tracks."

The symbol emblazoned on the side of each was a stylized red dragon, European type, not Chinese, and the lettering under the dragon was in characters that resembled N E A in some outlandish variation of the Roman alphabet. Other characters, that might have been derived from Arabic numerals, were painted below.

Beyond the vehicles were the other buildings you'd normally associate with a farm: a barn, now converted into a combined barrack and garage; a silo, empty save for a few wooden crates that seemed to contain ammunition and other military supplies; several sheds converted into workshops, excepting one under which sat a vehicle that looked very much like a farm tractor, but which appeared to be damaged and badly rusted; and a structure that might have been quarters for hired hands and/or servants, now converted into what might best be called a "beer garden," a place to which the enlisted personnel flocked at night after the day's duties were done.

There was always activity out there in the yard, olive-clad men and women, the men all bearded if old enough to grow them, the women all with pigtails, going about one sort of business or another, or drilling in classic military formation to the barking of non-commissioned officers.

There were no signs of the animals usually seen around a place like this had once been, except for several large dogs of indeterminate breed. I supposed that all the chickens and pigs and cows had long since been butchered and eaten. Such fresh meat wasn't in *my* diet.

And now and again an individual of strikingly different appearance would stride through the area, getting respectful, even fearful glances from the others.

He was shorter than most of the whites, this man whose skin appeared to be copper in certain light, who wore his black hair done up in pigtails not unlike those of the women. He wore a handful of feathers in the band of his wide-brimmed hat and a brightly colored poncho. His trousers and shoes were of soft brown leather. His chest was crossed with bullet-laden bandoleers. Upon his right hip he carried a pistol like that worn by the officers and upon his left a long knife of stainless steel. And from what I could make of Freya's words when she spoke of him, this one's name was An Mona Steorra and he was a "Skralang."

Sometimes, especially at night after the beer garden had closed and the farmhouse was quiet save for sentries walking their rounds outside and occasional sounds from the improvised workshops where a job hadn't been completed during the day, I would hear a remote booming, a series of rumbling sounds very much like distant thunder, but equally like the roar of heavy artillery beyond the horizon. We apparently weren't too far from an actual combat zone, though whether it was moving closer, drawing away, or remaining in the same place, I couldn't tell.

And try as I might, when with the lovely Viking Freya or with the young officer who could have been Freya's brother, Leufan Halga Hrothgrason, or with one of the enlisted men who sometimes guarded me, I couldn't pick up more than a few isolated words of their language, though I was soon certain that I knew something of its origins, and believed that they called themselves Anglianers, or, when speaking more formally, Niew Est Anglianers. I believed their language to be called Anglisch. And if that were so, then the language should be quite easy to learn once I'd grasped its basics. I set out to do that.

7
Count Albert von Heinen's Return

On the morning of the fourth day after my "recovery" I was again allowed to breakfast with the officers, and after the meal we sat at the table, drinking from dragon-symboled procelain cups a strange brew that was more like tea than coffee, though from what plant it came I wouldn't venture to guess. Sufficiently sweetened it wasn't bad.

Aelfric, Freya, Wexstan, and Halga were involved in some discussion I couldn't follow, though I thought I recognized certain landmarks on the rough map Aelfric drew on the tablecloth with a stick of charcoal; the geography of this place, of course, was identical to that of the Georgia I'd left behind in Tar-hortha's skudder. Aelfric was indicating something apparently some miles to the south and talked about it in angry tones, making motions of destruction with his hands.

His words were interrupted when a young enlisted man came up to the table and, in an apologetic tone, spoke to him. All I caught was the name "An Mona Steorra" and the phrase *"an Sclavanianer."*

A smile suddenly came across Aelfric's face and he spoke a few words to the others. Freya looked at me and then back at him as if asking a question. Aelfric pondered for a moment, twisting the end of his ash-blond mustache between the thumb and forefinger of his left hand, then shook his head, said, *"Nan."*

The others rose, though Freya gestured for me to return to my broom closet of a room.

It wasn't until later that I learned that the Skralang had brought back an enemy soldier from a brief raid across the border. The captive, it turned out, was tortured for information he didn't possess. An Mona Steorra's delight at the sadism he inflicted on the captive, Freya told me later when I could understand her, was not a pleasant thing to behold. I suppose it's just as well I was denied permission to witness it.

For some time I sat alone, smoking vile-tasting cigarettes from a pack given me by Freya—it seemed that in this world tobacco hadn't been given the care and concern it should have—leafing through a magazine entitled *Foegift*, trying to decipher some meaning from it. The pictures were clear enough, scenes of people and places in a world in the middle stages of heavy industrialization, a Victorian, puritanical world dominated by the Church and the Aristocracy, a world perhaps ready for a sudden, chaotic leap into post-industrial civilization.

I recognized the relationship between some of the words printed on the magazine's pages and some of those in the version of English I'd learned from my Timeliner assignment in RTGB-307, Sally's Line. And I was still convinced that I was about to stumble on to the keys to the language and a lot of it would then fall into place.

Then, as I was crushing out a cigarette in the tin-can ashtray provided me and wishing that I had some of the beer ration that would be served with the evening meal, there was a knock on the door and Freya, without waiting for an answer, came in, excitement on her face, speaking words I found impossible to comprehend.

At last, through a few simple words—*cuman* and the like—and some equally simple hand gestures, I did understand that she wanted me to go some place with her.

With Freya leading and the two of us following several other clusters of the olive-clad company, I went outside of the farmhouse-cum-headquarters for the first time since my unconscious arrival.

And outside I saw the reason for all the excitement.

Two more of the armored, tracked vehicles were there now, even at that moment rumbling to a halt in the grassless area before the whitewashed farmhouse. Both had obviously been in recent combat; both showed scars of bright metal and areas of blackened, blistered paint, and the engine of one was clattering so loudly that it was hard to hear the welcoming voices above its noise; the threads of the other looked so damaged that I doubted that it would have been able to travel much farther, and I wondered how far they'd come; how distant was the place where they'd been fighting?

The engines of the two vehicles roared more loudly for a few moments. Then their ignition switches were cut off and they grumbled to silence.

The men who climbed out were as battered as their vehicles, their clothing tattered, their wounds bandaged with dirty rags, their eyes red and weary. Yet they were smiling and I knew they hadn't come back in dishonor and defeat.

The officers of this group, beneath their tattered and soiled clothing, wore what appeared to be a kind of body armor akin to the chain mail worn in an earlier era, and carried upon their hips, in addition to firearms, short swords that reminded me of those of the soldiers of Imperial Rome, when there had been an Imperial Rome. And a few of them wore steel helmets decorated with dark, curving horns that could have come only from American Bison. An odd admixture of military accouterments from different eras, it seemed to me, but then I was standing on the outside looking in, not judging this culture from within its own context. I didn't know enough about it yet to accept it on its own terms. But then maybe I wouldn't be there long enough to do that.

I stood beside Freya as the men clambered from the war machines and felt her mounting excitement. There was something, to her at least, very special about one of these returning soldiers—and in a few moments I began to realize why. And who.

Had I not been thinking of him, had I not thought I'd seen him not long before, I wouldn't have recognized the third man to climb from the first vehicle and plant his jackbooted feet on the dry, dusty soil.

But I *was* looking for him and when I saw him, despite the bandage wrapped around his forehead, despite the grime and beard upon his face, I recognized those features of Teutonic nobility. . . .

Feldmarschall Graf Albert Frederick Maximillian Joseph von Heinen, late of the Armies of His Imperial Majesty, Franz VI, by the Grace of God, Emperor of the Romans . . . but then that was in another world.

Von Heinen spoke a few words with Ufan Aelfric

Dagrefson, closely and confidentially, and then turned to face me—or rather face Freya first. He only seemed to notice me after he had reached her, took her hands in his soiled ones, kissed her soundly on the lips and let her bury her head for a moment against the dirty uniform blouse that covered his chest, the words she tried to speak broken by sobs of what I took to be happiness.

His reunion with Freya finished, or at least the first, public stages of it, he turned to face me and said in *his* Outtime version of the Enlish language. "So you lived after all, Mathers. I had my doubts. I heard Kar-hinter was no easy one."

"I lived."

"But then you're a tough bastard yourself, for what I've been told."

"You don't appear to be any too soft, Graf," I told the man who not so long before had been one of the highest ranking officers in the Army of the Holy Roman Empire, circa A.D. 1971, Timeline RTGB-307.

"You expected me to be a cripple?" Von Heinen asked, his voice touched with bitterness. "Your aim wasn't all that good, Mathers."

"It was dark," I said, "but I'm glad to see that you recovered." Then I added: "I think." Despite the glibness with which these words came to my lips, despite my gratefulness at finding someone who could speak a language I knew, I was still disturbed and even a bit frightened at finding him *here*, in this where-and-when. Coincidence I can accept, but this seemed a bit too much for coincidence—but then, I asked myself, what else could it have been?

"I believe we have a great deal to discuss, you and I," Von Heinen said, "but that will have to wait. I have some, well, what you might call 'debriefing to go through. We've just returned from a rather important mission, and a somewhat successful one, I might add, and I *am* expected to report to Ufan Dagrefson, though not as an underling. And you might be interested in hearing about what we've done. Later."

"I might be," I said, "if I knew who the hell was fighting whom, and why."

"Of course," Von Heinen said with a laugh, "you *don't*

know, do you? We're 'Anglianers,' at least that's what the others are. Anyway, the Independent Constitutional Thanedom of New East Anglia, headed by Thane Leo IV and Mootan First Speaker Hama Halgason, a loose member of the Anglish Commonweal"—now his tone was pedantic, like an old German schoolmaster he might have learned under his youth—"is fighting to preserve its territorial integrity against a limited invasion by the Franks of Neustria from the north and their allies, the armies of the Imperial Colony of Sclavania to the south. They are trying to crush 'us' between them and divide Niew Est Anglia among themselves. We're trying to stop them"—his voice was shifting to a more conversational tone—"and it's beginning to look as if we just may succeed."

"And who else is involved?" I asked.

Freya, standing at Von Heinen's side, looked anxious and confused. Aelfric, a few feet away, looked anxious and annoyed. That neither of them spoke I considered to be a compliment to Von Heinen or an admission of some authority he held.

"Who else?" There was now a teasing sound to his words. "Well, on this continent the Saxonites from the far north and the Skralang Nations to our west are allied with New East Anglia, as, of course, are the member countries of the Anglisch Commonweal—it's not an empire here, you know—but then the Dual Allies, as Neustria and Sclavania call themselves, have assistance from Europe as well. The Empire and Franklande are on their side." He paused, maybe to catch his breath. "But that isn't really what you're asking, is it?"

"No, not really."

"The Timeliners and the Paratimers are both involved too, of course."

"Of course," I said and nodded, not surprised. How else could Von Heinen have gotten here had there not been Outtimers involved as well? But exactly why was he here? I wondered. "And which side are you on?" I asked pointedly.

"Which side, Mathers?" he said, repeating the question, then answered cryptically, "My own, of course. I really must get on with Ufan Dagrefson. He has his own superiors to report to. We'll talk later at greater length, Mathers, if you behave yourself."

After a quick kiss of Freya's cheek and muted words to her in Anglisch, he joined the other officers with whom he'd been in combat, none of whom wore the silver earrings I'd seen so frequently at the farmhouse, and with Aelfric they went inside and closeted themselves in Aelfric's office for several hours.

Freya's eyes followed him worshipfully.

So, I told myself, maybe I didn't know a great deal more than I'd known before, but perhaps I knew some of the questions now.

There were some things I had to do and just maybe Feldmarschall Count von Heinen could help me do them.

He'd come from Outtime, but unlike myself he'd come to this Line willingly. He'd known how to leave it. He'd know the location of a skudder, a sautierboat, a transtemporal device.

At least I was counting on his knowing.

"It's hard to remember the exact date now, the days had all begun to run together, but it must have been the first part of November when Von Heinen and I finally had our talk.

It was late one evening and I was fumbling my way through a rather simple child's history text under a bare light bulb behind the heavily shuttered windows of my broom closet. Nursing the last of my warm evening beer, I was having trouble concentrating.

I'd been disturbed on Jock's world when I'd thought about things, even though I'd had Sally to keep me company and some feeling of security.

There was none of that here. Sally was gone— Tar-hortha had her now. Somewhere. Somewhen. And my sitting here wasn't going to do her, or me, one bit of good. So much for the noble ideas I'd had when I decided to escape from a moving skudder. Sally must assume me dead by now.

And I was convinced that my ugly acquaintance, Tar-hortha, not really hurt in the scramble in the skudder, wasn't sitting on his tailed rear end. My hidden transmitter was still lodged somewhere inside me and still

beeping out its telltale signals, and I was certain that the
Kriths and the Timeliners were searching up and down
the Lines for it again—and they probably had a fair
idea of where to look.

How much time did I have?

And, well, there were things I had to do, and before
I finished them a lot of time might pass, time whose
seconds could be as precious as rare jewels—or drops
of human blood.

I'd been doing a lot of thinking during those long,
lonely nights in bed by myself in that farmhouse, and
I'd made up my mind that I wasn't going to sit back
much longer and let things *happen* to me. There were
still a lot of questions I wanted to ask, and about the
only ones who could give me the answers were the
Kriths. And they weren't likely to give them willingly.

If I were ever going to know just what was going on
across the Timelines, if I were ever going to know what
the Kriths were up to and what the Paratimers were up
to and exactly why the two were at war—and if I were
ever going to do anything about it all—then by God, I
was going to have to get moving.

Maybe old Albert von Heinen could help me do that.

I put the book down, finished my warm beer, lighted
a cigarette, coughed and sputtered a couple of times—and
told myself again that the local cigarettes must have been
made of grass, burlap sacks, and horse manure. Maybe
they really were.

Just as I'd buttoned my shirt, brushed back my hair,
combed my three-week beard with my fingers and re-
hearsed the words I'd say to the guard who stood just
outside the door, somebody knocked.

"Yes, who is it?" I asked in my best local Anglisch,
which wasn't yet worth a damn.

A voice answered in a version of English I could
more easily understand: "It's Von Heinen. I want to talk
to you, Mathers."

"How's that for perfect timing?" I said, twisted the
knob and opened the door.

Count Albert Frederick Maximillian Joseph von Heinen
was dressed in three-day-old fatigues with all the starch
gone out of them. His hair and beard looked as though a

family of rats had moved in for the winter though there was a big gun on his hip and strength in his eyes above the bags of weariness. "How's that?" he asked, his English only slightly flavored by an aristocratic Imperial High German accent.

"Nothing. Strictly rhetorical. Come on in."

"Would you like for us to have our talk now?" he asked politely, maybe meaning it seriously.

I laughed, sat down on the edge of the bed, offering my visitor the room's only chair.

"I do think it's time we talked, Mather," Von Heinen said, drawing a large cigar from his breast pocket and then lighting it.

"I've been waiting."

"And I've been busy. I'd meant to talk with you before, but there just hasn't been the time."

"Decent of you to think of me."

"Don't get smart, Mathers! I could still shoot you out of hand or turn you over to One Moon Star." He paused. "And I might yet."

It didn't seem polite to make a wise answer to that. I let him have the floor.

"Well, what do you think of Scragheafod?"

"What?"

"Scragheafod," he repeated. "That's what old Gawolf, the fellow who ran the Marauders before Aelfric, called it. This place here."

"I'm withholding judgment until I know more."

"I'll do what I can to fill you in, but there are some things I want to know first."

"Like what?"

He didn't answer immediately, but sat in the chair looking worn and tired, rubbing his chin through his dark beard. Finally he spoke, "Your being here is one of the strangest things I've ever encountered. I can't believe it's just coincidence, but I can't figure out what else it might be. I know you're no Krithian agent and you said enough in your delirium for me to have a pretty good idea of what happened to you, but I'd like to hear it in a little more coherent form, if you don't mind."

I attributed his abrupt reversals of mood and attitude

to his fatigue, and to the fact that he was trying to convince me that he was my friend, or least ally, but still held the power of life and death over me.

"Okay," I said after too long a pause, figuring that if I gave him information he'd reciprocate. "Where do you want me to start?"

"Well," he said, pondering for a moment, "I know about your stay in Staunton, of course, and your escape. I know that the Kriths gave you my wife as a reward for your services to them." I'm not sure how much bitterness there was in his voice, after all Sally had been his wife in name only, a political alliance, not one of love or sex. "And I know that finally you became disillusioned with them, though I don't know the full story of that. I'm not certain any of the Paratimers do."

Does that mean that old Albert now considers himself a Paratimer? I wondered.

"It appears," he went on, "that you and Sally tried to get to the Albigensian Lines to confront the Paratimers on their own ground and ask them why the Kriths were telling their 'Great Lie' about the alien invasion in the future. Right so far?"

"Essentially."

"The Krith named Kar-hinter and some of his cronies caught up with you before you got there—I didn't correct him—"and there was apparently something of a fight. You and Sally and the Krith's bodyguard were apparently the only survivors, and you and Sally dropped out of sight for months. Then suddenly you turn up here, of all places." He puffed on his cigar, went on. "Some of the Skralangs found you and, seeing your blond hair, thought you were an Anglianer and brought you here to Scragheafod. Aelfric was ready to throw you to the wolves—literally!—when I thought I recognized you. You know the rest." He paused again. "How I'd like for you to tell me what actually happened to you between the time you had the gunfight with Kar-hinter's gang and when you got here."

"That's really not too much of a story," I began.

I didn't know how much I ought to tell him. I knew he wasn't on the side of the Kriths, but if he were working with the Paratimers now, would he believe me if I told him that theirs was no more a *human* organization than was that of the Kriths? I decided to play it slow and easy and wait to see just what he was going to tell me. So I told him the bare bones of what had happened since the shootout in the Albigensian Lines, though I didn't mention that half of that shoot-out was between me and some blue-skinned characters who didn't look much like my kind of people, but then maybe he already knew that.

There was a twisted smile on his face when I finished.

"So here I am," I said, "lost on some Godforsaken Saxon-British Line and the Kriths have whisked Sally off for interrogation somewhere way in the T-East maybe all the way to their Homeline."

"So what are your plans?"

"I'm not in a position to make many plans right now."

He smiled again. "No, I suppose you aren't."

"But maybe I could if I knew what you're doing here and just where you stand."

Once more he smiled that twisted, weary smile. "It may be that you're not the only renegade along the Lines, Mathers. Have you ever considered that?"

"Well, I never did think myself to be what you'd call unique," I said, feeling a glimmering of hope. Could Von Heinen . . . ?

"I'll indulge you," he said, knocking a long, gray ash from his cigar into the tin-can ashtray on the table beside the bed. Then a thought seemed to cross his mind; his weary eyes brightened. "Mather, would you care for some schnapps?"

"Would I?"

He rose, stuck his head out the door and barked an order in Anglisch. In a few moments an orderly came darting into the room with a bottle of what appeared to be some Outtime bonded bourbon, two glasses, and a bucket of ice.

"We can at least be civilized about this, can't we?" Von Heinen said as he poured himself a drink. "Over ice?"

"Is that really what it looks like?"

"Exactly."

"On the rocks, please."

With a bit of warmth inside us now, he began to talk again. "I said I'd indulge you. As you may recall, I wasn't in very good shape when the Paratimers took me to Staunton."

"I recall," I said, remembering how I'd put a big .62-caliber slug in his stomach one night, but that was in another world, in more ways than one.

"They kept me there for a while, a couple of weeks, and then transported me to a Line where I could be given better medical treatment. That's how I happened to be absent when you made your dramatic exit from Staunton."

"I can't say that I was in very good shape when I left there myself."

"So I understand," he said, sipped at his whiskey. "After the blow up of Staunton the Paratimers decided that I'd served my usefulness on that Line and proposed that I go to work for them Outtime."

He sipped whiskey again. "The Paratimers seemed to consider me a potentially valuable agent for them, and contact with them had made me anxious to see some of the other worlds for myself," he said. "I accepted their offer. Anyway, things didn't look at all good for the Holy Roman Empire with the Paratimers pulling out and the Kriths still backing the British. If I'd gone back home to the Empire, I'd probably have gotten myself killed in combat or been tried for war crimes when the British finally won—as I suppose it's certain they will, there." He wasn't happy with that idea, but he'd accepted it.

"With the Kriths' help," I said, and then asked, hoping he'd give me a negative answer, "So you're a Paratimer now?"

"In a manner of speaking."

"Will you explain that?" I asked when he didn't speak again for what seemed like a long while.

"Well, I was sent here by an old acquaintence of yours," he answered at last, "an Albigensian named Mica. I'm certain you remember him."

"I do. He's still alive?"

Von Heinen nodded above the rim of his glass. "More of the Paratimers escaped from Staunton than you might think. But, as I was saying, Mica sent me here as an 'adviser' to the New East Anglianers. The Paratimers are backing them on this Line. The Kriths are aligned with the Imperials, or more particularly the Colonial Sclavanians down in the area known as Florida back in my Homeline."

"Just like RTGB-307," I said, thinking that there must now be a number of worlds on which very similar situations existed. "Hidden Kriths waging war with hidden Paratimers and most of the dying being done by ignorant locals."

"Yes, and also like on my Homeline, we don't think that the Kriths and their Timeliners are aware of the presence of the Paratimers. It seems that only a few Anglianers and Sclavanians are aware that Outtimers are assisting them. I don't think even King Edmund IV of the Anglisch Commonweal nor Emperor Conrad VIII know about the aid they're getting, only a few of the highest political and military leaders in Nordniwerda —North America—and a few lower-ranking people in very 'need to know' positions, like your friend and mine, Ufan Aelfric Dagrefson." The final words were spoken with sarcasm.

I nodded and let him continue.

"The Outtime forces here are struggling for control of the Line and New East Anglia has become the place of their contention for it. It does have considerable importance, on this world, at least."

"New East Anglia? How's that?" I asked.

"Let me explain: If you were to take a map of North America here and now and draw a line from the western end of Lake Erie down to Mobile Bay, you'd have to the east of that the area that has been settled by Europeans." There was a touch of the German schoolmaster in his voice again. "To the west are the Skralang Nations. Now, if you'd draw a line west from the bottom of Chesapeake Bay you'd have New East Anglia and then Sclavania below it and Frankish Neustria and then the Northern Alliance above it. With me so far?"

"I think so." I did wish we had a map so that I could see what he was describing a little better, but I had an idea of how this North America was laid out politically, though I wondered who ran the Far West. Skralangs? Chinese? But I didn't ask.

"As I told you, Neustria and Sclavania want to divide New East Anglia between them, but because of a number of conditions imposed on them from the outside, Imperial considerations, and the opinions of both the Popes—the one recognized by the Empire and Franklande and the one recognized by the Anglisch Commonweal and some other nations—all out war on the North American continent is unthinkable. So far the extent of the war has been some rather intense border clashes, very concentrated firepower in very limited areas, in terms of the local military technology."

"Okay," I said, as he refilled my glass.

"Mainly the hope on the part of Neustria and Sclavania is to wear down New East Anglian resistance, get some territorial concessions from the Mootan— the New East Anglian parliament—and then, when the matter of Papal succession is settled in Europe, hopefully for them with Benedict XIV being recognized as the Pope by all the churches, they'll continue to carve New East Anglia into smaller and smaller pieces until it really no longer exists."

He refilled his glass, took a long sip before he continued.

"Well, it's a long-term thing, maybe twenty years, but if the Kriths can eventually whittle New East Anglia into nothingness, Neustria and Sclavania will effectively have a common frontier, a common border. From what we've been able to learn, the Kriths believe that in such a situation trade and cultural exchange between the two powers would greatly increase and some time in the future, maybe within the next century, they would form a confederation, push westward and eventually come to dominate Nordniwerda and become a major power in their own right—*its* own right, whatever this combined nation might be called."

"Then the Kriths would use this New World continental power to help direct history toward their own ultimate goals?" I asked.

"Yes, that and more. We believe they'd then bring in a lot of Outtimé technology and make this Line one of their staging points for the invasion of other 'nearby' Lines. This would become a Krithian Prime Line and from here they'd seek to dominate a whole series of related world sectors."

"I see." I saw. I felt a chill.

"On the other hand the Paratimers want to prevent the establishment of a Prime Line. They believe that the best hope for ultimate freedom and strength for this world"—I wondered if the Paratimers cared any more about human freedom than did the Kriths, but I didn't say so—"is a balance of powers in the New World, small, independent nations biding their time while the European powers, already decadent, crumble and collapse under their own dead weight. They feel that within a century to a century and a half there'll come a renaissance in the small nations of the New World."

"And what would this 'renaissance' bring?" I asked.

"A world of truth, justice, light, and peace," Von Heinen said, sarcasm suddenly thick in his words.

"Then you don't believe it?"

"Should I?"

"Then why fight for them?"

"Whoever said I was fighting for *them?*"

"I see."

"I'm doing a job, that's all," he said, though there was little sincerity in these words either.

Again I said, "I see."

He took a cigarette from the pack I had on the table to replace the soggy, burned-out butt of his cigar, lighted it, inhaled deeply.

"Gawolf's Marauders—the commando group that Aelfric now heads—have been given a special assignment," he went on slowly. "I'm to advise them and help lead them as one of three elements which will attempt to take command of the Krithian headquarters for this Line, which is believed to lie only a hundred or so miles south of here, just across the Sclavanian border. I think we can do it, and if we do, I think we can just about put the Kriths out of business on this Timeline, as well as capture a lot of valuable equipment, if our timing is right."

"If you make it, then it'll be a Line won for the Paratimers," I said.

"Rather to offset the loss of the Line you call RTGB-307, you might say."

"Okay, then explain yourself," I said, deciding it was time we put some of our cards on the table. "Just why are you telling me all this? You know I'm no friend of the Paratimers."

"You're no friend of the Kriths either," he said.

"Maybe I'm nobody's friend."

He smiled his twisted smile again. "Maybe you're mine, Mathers. Or could be." He sipped at his whiskey. "I said that I'm a Paratimer in a manner of speaking. True, I'm here on an assignment from Mica, and true I'm carrying out the ostensible purpose of that assignment. I want to see that Krith HQ knocked out."

He took a long pause, finished what was left in his glass, poured another. I dropped new ice into my own empty glass and let him refill it once more.

"I've seen some things that bother me, Mathers. Some things that scare hell out of me."

There was another long pause as he turned things over in his mind, and for the first time since I'd known him I could almost tell what he was thinking. Almost.

"Mathers," he began slowly, carefully, "we both know that the Paratimers the *real* Paratimers, are no more human than the Kriths. The real Paratimers, the ones who call themselves Albigensians, are just made up to look like people."

I lighted a cigarette of my own and as I did I remembered the ones I'd seen, vaguely and indistinctly, on a ruined world where the true Albigensians had once lived.

"Then what are they?" I asked Albert Von Heinen. Maybe he *did* know.

"I don't know how to put it," he said. "They're alien, I guess you'd say, but they're Earthlings too, just like the Kriths claim to be, evolved on a world a long, long way across the Lines."

I nodded.

"I saw some of them once," he said slowly, as if in fear and awe. "I wasn't supposed to and they didn't know

I saw them. It was when I was in a hospital on some Julian-Roman Line where they'd transferred me from Staunton, just before they asked me to join them."

I nodded, listening to him, drawing on my cigarette and then sipping at my whiskey.

"They came into the room where I was," he went on as slowly as before, "and they thought I was alseep. They just stopped for a minute to look at me and then went on. They didn't say a word among themselves."

He looked at me, something close to a plea in his eyes, a very strange thing for *this* man. "They were about the height of a normal person and they had two arms and two legs and all, but . . ." His voice broke and he came to a stop and I remembered how it had been when Hillary Tracy had tried to describe them to me just before the Kriths killed him.

"I don't really know what they are," Von Heinen went on after a long silence. "But from bits and pieces I've gathered that they'd contacted humans before they ever left their own world. This is crazy, but I've got well—the idea that they were—dammit!—artificial!"

"What do you mean by that?" I asked, puzzled.

Von Heinen was obviously badly agitated, even frightened, and he hated for me to know it, but now he wanted to talk. I wasn't going to let him stop.

"Androids, maybe," he said. "Is that the word?" Some self-control seemed to come back to him. "I've got the idea that originally they were the result of some experimentation on a very high-tech world a long way to the T-West. They, or rather their ancestors, were created as slaves or domestics or something on that order to do the work that the people of that civilization felt themselves above doing. A race of flesh-and-blood robots created in laboratories, but fully alive, self-reproducing, and all that." The words began to pour out of him in a torrent, tumbling over each other.

"Well, Mathers, if I'm reading things right, if I understand any of it, the slaves soon began to outnumber their human masters, developed self-awareness, consciousness, and even the ability to genetically increase the abilities of their offspring. After a time they just took control of *that*

Earth and killed their masters, the humans who'd made them."

He paused and gasped for air like a landed fish. "Does any of this make any sense?" he asked.

"I don't know," I told him. "It's crazy, like you said, but then so's everything else in this damned universe. Go on."

"Remember, I don't know any of this for a fact," he said, speaking slowly once more, "but I think there's a lot of truth in it."

"Okay."

"Well, after the androids had complete control of their world, they stumbled across the 'facts of Paratime,' as they call it—or maybe someone from another Line with cross-Lining facilities found them. I don't know, but they got their hands on skudders—sautierboats—and set out across the Lines themselves."

"With what in mind?"

"Damned if I know. Maybe nothing. Maybe they just decided they'd see how many worlds they could take over. Their hatred of humans was pretty intense by then, I suspect."

"Then they discovered the Kriths?"

He nodded. "But before that they ran into the real Albigensians. They had a vey high-tech culture themselves, maybe one of the highest in all the human Lines. And there was a war."

"I saw the results."

Von Heinen nodded again. "I figured you'd actually gotten all the way to the Albigensian Lines. Pretty bad, wasn't it?"

"It was."

"It was right after their war with the Albigensians that they found out about the Kriths. That's when they started disguising themselves as humans—no mean trick!—and infiltrating worlds in the same manner as the Kriths. They want the same thing as the Kriths. I guess, total domination of all the human Lines."

"You think so?" I asked.

"Of course. Don't you?"

I shrugged. I didn't know, but somehow I didn't think it was all that simple.

A new sternness, or a return to his older sternness,

came over Von Heinen, and perhaps something of shame in his having let me see the fear he felt at the beings who called themselves Paratimers.

He looked at me almost coldly, sipped at his whiskey, then got another cigarette from my pack.

"Enough of this kind of speculation. Current reality is what matters now. I want you to help me knock over the Krith HQ I told you about. But certainly not for the Paratimers. I want some of the equipment for myself."

I sipped again at my own drink, thinking. . . . So Von Heinen was, or claimed to be, a renegade just like me, an enemy of both Outtimer groups, though nobody knew about him yet. No public enemy he. Not yet. Though he wanted one to join him.

And then what?

We had the rest of the night to talk about that.

And before the night was over I intended to get a few more hard answers.

Von Heinen raised his glass in toast and said, "Hail, brother."

8
The Night March

On the third night of the march south the smell of rain to
come was heavy in the air, though now and then the clouds
would break for a moment or two and through the break
I could see the stars. The ground under our feet was rough,
uneven, a crude path beaten into the earth by the passing
of animals and men, hardly a superhighway, but then
we'd left our vehicles far behind us. There were great
masses of dark trees, huge pines, towering oaks to our left,
and to the right smaller vegetation, less massive, but just
as forbidding.

Up ahead Von Heinen spoke with Aelfric, Wexstan, and
another officer named Harold Winfredson, one who didn't
wear the silver ring of the Marauders in his left earlobe,
though all wore the anachronistic body armor under their
fatigues and carried swords they never used. The three
of them, and An Mona Steorra who was farther ahead then
they, led the party of nearly two score men and pigtailed
women, all in the uniform of the Army of Niew Est Anglia,
toward a destination somewhere south of us. Beside me
Freya was silent, as were most of the others who followed,
excepting Faeder Baldwin Edgarson, the Gregorian Catholic priest of the commando force, who was giving a worried soldier a late-night blessing, speaking softly in a
strangely accented Latin.

As we made our way during the long night march there
was a November feel to the air, to the countryside, for it
must have been November by then—the name the locals
gave this month sounded something like "November",
though I'm not not certain how closely the local calendar
agreed with any I was familiar with. There was a feel of
winter in the air, a cold, chill winter, and one that I
thought would be unpleasant in more ways than one.

Von Heinen must have come to trust me by then, for
this was more than just a minor patrol—this was the begin-

ning of the "big one"—and he had given me weapons.
Now I carried on my hip a big revolver, a heavy, ugly
weapon called a Slean that reminded me of the Harling I'd
once carried and wished I still had. But this pistol would
probably do; I liked the feel of it. And slung across my
left shoulder was a smaller caliber but quicker firing semiautomatic Fiurer carbine which I'd never had a chance to
really practice with, but that seemed like a simple and effi-
cient weapon. I figured I could do some damage with it at
close range.

After a while the path we followed took a sharp turn to
the south and plunged into deeper and darker woods. The
trees bridged above us and hid the cloudy skies, and the
smell in the air was that of moist earth, rotting and disturbed vegetation. The sounds of nighttime insects filled
the air and now and again came the cry of an owl. Noc-
turnal beasts roaming the forest fled at the sound of our
approach.

The party grouped tighter as it followed the dark path
and Freya walked closer at my side, our arms brushing
through the heavy clothing we wore. I could sense the
tension in her—and I shared it.

As I was about to speak to her, to say something to
lessen the tautness of the night, the blackness ahead shifted
and something loomed in front of me.

Von Heinen had stopped and was waiting until we
caught up with him.

"Mathers," he whispered, "I want you to take the point
with me."

I followed him as he set a pace that soon put us out in
front of the others. We slowed again, alone in the lead except for An Mona Steorra who was some distance ahead of
us, invisible in the night.

"We're nearing the Sclavanian border," the German
whispered to me in Outtime English. "It'll be another fifteen or twenty minutes before we get close enough to run
into any scouts or border patrols, probably, but I don't
want to take any chances. And you're our chief weapon,
you know."

"How's that?" I whispered back, trying to see his face in
the darkness. All I saw was a black oval with two little
glints where his eyes were.

"You're the only Augie we've got."

"Oh." I should have known.

"Just keep your eyes and ears open, and be ready to go into augmentation at the first sign of real trouble. I hope there isn't any. I hope we can get there without having to fight. But be ready."

"I understand."

Our destination was somewhere on the other side of the Sclavanian border, outside of the New East Anglian constitutional thanedom of Beo IV. We were now some distance south and to the west of where the fighting was taking place, concentrated in border clashes as the rules of this war demanded, and we didn't expect to find ourselves in a real combat situation, although neither did we expect to be able to just walk across the Sclavanian border without opposition.

On the other side of the border that separated New East Anglia from the Imperial Colony of Sclavania, south and west of us, was a military installation that the Anglianer high command was convinced was the Krithian headquarters in the Timeline, the place from which they initiated their efforts to aid the Sclavanians and their Neustrian allies in their war against New East Anglia. Our present destination was a rendezvous for the personnel who would comprise one of the three elements of the force that would attempt to capture that headquarters. The attack itself, or more properly raid, was to be a sudden, swift surprise effort by small, highly mobile units rather than a massive frontal attack and was planned for three nights hence.

Even then I had no real plans of my own. For the time being I was going along with Von Heinen. Right then his plans suited me. He wanted to get his hands on Krithian transtemporal equipment, not for the benefit of his Paratimer employers, but for his own purposes. I suspected that he had in mind doing a little theivery here and there once he had the equipment for flickering from Line to Line, stealing wealth and materiel, and then finally settling down in some backwater Timeline where he could be cock of the roost with Outtime wealth and technology to help establish and maintain whatever kind of empire he wanted. He wouldn't be the first to try that. The idea even appealed to me. Maybe I was a fool for not doing it.

But then I had other plans, vague as they were, and maybe they were even more grandiose than Von Heinen's, but going along with him just might enable me to get my hands on a skudder. That's what I wanted. And preferably one of the newer ones outfitted for spatial locomotion like the 'sautierboats" of the Paratimers—Von Heinen had informed me that he'd already seen one such Timeliner craft in operation.

Some time had gone by when Von Heinen signaled for us to slow. I didn't know how he knew it in the darkness, but the Sclavanian border was now only some few hundreds yards ahead of us, beyond a rise in the land that swelled and crested like an ocean wave.

We came forward to a clearing in the forest and then he commanded the group to stop, giving the order as if he were the chief Anglianer officer.

During the three nights of the march Ufan Aelfric Dagrefson had shown deference to Von Heinen, though grudgingly. Apparently someone farther up in the chain of command had given him orders to let the Outtimer run this particular show—orders that must have been inspired by the Anglianers' Paratimer allies.

When the march halted Von Heinen took the officers and myself to one side.

"Mathers, Ufan Dagrefson, and I will go ahead and scout things out," he told us in a whisper. "We'll see just what the border's like here and what it'll take to get us across. The border's bound to be guarded, but I doubt heavily. The Sclavanians haven't the manpower to guard every mile of it and most of their men should be farther east since that's where the fighting is. Acceptable, Ufan Dagrefson?"

"Acceptable," Aelfric muttered. He didn't seem to be taking his inferior position to Von Heinen with very good grace.

"I didn't know for a fact where An Mona Steorra was at that moment, but I assumed that Aelfric, to whom alone he seemed loyal, had sent him ahead scouting.

"Let's go then," Von Heinen said, rose from his crouching position and turned toward the rise that separated us from the border.

The clouds were darker and heavier now and the stars

were gone, though there was a moonglow creeping up from the horizon through the overcast. There was a heaviness and an invisible gloom in the air, growing stronger, and I was certain it would begin to rain before another hour had gone by. Maybe some rain would be in our favor. Anything that would help conceal us would help.

We reached the crest's top, crossed it, and then as we slowly crept down the southward side of the slope, aware that the trees and brush, all the larger stands of vegetation had been cleared, we saw headlights approaching from the west, bouncing up and down as the vehicle on which they were mounted rumbled across the rough terrain.

"Motorized patrol," Von Heinen whispered.

As the headlights grew nearer they revealed a strip of land maybe a hundred and fifty to two hundred yards wide that had been cleared; we were on the northern edge. Down its middle was a twisted, tangled mass of coiled barbed wire, ugly and glittering in the headlights, freshly galvanized metal, the wire newly laid down. They'd learned the barbed wire trick here too and had put it to good use.

As the vehicle grew closer—though at its closest it was still on the other side of the wire, some distance away —I could make out some of the details in the light reflected back from the ground. It was a terribly ordinary-type military vehicle, a common design on a lot of worlds at this technological level: rectangular of shape, boxy and unesthetic, with four wheels, two seats in front and two in back, two headlights with yellowish auxiliary lights below them, a spare tire and a spare petrol tank mounted on the vehicle's rear, a heavy weapon that looked like a machine gun, and three occupants—the driver, the gunner, and a man with a rifle in the back seat. He was probably the officer in charge.

The vehicle—I want to call it a "jeep"—was doing something like twenty miles an hour, and that was probably fast enough considering the ground. The headlights were covering a large area, throwing everything into sharp relief, though in this case "everything" consisted of nothing more than the rough ground and the barbed wire. I noticed that there was a spotlight mounted near where the officer sat, but he wasn't using it.

We hugged the ground as the car came as close to us as it would and then roared on, though we were far outside the range of its lights.

"About what I expected," Von Heinen said softly as the car swept away, its headlights dwindling. "They're not too concerned with this area and haven't the manpower to patrol it well. They don't figure we'll try anything here."

"I wonder how often it comes by," Aelfric pondered aloud.

"Hard to say," Von Heinen replied. "It must be pretty often or it'd have no effectiveness at all."

"Then we can assume the car doesn't have a large area to cover," Aelfric said.

"I think that's right," the German Outtimer said. "A ten-mile stretch, not much more than that. Of course, that would make it a twenty-mile round trip."

"Then it could take as much as an hour to make that round trip," Aelfric said in a whisper.

"It *could* take that long, but it might not," Von Heinen replied.

"I'll get the others," the Anglianer officer said. "Time *is* of the essence." And without another word he slipped off into the darkness, hardly making a sound.

"If we were all augmented like you, I wouldn't worry," Von Heinen whispered in Outtime English. "We could just go augie and cut through the wire and slip across in no time."

"It's not really that simple."

"I know." But he didn't explain what he meant by that remark.

Very little time had gone by when Aelfric and the others returned. The party was together again—except for An Mona Steorra who hadn't rejoined us. And right then I wished the Skralang was with us. I didn't like him, but I thought it would be good to have him on your side in a situation like this. If I'd judged right.

"We're going to have to move fast," Von Heinen said after Aelfric told two troopers to get their wire cutters out. "We can't be certain how long it'll be before the patrol comes back, but we'd better be across before it does."

Nods and grunts of affirmation.

"Then let's get moving," Aelfric said quickly as if to get it out before Von Heinen did.

As we moved down the slope I became more aware of the faint moonlight that seeped through the clouds, the nakedness of the slope, and I felt terribly exposed. It would have taken very little light to reveal us there.

The two enlisted men with wire cutters had started ahead of us, acompanied by Wexstan and a non-commissioned officer named Efor, both of whom now carried hand torches they covered with their palms until they reached the tangle of wire. The rest of us stopped a few paces from the barbed coils, knelt on the cold ground, peered off into the darkness and hoped that there'd be no sign of headlights until we'd all gotten through the wire.

For a while the only sounds were those of the cutters' snick! as they cut through the thick, twisted strands of galvanized metal. Gloved hands, those of Wexstan and Efor, pulled away the severed sections and the two men with cutters inched forward again. It was slow going; the wire was terribly thick and tangled, rising half again as high as a standing man, and if that machine-gun carrying car came back before we got through, our damage to the barbed coils would be obvious. We'd be the proverbial sitting ducks for the Sclavanians' spotlights and bullets if we weren't able to get out of there in time. I didn't like it, but then nobody'd asked my opinion.

The feel of the rain had grown stronger and a chill had entered the air, a breeze carrying more dampness, and after a while Von Heinen came creeping back through the darkness to where I knelt.

"Mathers?" he whispered loudly.

"Here," I answered in the same sort of voice.

At a crouch, as if ducking under low-hanging branches or to avoid gunfire, he came to where I was, stopped, peered at his luminous wrist watch dial. "They're better than halfway through, but it's been almost fifteen minutes since they started. I'm worried about the time."

I grunted an affirmation, anticipating his next words.

"I want you to finish the cutting."

I nodded to myself. "In augmentation," I said aloud. It wasn't a question.

"In augmentation," he echoed. "I think I've got an idea of how that drains a man, but even that's better than being dead."

"There've been times when I've wondered."

"Come on." He made a motion to rise.

With a sigh I didn't have the will to resist, I slung my carbine back across my shoulder and rose to follow him.

When we got to the maze of wire Wexstan called for those with the cutters to pull back. One of them gave me his gloves and his heavy wire cutters and I handed my carbine to the German; it would only get in my way as I crawled through the wire, but I'd still have that big revolver. I hoped I wouldn't need it on that particular night. Another time perhaps.

True to what the Count had said, Wexstan's men had cut something slightly better than halfway through the wire, but that had also taken them something close to seventeen minutes. Von Heinen was expecting me to better than double their combined rate. At X5 augmentation I thought I could do it, though I didn't like the idea of staying under that long. However, Von Heinen was right. *I* didn't want to be there when that "jeep" came back.

I crawled and willed the electrobiological controls into operation. There was a momentary sense of disorientation as the world around me slowed, but not as much as usual since there wasn't a great deal of sensory data coming to me right then anyway.

I glanced down at the dial of the watch given me before leaving Scragheafod and saw the terribly slow creep of its second hand, moving more like a minute hand now.

I started cutting.

Snick! Snick! Snick!

Three minutes times five is the equivalent of fifteen minutes and that's about how long I'd been at it when I thought I caught a glimpse of light. When I turned to look there was nothing there and I supposed that I'd just imagined it or that it'd been some random "noise" of retinal nerves giving my brain the impression of light.

But then I saw it again, bouncing above the earth, oddly slow, and saw that it was a pair of headlights, a long way off, coming toward me at one fifth of its twenty miles per hour.

I hadn't many more strands of wire to cut and figured *I* could make it before the "jeep" reached me, but I doubted that any of the others could. Without cutting out my augmentation, I made an effort to speak as slowly as possible, calling back to the others. "Cooomeee oon." I kept on cutting.

They must have understood me, for a few moments later I heard a series of bass rumblings that I took to be Von Heinen and/or Aelfric yelling orders. Some people claim to be able to understand spoken words in X5, but I don't see how. It all sounds like a Greek chorus of sick frogs.

I "snicked" on at the wire and in a few more moments had cut through the last strands. Dropping my cutters, I forced an opening as wide as I could and pulled myself through. Now I wished I hadn't left that carbine behind, as awkward as it might have been getting it through. But I had the heavy revolver, .441 caliber and carrying the equivalent of 240 grains, and maybe it would be sufficient. Maybe it would have to be.

As far as I could see the first members of the party were about to enter the tunnel through the wire, but there was a long line behind them and the progress through the tunnel would be slow. There were nearly forty of them and by the time the car got to where its occupants could see us, very few of them would have gotten through.

"Hurry up," I yelled, knowing full well they could no more understand me than I could them. I pulled the revolver out of its flapped holster, worked the mechanism. The six slugs in its cylinder would have to be put to very good use soon if . . .

I came fully erect and held the gun before me, left hand steadying right wrist, right arm only slightly crooked. The "jeep" was coming on with agonizing slowness, but the people behind me were moving even more slowly.

I waited. The car drew nearer.

I held my breath, tensed my body into stillness, felt a tremor of nervousness, tasted flat, dry metal in my mouth. It was always like that just before it started.

Then the time was up.

The report of the big pistol going off in my hand really didn't seem much deeper than usual, but it must have been, and I thought I could see the bullet as it moved toward the car, reflecting the light of its right headlight—until it met the headlight and shattered it.

I fired again as quickly as the mechanism of the single-action Slean would allow and was again amazingly lucky —the other headlight went out. I jumped to one side.

The car wasn't that near, but the slugs bursting from the machine gun slung over its hood were. The fellow manning that gun hadn't been asleep and he had damned good reflexes. I know he couldn't have seen me yet, but he nearly pegged me.

I rolled, came to my knees, aimed.

The officer in the back seat was awake too. He had the sense to flip on his spotlight as the headlights went out and began to sweep with it as the driver tried to brake the vehicle to a halt.

I fired . . .

. . . and hit the officer without hitting the spotlight, though the slumping of his body must have hit the handle, for it flipped skyward, beaming upward at the clouds like a glowing eye. I didn't waste any more bullets on him.

The flash of my weapon must have given me away to the machine gunner. His chattering weapon began sweeping in my direction again, vomiting light and smoke and bullets. I dived toward the earth again even though his sweep seemed slow, and I fired an awkward shot toward the vehicle. I didn't think I'd hit anything.

Coming to my knees, no more than a few yards from the slowing car, I could have seen both living men had there been decent light. There wasn't, so I put my next shot through the door of the car where I thought the driver might be. I didn't know whether I'd hit him. I didn't have time to check.

The machine gunner was fast; I'll give him credit for that. But he wasn't as fast as a man in X5. He continued to swing his gun toward me, my location again revealed by the Slean's muzzle-flash, but, coming to my feet and breaking into another run, I outdistanced the sweep of his gun, came up on the other side of the "jeep," and put a bullet in the back of his head before he knew I was anywhere close to him.

I was about to turn my attention to the vehicle's driver, but discovered it wasn't necessary. Out of the darkness came an indistinct figure I was certain was clad in poncho and leather pants, moving with the quick, graceful quiet of a cat; I could doubly appreciate An Mona Steorra's movements in my augmentation.

The Skralang had leaped into the vehicle's front seat, landed at a couch beside the driver who fought to bring up a pistol, and deftly slid a knife into his left breast.

Cutting out the augmentation, I felt a wave of fatigue sweep over me and a sharp pain in my right thigh. I'd been in augmentation in excess of eight minutes, I thought. It had taken a lot out of me, how much I wasn't yet sure.

I noticed that it had started to rain.

An Mona Steorra climbed out of the car, said something to me that I couldn't understand. I grunted back to him as pleasantly as I could and leaned against the side of the car, and waited for Von Heinen and the others.

The Skralang signaled to them with the vehicle's spotlight.

It was while we waited that An Mona Steorra and I simultaneously noticed the box slung under the vehicle's dashboard to the right of the dead driver, a box with a glowing pilot light and a grille from which came words in a guttural language I didn't recognize—which wasn't at all unusual of late. But then this was a military patrol car of the Imperial Colony of Sclavania.

What the words meant I didn't know, but their tone was urgent and I suspected that they were directed at the car's deceased occupants. Someone on the other end of the live radio may have known about my attack, must have heard the sounds of shooting and death.

We hadn't time to waste now. Whoever was on the other end would probably very shortly send somebody to find out what was going on, a number of some-bodies, armed.

While An Mona Steorra deliberately drew his side arm and put a bullet through the radio's pilot light, chuckling as he did, I called to Von Heinen, "We'd better get out of here while we can. This car's equipped with—"

Then a wave of grayness came over me. I staggered, wavered, realized blood was running down my right leg, then gave up the fight.

The People of Tapferkeitenhaven

The place of rendezvous was a small fortress, a miniature marble castle out of medieval Germany, though built less than a century and a half ago by a Sclavanian nobleman to defend the ill-defined border between Sclavania and New East Anglia as much as it had been to guard against attack from the Skralangs, who at the time weren't at all amicable toward the Imperial colonists. Neither were they at present.

We arrived there as dawn brought the sky from black to gray. The thick overhang of cloud and the rain that had begun to fall from it gave the world below a pale, washed-out, shadowless appearance and effectively hid our party as we reached the "castle."

There had been little difficulty getting from the barbed-wire border crossing to the fortress, which I later learned was called Tapferkeitenhaven, except that for the first mile or so I required assistance in walking. Wexstan and the priest, Faeder Baldwin, took turns half-supporting me, allowing me to lean on their shoulders as I recovered from the shock of being too long under augmentation, as I adjusted to the pain from the flesh wound in my right thigh. Finally enough strength came back to me to allow me to walk alone, unassisted, and still keep up with the rest of the company, though I knew it would take several good meals and some long hours of sleep before my metabolism fully recovered. That's the price you have to pay for such advantages as augmentation.

The wound in my thigh had bled copiously, but wasn't serious.

During the final two hours of the march Freya was never far from me, again taking on her role of nurse and remaining solicitous of my health.

So with dawn a grayness streaking the cloudy sky and

the long expected rain a drizzling reality, we came out of the forest at Tapferkeitenhaven and were met by two men in civilian clothing who carried military rifles and spoke Anglisch with accents that made it almost impossible for me to understand them. Von Heinen and Aelfric spoke with them, apparently established the identity of the party, for the guards finally indicated that we were to go on toward the fortress.

I believe I saw glimpses of a dozen or so more men hidden in the trees and brush on the edge of the forest, steel eyes watching our movements closely.

With Aelfric in the lead, we walked single file down the path the guards had indicated and reached a set of massive wooden gates in the castle's stone wall. The spiked porticus was raised and the gates were opened for us and inside we were greeted by more armed men who didn't wear military uniforms, though several of them wore a distinctive, medieval-looking livery of black and orange.

After a few minutes of milling around in the courtyard, we were taken into a large room within the fortress' main keep where there was a roaring fire in a huge fireplace and a large oaken table covered with platters of cold cuts and pitchers of beer. The man who appeared to be the senior of the castle's liveried guards told Aelfric that we should eat and dry ourselves before the fire. Soon the *Herr* would be about and would meet with Aelfric and the other officers.

Freya requested fresh, dry bandages for my wound, which were delivered at once. She and Faeder Baldwin saw to the injury, cleaned it, rebandaged it. When they finished it seemed to hardly bother me. We addressed ourselves to other matters.

To me, and obviously to the others, the cold cuts, black bread, and thick, tangy beer were more than welcome. I devoured three sandwiches as quickly as I could, washing them down with the lukewarm beer. I must have looked half-savage, wolfing down my food, and Faeder Baldwin did comment on my haste in eating, but when I was finished and sat by the fire with my fourth mug of strong beer, I felt that I just might survive the ordeal. The only thing I needed now was ten or twelve hours of sleep, but I rather doubted they were likely to come any time soon. I was right.

When most of us had finished eating and sat in a half-circle around the fireplace drying ourselves, Faeder Baldwin announced he would hold a "short mass" in one corner of the large room for those who felt a need to thank God for our safe passage.

About half of the Anglianers expressed a desire for the holy sevice. Faeder Baldwin converted a table into an altar by the use of draperies, candles, and other paraphernalia he'd brought with him, but had said hardly more than *"Credo in unum Deum,"* when a man entered the room and told Aelfric, in thick accents, that the "Herr" was ready to see him, Von Heinen, and the other officers.

Aelfric nodded, directed that Von Heinen, Freya, Wexstan, Harold Winfredson, and I accompany him. I was only half-surprised that I was asked to go along to the meeting; Von Heinen's plans for me, I strongly suspected, had just begun.

Although there had been electric lights in the hall where we had eaten our cold-cut breakfast, there were none in the long hallway down which we walked after leaving the room. The hall was dim and sooty, lighted by torches spaced some distance apart. There was a chill in the air, a dampness, and a patina of moisture on the walls. This place was an excellent reproduction of a medieval castle, I thought, right down to the inconveniences. I wondered if it had indoor plumbing, and thought I'd probably find out sooner than I wanted to.

When the hallway ended we mounted a flight of stairs that led up one floor and down another torch-lit hallway to a pair oaken doors bracketed by two guards in black and orange livery, carrying automatic rifles. The guards didn't speak as the multi-clad man who led us opened the doors and admitted us to another large room.

This room didn't have the austerity of the one we'd left behind. It was lighted by a brace of elaborate electric chandeliers that depended from the high ceiling and cast their light over the room's rich furnishings and luxurious appointments. It had more the appearance of the parlor of a sixteenth-century French king than that of a sixth-century border lord.

There were six people waiting there for us, six people whose names and positions I soon learned, and who were to play important parts in the events of the days to come.

They were:

Herr Jurgen Matthausen, a Sclavanian and the lord of Tapferkeitenhaven. He was a large bear of a man with heavy Teutonic features, hair more gray than blond. There was a ragged scar on the right side of his face, running from temple to jawbone, and there was a slowness to the movements of his left hand that indicated some sort of impairment. What had caused these I never learned, though I didn't believe they'd come from war. More likely from a hunting accident; Herr Jurgen was a great one for the hunt as the trophies on his wall indicated. As he greeted us in almost flawless if slightly condescending Anglisch, he was dressed in an elaborate smoking jacket of blue trimmed in gold, with silvery brightwork, and was smoking a large cigar that could have only come from Cuba, or whatever it was called in this Line. On the table beside the chair in which he'd been sitting was a brandy snifter, all but empty.

Herr Jurgen had once been a loyal Sclavanian and subject of his Imperial Majesty Conrad VIII, but events during the past few years had turned him against both the Emperor in Wursburg and the Colonial government in Neu Fulda, a city on the coast of an area known as Florida on some Lines. What was most important to Herr Jurgen, besides the Emperor's alliance with the "damned Franks" and some of the political machinations of the Emperor and his cronies, was the recognition by the Empire of the "Godless and unholy Antipope," Benedict XIV, who was now in sanctuary in one of the Emperor's palaces in Wursburg, surrounded by his "renegade bishops and false cardinals." Herr Jurgen was loyal to the "true heir of St. Peter," Pope Gregory XVII.

Although Herr Jurgen may have dominated the room, his powerful presence wasn't enough to totally distract from the others, the most striking of whom was a short, dark-haired woman in her twenties, now dressed in tan quasi-military slacks and blouse, an outfit that one might wear on an African safari on some other world than this.

Gwendalfa Halgason, as I soon learned her name to be, was a very attractive woman, in her own distinctive way as lovely as Freya, though there was a hardness and a bitterness around her brown eyes and an angry quickness to her movements. Now, as she sat in Herr Jurgen's luxurious parlor dressed in masculine clothing, her long, dark hair tied up in a bun on top of her head in a manner as harsh and masculine as her clothing, her femininity was betrayed by the curves of her body beneath the clothing she wore.

And although she was unarmed now, she wore a web belt in addition to the leather belt of her trousers, a belt obviously designed to carry a holster and ammunition.

Gwendalfa, I also learned not too much later, was the niece of Hama Halgason, then First Speaker of the New East Anglian Mootan, daughter of the late Halga Halgason, formerly First Speaker, assassinated by a Neustrian agent some months before, and sister of the late Maufan Anslem Halgason, an Anglianer officer who'd died in a very brutal way at the hands of one of the Emperor's most expert torturers. She *was* a bitter young woman and had come into Sclavania as an agent for Anglian military intelligence in order to satisfy some of that bitterness.

The third person in the room was a middle-aged, pot-bellied, red-faced man who looked as if he should be a journeyman carpenter or an innkeeper, but he was actually another Anglianer agent carrying the rank of maufan—major or its rough equivalent. Artos Alaricson, bearded and jovial, though a shrewd military officer, had been working behind Sclavanian lines for some three years now and spoke the language perfectly.

It was only later that I learned that his "cover" actually was that of an innkeeper in Trier, the city nearest the military installation believed to be the Krithian headquarters for this Line.

Geoffry Dunstanson, a handsome, beardless young man also in mufti, carried the rank of ufan and was, like Aelfric, the leader of a company of commandos working across the Sclavanian border. He'd brought with him a party similar to ours, though smaller, which was now quartered in Tapferkeitenhaven. They'd arrived the night before last, having a shorter distance to come than we. They were to supplement our force when the raid took place on the base near Trier.

And the other two—I should have been expecting men like them. . . .

One was named Devoto Baugh. He was a quiet, aloof man, small of stature, swarthy of skin, unhandsome in the manner of a rodent, though, as I was to learn later, tough and quick-witted. Like myself and Albert von Heinen, he wasn't a native of this Line—he was Paratimer, though he didn't claim to be an Albigensian. He was the co-ordinator of our phase of the raid on the Trier installation, Fort Lothairin.

Kjemi Stov looked like an Irishman, but wasn't. Just below middle height and stocky, a man of apparently great physical strength, with blue eyes and hair almost impossibly red, he was Devoto Baugh's lieutenant and was later identified as being from a "Norse-American" Line not greatly distant from the Saxon-British Line we were presently on.

I'll admit that when I discoverd that there were two other Outtimers, two *Paratimers,* in the room, I was startled, shaken. Right then I had no desire to be "discovered" by the Paratimers. They had no more love for me than I had for them—but Von Heinen had prepared for this, though he hadn't told me so. His idea of a joke?

"This is Franz Anselem, of whom I told you," Von Heinen said as he introduced me to the Paratimers—and so I was to be, a Frisian Saxonite from the Northern Alliance, an area that extended from where upper New York is on some Lines to the location of Quebec. This accounted for my accent and ignorance of local customs. The members of Aelfric's commando squad had apparently been briefed, for they showed no surprise. And I wondered why Von Heinen hadn't warned me—maybe he enjoyed the joke he played on me. That wouldn't have been out of character.

Once the introductions were over, Herr Jurgen offered

us chairs through the person of an elderly servant, and brandy with his own voice. Aelfric, speaking as the officer in charge of the Scragheafod group, declined politely. Both Von Heinen and I might have accepted, but neither of us did, for differing reasons.

"Welcome to Tapferkeitenhaven," Herr Jurgen said again when we were all more or less comfortable. "I may say that I'm delighted that our Saxonite allies have seen fit to be represented in this endeavor." He was referring to me. "The ultimate result of our activities will benefit all honest and God-fearing men the world around. These heathen monsters—your Krithian *things*"—he spoke these words to the Outtimers—"must be banished from our world. It's God's will, so I'm certain, that we work our destinies out in this world, and not have them imposed on us by outsiders *who aren't even human beings*." The emphasis placed on these last words suggested to me that Herr Jurgen, good Catholic by local standards as he was, might well consider the Kriths to be agents of His Satanic Majesty, as an old man in another Line must have done before he was murdered by them.

"But enough of this talk," Herr Jurgen said, having sipped away the last of his brandy and nodding to the old servant for a refill. "I'm merely acting as what you might call an innkeeper for more active and daring men than myself. I'm merely providing a place from which to begin your efforts to rid our world of this menace." This self-deprecation was totally false and obvious to everyone. "Therefore it would be best if I were to turn this meeting over to Master Devoto Baugh and let him outline your plans. Master Baugh?"

Devoto Baugh wasted no time on preambles, but unfolded a map which he spread out on a table provided by Jurgen's elderly servant. It was a map of the lower portions of North America as politically arranged on this Line, New East Anglia to the North and the Imperial Colony of Sclavania to the south, stretching to and then swinging southwest like a crescent around the Gulf of Mexico, taking in the peninsula of Florida as well as the southern portions of what were Alabama and Georgia in Jock's world.

As we clustered around the table I saw that several

places had been circled in red and labeled in a neat hand-writing, among which were Scragheafod, from which we'd come in the north, Tapferkeitenhaven, our present location, and to the southwest the city of Trier and the nearby installation, Fort Lothairin. There were other red circles, both above and below the border west of Trier; he didn't identify these at once.

"We are presently here," Devoto Baugh said in a voice pitched lower than one might have expected from a man of his small stature, tapping the red circle that represented Tapferkeitenhaven with the eraser end of a pencil. "Our objective is here." The eraser tapped Fort Lothairin. "On the third night from tonight we shall make our raid, which will be co-ordinated with simultaneous raids by anti-Krith forces"—he was careful not to say "anti-Sclavanian" or "anti-Imperial" forces, for Herr Jurgen didn't consider himself a traitor to either; perhaps more of a true patriot—"operating from here and here." He tapped two more of the red circles on the map, one almost directly west and another more northwesterly of Fort Lothairin.

"The raiding forces will consist of three elements which will originate from these points, headed by Paratimer officers working in close conjunction with local officers. Each element will consist of three units, about which I shall tell you more later." He paused, surveyed the group, continued. "I shall be the superior Paratimer officer of this element, designated number one, with Kjemi Stov and Count Albert von Heinen as my executive officers. We will work through Ufan Dagrefson and Ufan Dunstanson who will be in charge of their respective Anglianer groups. Is that understood?"

Von Heinen, Stov, Aelfric, and Geoffry Dunstanson nodded their understanding.

"Herr Jurgen has kindly offered us his services as Quartermaster and Chief of Logistics for element one.

"Now each element of the strike force," Devoto Baugh went on, tapping his pencil against the hard oaken table, "will have a specific goal, or to be more precise, several specific goals, each of which will be essential to the success of the mission." He paused as if pondering for a moment, then continued. "It would be well to make clear now that our objective is the *capture,* not *destruction,* of the Krithian installation at Fort Lothairin. Destruction will be a last alternative if capture proves impossible. This responsibility, should its need arise, will be in the hands of another element.

"*Our* goals, ladies and gentlemen, are twofold.

"Firstly, the temporary disruption of service from the main power plant which supplies electricity to Fort Lothairin. It is a steam-powered generating plant located on the reservation and no great distance from the Krithian skudder shelters and communications center. I have maps of the area and some photographs taken from reconnaissance balloons which you will be required to study prior to our departure.

"Our second goal, due to our proximity to them, will be the capture of both the Krithian skudder shelters and their skudders, should any be present, and the capture, if possible, of their communications center. The highest priority lies in the capture of the skudders, which we understand are of the newer type provided with locomotion facilities—putting them nearly on a par with our sautierboats. The communications center is of lesser importance and may be destroyed if capture presents significant problems."

He paused again, looked at the faces around him, particularly at those of Von Heinen, Stov, the two ranking Anglianer officers and me.

The look that Devoto Baugh gave me, as might be expected, was one that asked for agreement with the plan he'd outlined, the supposition being I was a Saxonite ally. But mixed with that was an inquisitive look that I wasn't supposed to see, a look that made me wonder if he'd wholly swallowed Von Heinen's story that I was from the Northern Alliance, a local comrade in arms.

"I am certain that you all have a number of questions at this stage," Devoto Baugh said momentarily, sitting back down in the chair he'd occupied earlier. "If Herr Jurgen would be so kind as to provide us with coffee and his inestimable cigars, should the ladies have no objection, I would be glad to answer them wherever possible."

Herr Jurgen "harrumphed" at the elderly servant who scuttled from the room and then suggested we make ourselves comfortable. Cigars and coffee would be coming soon.

I tried to do as the Sclavanian border lord suggested, then and during the several hours that followed while more details of the planned attack on Fort Lothairin were divulged, though what I wanted most desperately was sleep, good, sound sleep to allow my body to recover from the stresses through which it had gone.

Eventually I got that sleep, in a small, comfortable sleeping room which Von Heinen and I were to share during our stay at Tapferkeitenhaven, but not before I had some further words with the German count.

"Well, what do you think, Mathers?" Von Heinen asked as each of us sat on our beds, unlacing our black combat boots. "Can we pull it off?"

"If this Devoto Baugh of yours is right," I replied, dropping the butt of one of Herr Jurgen's cigars into a large ceramic ashtray, "and if the Kriths have no idea that there are Paratimers on this Line, and if they believe that the location of their headquarters *is* secret, it *might* work. Surprise should be in our favor if they're really not expecting to be attacked."

"You don't sound as if you're altogether sure."

"I think it'd be dangerous and stupid to underestimate the Kriths at this stage of the game," I said. Since entering the privacy of the sleeping room we'd been speaking the English native to Von Heinen's Line. It was easier for both of us than local Anglisch.

"You think they might be aware of the Paratimers here?"

"They could be."

"What do you consider our chances, yours and mine," he asked, "of stealing a skudder and getting the hell off this Line?"

I thought carefully for a moment before answering. "Well, if everything goes okay, there should be no great problem." We'd hardly discussed our plans after getting into the Krithian skudder pool, but I believed we'd been thinking along the same lines. "I'll be in augmentation and I doubt there'll be many Augies besides me around. There'll be plenty of confusion, as there always is, and *we* should have the element of surprise on *our* side. It should work, if everything else does." I paused, then posed him a question: "Where do we go once we leave this Line?"

"I haven't really decided my destination yet," he answered slowly. "You can probably offer me suggestions. We can work that out when the time comes. Agreeable to you?"

"I guess it would be best not to count too many chickens yet," I said. "We can work out something when we need to."

"Very good."

There was something else in the back of my mind that I'd considered telling him: the transmitter Kar-hinter's physicians had placed in my body was still functioning as far as I knew, broadcasting a signal that even now Tar-hortha's crew was probably trying to track down. And that transmitter put me in danger; Von Heinen as well. Maybe I should tell him of the disadvantages of having me around, as well as of the advantages.

But what good would that do? I wondered. The medical science of this Line wasn't such that I'd want their doctors probing around inside me trying to find a device that was probably no larger than a pea. They just might kill me before they found it, or take out half my augmentation by mistake.

And when I thought of being killed, I considered that it might not be by accident. Von Heinen might decide that I was more of a liability than an asset with that thing on me. Cremation wasn't an unusual funeral practice on this Line, and an excellent means of certifying that the transmitter stopped broadcasting my location.

No, I thought as I drifted off toward sleep, I'd just keep that bit of information to myself. Things were bad enough without bringing that up.

The much-needed sleep into which I drifted was one disturbed by dreams of Sally and Tar-hortha and of the things the Kriths might be doing to her in order to extract information from her, information she might well not have.

My sleep was not as sound as I would have liked, nor as long.

10

Dinners, Lessons, and Agents

We were awakened an hour or so after dark by one of Herr Jurgen's multitudinous servants, this one a young blond girl named Fredericka, dimpled, full-busted, long-legged, who didn't look to be over sixteen, but whose beauty must have made her the goal of every male under thirty in the neighborhood, and a good number over that age. Would her parents demand a high bride-price!

Mein Herr Jurgen, we were informed in halting if correct Anglisch, was expecting us for dinner, which was at eight of the clock sharp. The attire would be formal. She pointed out for us clothing that had been brought in while we slept.

When the girl departed I found, after a short search, that Tapferkeitenhaven, despite its antique appearance, was equipped with such amenities as indoor plumbing. After using the chrome and tile facilities, I returned to the sleeping room to find Von Heinen talking with a portly, middle-aged man in the black and orange livery of Herr Jurgen, who was to serve as our valet while we dressed in the proper clothing in the proper manner—which seemed like an odd occupation for a man with his flintlike eyes. And I wondered how it was possible for Herr Jurgen to keep any secrets with this number of people running loose. I figured that either they were awfully loyal or half of northern Sclavania would know of our presence by then.

While we dressed, the valet, whose name turned out to be Otto, kept up a running conversation, or more correctly monologue, since Von Heinen and I were hardly given a chance to speak during the time he was with us. He informed us, among other things, that Herr Jurgen *always* expected his dinner guests to be in proper attire. Rebel though he might be against some of the practices and religious positions of Emperor Conrad and his nobles, Herr Jurgen believed in keeping up the traditional standards.

111

Too many of the nobility, Herr Jurgen believed, had tended to "go native" after settling in the New World, a fate that would never come to the House of Matthausen.

As the last touches were put on our clothing, elaborate blouses, coats, and trousers of bright-colored silks and linens, Otto informed us that a person whose presence had been wished at this dinner had been unable to attend, that worthy being one Mistress Chlodwilda Johannes, a young lady of a wealthy loyal family who'd recently become betrothed to Herr Jurgen, whose first wife had died some two years previously. Her absence was regretted, Otto said. She was a bright and cheerful young person who added sparkle to any gathering.

I thought this gathering would need all the "sparkle" it could get.

Unfortunately I was correct. The meal, though of excellent quality, if not cooked to my taste, was dull and uninteresting, everyone save Herr Jurgen seemingly too inhibited or too concerned with the future to talk freely. While the lord of the castle drank wine with his meal, the rest of us, at Devoto Baugh's "suggestion," had only water. It seemed that there was work for us to do later and we didn't need wine "dulling our wits."

When the table had been cleared of the last course, when the coffee had been drunk and the cigars smoked, Devoto Baugh asked Herr Jurgen to excuse us and we went to that work, which consisted of three full hours of careful study of aerial photographs and maps of the Sclavanian military installation and the suspected layout of the Krithian HQ.

Exactly where the Paratimers had gotten their information about the Krithian base Devoto Baugh didn't say, though from his admitted uncertainty about some areas I suspected that it hadn't come directly from spies in the pay of the Paratimers or the Anglianers. Rumors, gossip, and hearsay may have been the only basis for the data, though as things turned out it was largely correct. I learned more of one of those sources later.

The studies of the photos and maps took place in a large room below the gound floor of Jurgen's castle, something that could have once been a small gymnasium—or a dungeon. In it now were only the tables and chairs we used, a

stand on which a large pot of coffee gurgled as it perco-
lated, a large map of Sclavania on one wall and an equally
large blackboard on another. Devoto Baugh, assisted by
Von Heinen and Stov, led us, pointing out certain things
on the large map and sketching out quick, draftsmanlike
diagrams on the blackboard.

We'd been divided into five teams of two each, each
team at a separate table with its own set of lithographed
maps and photos. My luck, good for the first time in
longer than I cared to remember, was to have me paired
with the lovely, if dangerous-looking lady called Gwendalfa Halgason.

We listened as Baugh told us how unit one, the largest,
led by himself and Stov, would attack the power plant.
Immediately prior to this one of the other elements, from a
site directly west of the fort, a force consisting of New
East Anglianers, Skralangs, and Paratimers, would create
a diversion which should attract attention away from our
targets.

When the power plant was reached by unit one, units
two and three would move in. Unit two, led by Von
Heinen, had as its goal the capture of the Krithian skudders. Unit three's goal was the communications center,
which was to be hit the moment the power died. It was led
by Aelfric and would consist solely of his own people.

When the power plant was under control and had been
temporarily shut down, Devoto Baugh would leave a skele-
ton force to guard it and come to the assistance of units
two and three, should they need it.

"Well, what do you think of the plans?" I asked Gwendalfa when Baugh, at Von Heinen's suggestion, allowed us
a short break for coffee and cigarettes.

She smiled back at me with her lips, though not with
her eyes, and said across the rim of her coffee cup, "I believe it will be successful. Don't you?"

Speaking slowly and choosing my words carefully from
my still limited lexicon, I said, "I have every reason to believe it will. It seems to have been some time in the planning."

"It has," she said, her words chopped short as she
turned to gaze—or more nearly glare—at Devoto Baugh.
When she turned back to me a few moments later, she

said, "Many good men gave up their lives to make this possible. It had better be successful." Then suddenly she drew one of the maps near her and pointed with a long-nailed finger. "What exactly is this? Do you know?"

"It's one of the transformers fed by the . . ."

As I gave her what information I had about the type of power-generation systems used at this Line's level of technology, in this case a steam-driven turbine, I wondered if all the hatred in her were directed at only Devoto Baugh and his Paratimers, or did he and his kind share it with the Dual Allies and the European powers supporting them?

I'd learned that her brother had been an agent of New East Anglian military intelligence somewhere in this area when he was uncovered and taken, ultimately to be tortured to death by the Imperial Sclavanians. Did she feel that Devoto Baugh was responsible for her brother's death?

All I could do then was speculate, for she wouldn't speak further on the subject.

It was nearly midnight when Devoto Baugh finally rapped on the table at the head of the room and said, "This should suffice for tonight. I suggest that all of you get to bed at once and get what sleep you can. The day will begin early tomorrow. There is much to be done." He rose and added, as if as an afterthought, "Good night."

Over what I thought to be the final cigarette of the night, I asked Von Heinen about Gwendalfa.

"It's true that she has little love for Baugh," he admitted, "and not much more for me or Stov. She doesn't like Paratimers and their sort mucking around with her world, if you follow me."

"I'm not certain I do," I told him.

"I think you understand enough of it," he said, and that was all, virtually ordering me to turn out the light.

I didn't reply. I turned out the light.

Though I'm certain that I was as tired as Von Heinen, perhaps more so, I couldn't sleep. Too many thoughts were churning in my mind, too many questions unanswered.

As I lay back on the soft bed, staring at the white ceiling, my eyes becoming adjusted to the darkness, I wondered how many plots were going on in this vast castlelike home of Herr Jurgen's, how many different webs were being spun and broken, how many . . .

Then, almost imperceptibly, I seemed to become aware of another presence in the room, someone other than Von Heinen and myself, yet I could see nothing and I'd heard no sounds of entry.

It was a sensation I'd felt before, when I'd seen, or thought I'd seen, the shadowy, insubstantial form that I'd called "the shadowy man," a thing I thought had come to warn me or advise me several times during the past months, something that had almost made me doubt my sanity. And it was there again, though not a word was spoken, a sound made.

A greater tension filled me as I heard the sounds of movement just outside the door, one voice speaking to another in tones too low for words to be distinguishable.

Had I been warned again? I wondered.

Slowly, carefully I turned my head on the pillow and saw the rectangle of light that seeped around the edges of the door. At the bottom the strip of yellowish light was broken in four places. Two pairs of feet. Standing just outside.

Between the beds that Von Heinen and I occupied was a small, two-drawer night stand and in the second of those drawers I'd placed my personal belongings, which now included a .441-caliber Slean revolver. Instinct told me I should get it, while good sense told me I couldn't be in danger here. Instinct won.

Without giving it much thought, save to know I might regret it later, I alerted my control circuits to prepare for augmentation, and then began a stealthy movement off the bed, my hand fumbling in the semidarkness for the drawer.

Then my knees were on the floor, the bed not having made a sound as I slipped from it. The drawer was open and my fingers were closing around the pistol's butt. Von Heinen was breathing deeply, slowly, regularly, with just a hint of a snore. I feared he might awaken rather abruptly soon.

I heard one of the voices, male, speaking distinctly now;

the words were: *"N'rachateur pa'thieral, natle. M'relim ad haang."*

The language was Shangalis.

Two Timeliners were about to come through to kill me.

A second voice spoke, one fainter and more highly pitched, the voice of a woman, and she was saying that she wasn't certain of the wisdom of their decision, that they should contact "headquarters" before they did such a thing; what real proof did they have that these men were Outtimers?

The male voice—which sounded very familiar—replied as softly, saying he was certain that he'd seen "him" or "his" picture, and it wasn't on *this* Line. Kill them first, he said. Investigations could come later when they'd notified headquarters of their coup, which was certain to get them both a promotion.

The female voice sighed, agreed, and the masculine one said, *"Mashalla na! Ba'tora Devoto Baugh han, Kjemi Stov han."*

When they'd finished with me and Von Heinen, they'd seek out and kill the Paratimer leader, Devoto Baugh, and his assistant, Kjemi Stov.

I went into augmentation, came to my feet as the door opened.

The world slowed, reddened around me.

Then the portly valet named Otto and a sweet-looking girl who appeared to be no more than sixteen stood framed in the yellow torchlight from the hall. Both had Timeliner energy pistols in their hands. Neither had apparently considered the personal danger sufficient to require augmentation.

They didn't until it was too late.

The big Slean exploded in my hand as I pulled the trigger, throwing a heavy leaden slug into the face of the valet. As his skull slowly dissolved under the impact of the spreading lead, I cocked the single-action pistol, pulled the trigger again and put the second slug into the full left breast under the white, starched blouse of the pretty little blonde. Fredericka staggered backward, living seconds longer than Otto, long enough to pull the trigger of her own weapon and send a burst of furious coherent energy coruscating across the room, above, my left shoulder.

I was temporarily blinded as I fired the third slug. Later I found that it had hit the girl just above the navel, exiting through a shattered spine.

As my eyes regained their sight and I came out of augmentation, shifting back to the world's normal perspective, Von Heinen was coming up from the floor to which he'd rolled during the shooting, crying in his native German, "What the hell's going on?"

In the English of RTGB-307 I said quickly, "Timeliners. They tried to kill us." I shoved the smoking pistol into his hand. "Tell them you did it."

"Why?" he demanded as feet came thudding down the hall toward us, voices yelling in the night.

"I'll explain later," I said. "Take the credit now."

Two liveried servants, closely followed by Geoffry Dunstanson appeared in the doorway, shocked and stunned. One of the servants had the presence of mind to snap on the room's lights; then they could clearly see the two broken bodies, and they could see Von Heinen and the gun he held.

"Enemy agents," Von Heinen stammered.

Then Baugh arrived, followed by Herr Jurgen, Kjemi Stov, and a handful of others.

"What is this?" Baugh demanded. He was dressed and in his hand was a weapon never manufactured in this world. Had the two taken us, they might not have been able to take him.

"They're agents," Von Heinen said, giving me a glance meant to be surreptitious. "I was forced to kill them."

The scarred frame of the window in the far wall, the scorched wall and the smoldering curtains were evidence of an Outtime energy blast fired into the room.

"So it would appear," Baugh said, stepping closer to the two corpses and bending to examine them. "But your aim was too killing. I would have liked to question them."

"I—I didn't have time to think about that," Von Heinen said.

"I see," the Paratimer leader replied, then turned to a breathless and pale-faced Herr Jurgen. "I hope you will excuse this, sir," he said. "A regrettable incident of war."

Herr Jurgen's mouth moved, but no words came out.

To Stov, Devoto Baugh said, "See about cleaning this

up," and to Von Heinen he said, "Come to my room. I want a full report now."

Von Heinen didn't look at me, nor speak, as he placed the pistol in the night stand's open drawer and followed the Paratimer out.

Halfway down the hallway, the Paratimer stopped once, turned back to the scene of the shooting and gave me a look that chilled.

How much *did* he know?

11
Lessons, Paratimers, and Blessings

It was nearly an hour, several cigarettes, and two brandies from a bottle donated by Herr Jurgen later when Von Heinen returned to the room we shared. In the meantime, under Kjemi Stov's direction, servants had removed the bodies, swabbed up the blood, and replaced the scorched curtains. The odors of burnt cloth, blistered paint, and cordite still seemed strong in the air.

The German Count came into the room slowly, closed the door behind him, and sat down on the edge of the bed across from me. his face expressionless.

"Well?" I asked in Outtime English.

"He believed me."

"Are you certain?"

Von Heinen shrugged. "I hope so. I mean, he knows there's something not right about you, but he's taking my word you're okay."

"Does he believe you killed them?"

He shrugged again. "He doesn't know how I could have reacted so fast, but I don't think he suspects you're an Augie."

"I see." I lighted another cigarette and poured two tumblers of brandy.

"He and Stov examined the bodies," he went on after taking a long drink of brandy. "They were both augmented, by the way. Timeliners without a doubt."

"The girl seemed awfully young."

"The girl was older than she appeared. You could tell that with her clothes off, though she wasn't so pretty with those holes in her." He took another drink of brandy and got himself a cigarette from my pack.

"What about Baugh's plans?" I asked.

"The raid? He's not surprised at agents being around. Sclavania's crawling with Timeliners, but he doesn't think

119

the raid's been compromised. He believes they really didn't know who we were or they'd have had a bigger force to deal with us."

"He's right. They were acting without orders or the knowledge of their superiors."

"You heard them talking?"

"That's how I knew what they were."

Von Heinen nodded. "Well, the raid's still on as far as Baugh's concerned, though he's going to check with his superiors before anything else develops."

"Who *are* his superiors?" I asked.

"Paratimers higher up in the chain of command. I don't know their names."

"Are you sure?"

"What do you mean?" he demanded.

I sat forward on the edge of the bed, giving him as hard a look as I could, but said nothing.

Shrugging away my gaze, and after sipping brandy again, Von Heinen said, "I've already told you what I know about the Paratimers. Now what can you tell me about the Kriths . . . ?"

It was nearly dawn before fatigue forced us both to sleep, brief though it was. And I still hadn't gotten around to asking Von Heinen why he'd really gotten himself mixed up with inhuman monsters like those so-called androids who only wanted to enslave and/or destroy mankind.

I did dream about it during what little sleep I got.

It could have been no more than an hour after we fell to sleep that servants rushed us both out of bed and hurried us down to the large room we'd first entered upon arriving at the castle. It was barely light outside.

No word was said about the agents who'd been killed during the night, but there was a tension in the air, about the people, and a sense that the security of Tapferkeitenhaven had undergone a stringent change during the past few hours.

An ample breakfast was spread across the tables, with officers, enlisted men and women, and outsiders like An Mona Steolla and myself sitting side by side eating as quickly as possible, Devoto Baugh, looking rested and eager, urging us on.

The Paratimers hurried us out of the room at quick-step and we stayed busy until dark and well past it.

Outside the castle keep in a large, paved courtyard, an area sufficiently large for the parking of a number of motor vehicles, though none were in evidence, some-one had marked upon the pavement with chalk a series of squares, with arrows leading from one to the other, each carefully labeled in Anglisch.

"This is not to scale," Devoto Baugh said as we be-gan to inspect the markings on the pavement. "Sufficient room for that is not available, but this should give you some idea of the area we will have to cover and the time we will have to do it in."

The markings on the pavement represented the area of the Sclavanian fort we were to penetrate, the roads, walkways, buildings, steam-turbine power plant, skud-der pool, and all. We were to walk through the operation.

Devoto Baugh and Kjemi Stov divided us into our three units: Baugh's which would take the power plant; Von Heinen's which would take the skudder pool; Aelfric's which would take the communications center. It was then that I learned that unit two was to be com-posed of Von Heinen, Gwendalfa, Freya, Harold Win-fredson, Faeder Baldwin, the non-com Efor, several others, and myself.

With Devoto Baugh's surprisingly deep voice barking orders, we went through our paces, each of us trying to pretend as best he could that the chalk marks were ac-tually structures.

We continued at this until shortly after noon, most of our movements at a dead run, the slowest at a trot. That he hadn't loaded us down with field packs must have been an oversight on Baugh's part, I thought at the time.

During the morning I'd noticed the Paratimer's eyes on me a number of times, though all he ever said to me concerning the event of the night before was: "Fortunate for you that Albert is such a light sleeper. Had those enemy agents been successful, they might have killed you as well, Franz Anselem."

Had there been sarcasm in his voice? I wondered.

The midday meal, which I managed to share with Gwendalfa, consisted of hot sandwiches and coffee in the courtyard where we'd been running through Devoto Baugh's script, and we were all grateful for the opportunity to sit down, grateful for the food and coffee.

"Well, what do *you* think of it *now?*" Gwendalfa asked me when we were halfway through our sandwiches.

"What do I think?" I said. "Oh, about the same as last night, I suppose. If we have the element of surprise in our favor, it ought to come off well enough, though I expect higher casualties than Devoto Baugh seems to expect, and I'm not as certain as he seems that New East Anglian forces can come in to relieve us after we've taken Fort Lothairin."

"Do you doubt the fighting abilities of New East Anglianers?" she asked.

"Not that at all," I said. "It's just that the logistics of the situation aren't right. And from what I hear, New East Anglia hasn't really a great number of troops it can spare from the fighting along the Neustrian border."

"You seem to know a great deal about this sort of thing," she said, a bare hint of something to her words I couldn't quite decipher.

"I've been in my share of combat situations," I said.

"I'm sure you have, though that's unusual for a Saxonite, wouldn't you say?"

All I could think of saying was, "Not necessarily," but she didn't seem to expect any answer anyway.

For a few moments of silence Gwendalfa sipped at her coffee, nibbled halfheartedly at her sandwich. "What do you think are our chances if they're expecting us?" she asked at last.

"Very poor," I told her. "It seems the only things we have in our favor are surprise and mobility. They're ahead of us in numbers, weapons, and position. If they know we're coming, they'll probably let us walk into a trap and then spring it."

"Do you think they know?"

"I have no reason to suspect they do, but it's stupid to ever underestimate your enemy. And sometimes fatal."

She nodded slowly, bitterly. After the passage of a few more minutes during which I finished my sandwiches and coffee and refilled both our cups, she said. "I'm sorry if I seemed cold toward you last night. I was upset."

"I think I understand."

"You know about my brother? Everyone does."

"I know he was captured by the Sclavanians and turned over to the Imperials. He died at their hands."

"Did you also know he was working on an assignment directly under Devoto Baugh at the time, something related to this mission?"

"I suspected. And you blame Baugh for his death?"

She nodded sharply, the bitterness tight around her eyes again. "I wish I could tell you the whole story, but I can't," she said. "And maybe they're right and I shouldn't feel as I do, but I can't help it. I hate the man and that's the way it is."

I nodded; there seemed no correct words to use.

"I'm sorry, Franz," she said suddenly, trying to smile. "I'm getting into one of my moods again."

"I understand."

"Do you?"

"I do."

As the afternoon wore on, each unit went through the movements it would follow after element three had created the diversion and we had breeched the fences of Fort Lothairin. And this time Baugh did see fit to load us down with equipment, weapons, and the packs we'd be carrying when we made our raid.

He and Stov ran us through our paces until we were ready to drop, and then allowed us to rest while the other units went through theirs—resting to the extent that we were off our feet, though he insisted that we spend our time memorizing every square foot of Fort Lothairin so that we could make our way through it blindfolded if necessary—it was possible that we might have to do the real thing under circumstances as bad.

* * *

The evening meal was pleasant enough, more relaxed than had been the one of the evening before, despite or perhaps because of the killing of the Timeliner agents for which Von Heinen seemed to be held in high honor. I didn't mind. Better the eyes on him than me. And during the meal Devoto Baugh didn't deny us wine when Herr Jurgen offered it, though he cautioned us to be moderate.

After two glasses of the heady wine I actually found myself enjoying the Imperial Sclavanian style of cooking.

When the meal was finished and Herr Jurgen's numerous servants had cleared the table, brandy snifters were placed before each of us and we were all but ordered by the nobleman to join him in a series of toasts that followed, toasts to, first of all, "the noble men from out of Time who have come into our world to aid us in our time of peril," to "our gallant neighbors to the north, the New East Anglianers who, like ourselves, recognize God's true Vicar on Earth," and to "our allies of the more distant north, the Saxonites and New Frisians of the Northern Alliance." He'd been looking at me when he said the last, he at least still firmly believing me to be what Von Heinen had claimed.

The toasts relaxed us all a bit more, excepting Devoto Baugh, who'd grown more tense and silent as the evening wore on, though he did have the presence of mind to offer a toast to "our noble host and ally, Herr Jurgen of Tapferkeitenhaven."

At last, more snifters of brandy later, as Herr Jurgen was in the middle of suggesting that we retire to the sitting room for coffee and cigars, Baugh came to his feet suddenly, half-spilling the brandy that sat at his right hand. Had he not had so little wine during the meal, so little brandy afterward, I would have thought him drunk. Perhaps he was anyway.

"I hate to put a damper on these festivities," he said slowly as if picking his words with great care, "but we must keep in mind that our raid on Fort Lothairin is tomorrow night. We must all be in the very best possible condition. Therefore I suggest that we decline Herr Jurgen's generous offer and retire to our respective apartments to rest. We must rise before dawn tomorrow."

There was no audible grumbling from anyone, but neither were there any sighs of pleasure. I wasn't unhappy with his suggestion; I'd hardly slept the night before and was feeling it.

"I am sorry this must be so," Herr Jurgen said, his florid face more flushed than usual, "but if it is necessary, so be it. I wish you all a good, good night, though first—Faeder Baldwin?" He addressed the diminutive priest who sat across the table from me.

"Yes, Herr Jurgen."

"As a priest of the True God and His True Pope, His Holiness, Gregory XVII, I would like for you to give this final meeting of ours the Lord's blessing."

"I would be most happy, m'lord," Faeder Baldwin replied. "First let us pray," he requested, half bowing his head, clasping his hands together and waiting for the rest of us to do the same. *"Orate, fratres. Dirigator, Domine, oratio mea. . . ."*

When the "Amen" was said and the prayer finished, Faeder Baldwin spread his arms as if attempting to embrace the entire table and said a few additional Latin words: *"Deo gratias. Pax Domini sit semper. . . ."*

"Thank you, Faeder," the Lord of the castle said when the priest resumed his seat. "Now I wish you that good night, and God's speed on your venture tomorrow. I have no doubt that the Lord, His Holy Saints and His Blessed Angels will be on your side."

12
Trier and the Sign of the Purple Cow

The Sclavanian city of Trier was located some forty miles
southwest of Tapferkeitenhaven and less than twenty
miles south of the Sclavanian-New East Anglian border,
had a population of sixty thousand, sat at an altitude of
212 feet above sea level, and was located on the Gray-
stone River.

The Anglisch-language pamphlets Baugh handed out
to us said that it was the business center for an agricul-
tural area devoted to diversified farming, most impor-
tantly, cotton. The raising of livestock and the packing
of meat were also important means of livelihood for the
local population. Industry consisted of textile mills, thread
finishing, cottonseed oil and fertilizer works, as well as a
small-armaments plant producing handguns, and facilities producing trade goods for the Skralang market. Trier
was also noted for the large quantity of excellent-quality
Skralang-made products, brought from the Skralang Nations to the west.

Historically the city had first been an Anglianer
possession, though at the time no more than a trading
post deep in territories controlled by Skralangs. In the
early 1800s Imperial colonists had displaced the
Anglianers and the city of Trier was founded and given
Imperial charter in 1836. In 1842 it was the site of the
signing of the Treaty of Die Rasiermeisse which established the border between the Imperial Colony and the
Skralang Nations, which still stood.

It was also noted as being the birthplace of the famed
colonial artist Adolph Gottfried in 1873 and of the
statesman Ernst Hugoner in 1902.

The city, composed roughly of the Old Town and the
New Town, was an interesting specimen of the mixture
of Old Imperial architecture and of the newer styles of
the twentieth century, we were told. More important was

127

the fact that Trier lay under martial law and was filled with both Colonial Sclavanian and Imperial troops. Martial law had been imposed some six months before when segments of the population of Old Town, fanatically loyal to Pope Gregory, had revolted when Benedictine priests had taken over the city's churches. Martial law had remained partly because of the nearness of Fort Lothairin and the belief that sooner or later the border war would shift in that direction. It was felt necessary that our element pass through Trier on its way to Fort Lothairin, and while there we were to conduct ourselves with the utmost discretion. Still, we weren't expected to be in Trier long.

After breakfast and the briefing we were told to take hot baths and prepare ourselves for the attentions of Herr Jurgen's barbers, who would shave off the beards of the men and shorten their hair, and would help the ladies rearrange their hair more in the Sclavanian style. There were some objections to this, but we realized the necessity of it, and I especially welcomed the prospect of being without a beard again; mine had gotten rather itchy. Finally we were given clothing and identification papers that Herr Jurgen had obtained for us.

In the end we hardly recognized one another and didn't think that Sclavanians would take us for Anglianers from appearance alone.

We were to leave Tapferkeitenhaven prior to noon in several groups and proceed to Trier by dfferent means. One party, dressed in Herr Jurgen's black and orange livery and accompanied by the lord himself and Devoto Baugh, were to travel in the Herr's personal vehicle into the city. Preparations for Jurgen's journey had been made days in advance; he was expected in the city, one of the more notable of the local gentry, visiting his bride-to-be, Mistress Chlodwilda Johannes.

Another group disguised as a miscellanea of local types was to take a railroad train from the nearby village of Conradin into the city.

And still another party, dressed as a surveying team and a road construction crew, was to proceed to the city in vehicles that looked remarkably like official Colonial Sclavanian Road Ministry steam trucks. It was in this latter group that I was placed, along with Gwendalfa, Freya, Wexstan, Harold, Faeder Baldwin, "Apel" Efor Columson, and, of course, Von Heinen himself, who would pose as the chief surveyor. The Paratimers had given him a good command of the local language, Alaman, as well as Anglisch.

When all was ready, Herr Jurgen asked Faeder Baldwin and his own personal priest, a tall, thin man named Faeder Johan, a "Gregorian Catholic" as well, to each bless our ventures and invoke God's assistance. Herr Jurgen saw what we were about to do as an attack not so much on the Imperials and the Kriths as upon the antipope who called himself Benedict XIV. That was okay by me. A holy war is a good an excuse for killing your fellow man as any, I suppose.

"Pax Domini, sit semper vobiscum . . . sed libera nos a malo."

The blessings given and God, the Saints, and the Angels securely on the side of truth, light, and justice, we began to leave the fortress in our separate ways.

Since the means of locomotion of Von Heinen's party was expected to be the slowest, we were the first to leave. Outside in the large, paved courtyard now sat three gray steamers, great trucklike affairs with canvas-covered trailers attached to the steam tractors which had metal-covered cabs perched atop their boilers. Those boilers were already hot and steam was hissing from valves in an almost musical fashion.

Locals, men loyal to the Gregorian faction of the Church and recruited by Herr Jurgen, dressed as employees of the Imperial Road Ministry, sat in the cabs of the vehicles. After instructing Gwendalfa, Freya, Harold, Faeder Baldwin—now wearing no visible signs of his profession—Efor and myself to climb into the back of the leading vehicle, Von Heinen entered the cab. The rest of the party mounted the remaining two vehicles.

After a few moments of waiting, listening to the "chug-chug-chug" of the steamers' engines, the order was given, the driver engaged whatever transmission system the vehicles used and it began to rumble forward. Looking out the back I saw great puffs of steam emitted by the other two steam trucks as they too began to roll.

Gates ahead of us opened; orange-clad servants of the Herr waved us "good-by" and we slowly left the grounds of Tapferkeitenhaven—forever, it was to turn out. For me at least. Some of the others may have returned, but I'll never know whether they did.

The steamers of this Line must have had some things to their advantage, inexpensive fuel, low maintenance costs, something, but whatever advantages they had, speed certainly wasn't one of them. During the trip to Trier the highest speed we reached couldn't have been much over fifteen miles an hour and frequently it was less than that. It was afternoon before we reached our destination, but I don't suppose we were in any great hurry. Not yet.

Faeder Baldwin, who at times seemed quite a resourceful man, produced a pack of cigarettes of a type I hadn't seen before—on the pack was a picture of a bare-breasted, brown-skinned girl wearing a big smile and a colorful sarong, behind her palm trees, and superimposed over the trees the name in Anglisch, *Happy Times*. When the priest passed them around I found them to be much better than I'd smoked before on this Line. Faeder Baldwin informed me that they were manufactured in one of the few remaining Anglisch colonies in Midniwerda—Central America—and were very difficult to come by.

While Gwendalfa, Faeder Baldwin, Efor, and I puffed on the surprising cigarettes, I asked the niece of the First Speaker of the New East Anglian Mootan how familiar she was with Fort Lothairin.

"I've never been on the reservation," she answered, "But I think I know it just about as well as any of us. I've heard enough descriptions of it."

She looked significantly at the maps Leufan Harold Winfredson had spread out on the floorboards of the steamer's trailer.

"You've spent some time in Trier, I take it."

"I've lived there for the past eighteen months."

I knew she'd said words to that effect before, though I had never heard her say what she'd been doing there during that time.

"I take it then that you're one of those who helped prepare the maps?"

Faeder Baldwin gave me a look that was sharp, piercing, but I couldn't imagine what he meant by it.

"I am," she said, though there seemed little pride in her words. "Artos and I and some others supplied most of the information."

"And none of you have been inside?" I asked.

"None who lived to tell about it," she said slowly, bitterly. "Since the Kriths' arrival the security around Fort Lothairin has been of the very highest. I'll give the Imperials that credit."

"Well," I began to ask, Faeder Baldwin giving me another look and a slight shaking of his head. I thought of cutting my questions short, though I couldn't understand why he felt I shouldn't ask them.

"Who'd we get the information from?" Gwendalfa said. "Was that your next question?"

I nodded.

"From our customers. Artos runs a tavern, you'll recall."

I nodded again.

"I have my own business," Gwendalfa said, a heavy bitterness in her voice.

Faeder Baldwin bowed his head. Freya and Harold suddenly seemed very interested in the maps. Efor looked as puzzled as I felt.

"A one-woman business," Gwendalfa continued, almost defiantly, "which deals exclusively with male military personnel." She paused, then said, "Do you think a lonely soldier would be willing to spend a few *tollier* for a night with me?" Her eyes challenged mine.

I started to say something like, "I'm sorry. I didn't mean to pry." But I didn't.

"I'm a common prostitute, Franz Anselem, if that's really your name," Gwendalfa said without allowing any of the bitterness to leave her voice, "though I believe I ply my trade more for the benefit of New East Anglia than for monetary gain."

I shrugged. "Women have been doing it for centuries, and not always for such motives."

"Oh, my dear Franz, my motives may not be as pure as you think."

I shrugged again. "I suppose that's your business."

"It certainly is!"

Faeder Baldwin crushed out the butt of his cigarette. Freya and Harold ventured to raise their heads from the maps. Efor continued to inspect his fingernails.

Gwendalfa, still with all that bitterness, said to them, "The ostriches can pull their heads up out of the sand now."

"I'm sorry," Faeder Baldwin said. "This is no business of ours."

"Isn't it?" Gwendalfa said enigmatically. Then she turned to peer into my eyes again, her brown ones bright even in the shadows of the steamer's trailer. "And what about you, *Franz Anselem?* Now you know what I am. What are you?"

The others, who knew me to be an Outtimer, shot me a startled set of looks.

"It's an open secret," I said, "except to Devoto Baugh. I hope it's closed to him."

"Then you're no Saxonite?" Gwendalfa asked. "I never thought you were."

I shook my head.

"You're a Paratimer like Devoto Baugh?" she asked.

"I'm neither a Paratimer nor like Devoto Baugh," I told her. "But I'm not from this world."

"And Baugh thinks you're a—a native?" she asked.

I nodded.

"Why?"

"Why is he kept in the dark?" I asked.

It was Gwendalfa's turn to nod.

The four others in the rear of the steamer became even more attentive. They apparently didn't know why the ruse was being pulled either. I wondered how much of it should be told.

"I suppose you could say I'm a friend of Albert von Heinen," I told them. "At least we met in another Timeline. Now it suits my purposes to work with him and it suits his purposes to keep my identity from his superiors."

"And what are those purposes?" Gwendalfa asked.

"I can't tell you," I said slowly, "though I assure you

that our interests don't run counter to those of New East Anglia. Neither of us have any love for the Kriths *or* their allies."

"I see," Gwendalfa said. "I think."

"I'm sorry, but it's best that I don't tell you any more than that," I said.

"Very well."

Faeder Baldwin passed around his cigarettes again and each of us took one this time, Freya and Harold included, and each of us accepted a drink of sherry when the priest passed a bottle of that around as well.

Then we relaxed as the steamer made its slow and ponderous way across the Sclavanian countryside under an autumn sun, chugged and puffed toward Trier, Fort Lothairin, and the darkness of the coming night.

In many respects Trier was an odd mixture of the medieval and the modern—modern by local standards. Although the city was only something over a hundred and fifty years old, much of its construction was of a style some centuries old even then: massive stone structures sat alongside buildings that were little more than barely habitable hovels; narrow, winding streets with hardly the width to pass a single vehicle the size of our steamers; business houses juxtaposed with private dwellings; lack of proper sewage and sanitation; Gothic and forbidding, the Old Town, it was called. The center of downtown Trier wasn't at all an attractive place.

Outside the heart of the city, however, concessions had been made to a more advanced technology. The streets were wider, most of them sufficient to allow two-way traffic and some of them even as wide as four lanes. Buildings were taller and composed of more modern materials: brick, concrete, steel, and glass combined in different and sometimes bizarre fashions as if the architects who designed the newer quarters of the city have been allowed to give their imagination free reign. Shopping areas, broad and well-lighted, were separated from office buildings; tall apartment houses helped relieve the overcrowded conditions so manifest in the center of the city; government buildings numerous, large, ornate, and conspicuous, as were the churches and a handful of cathedrals.

Conspicuous too was the city's larger number of both Sclavanian and Imperial soldiers. These were easily distinguished from the local citizenry who for the most part were dressed in rather simple clothing of dull colors, save for a few of the gentry who affected more striking clothing in what I was informed was the Continental Imperial style. Almost all the men were clean shaven.

That the city was under martial law had been told to us before leaving Tapferkeitenhaven, but if we hadn't been told we would have learned it when our three-steamer convoy reached the outskirts of the city and was stopped by a roadblock where Sclavanian soldiers forced us all to climb out and present our papers. We and our papers passed their inspection without difficulty—Herr Jurgen had seen that we were provided with good forgeries, may his God bless him.

Then we traveled into the city proper, through the outer, newer portions, and then into Old Town, hovels, stone, and stink. West of what Gwendalfa told us to be the very center of Old Town, the steamers pulled into a large government parking area, where Von Heinen, in his role as the government official in charge of the convoy, presented our papers again. He was told, so Gwendalfa translated for us, that we would be permitted to take on water and fuel and to park our steamers there for a while, but that they would have to be moved before the vehicles that normally used the parking facilities returned for the evening. He came back and told us we could climb out of the steamers' trailers.

In order to avoid being conspicuous and to avoid any possibility of our getting into trouble with the local authorities through ignorance of language, customs, and law, the majority of the party was ordered by Von Heinen to go a block or so down the street to a large cinema. They were to go in groups of two or three or singly and were told to leave the cinema over a period of fifteen to twenty minutes some three hours later. We would all meet back at the steamer park, eat a meal we would procure then, and leave the city, heading west toward our final rendezvous. He placed Harold Winfredson in charge of this operation, and told Gwendalfa and myself to remain with him.

When the others had started on their way to the cinema, the three of us stood in the shadow of the first steamer while its valves hissed faintly under falling pressure, our jackets pulled tightly around our bodies, for a cold wind was blowing through the city now despite the sunshine that created sharp, deep shadows. The clouds of the previous day were gone from the skies now, if not from our minds.

"Gwendalfa," Von Heinen said in Anglisch, "you're familiar with Artos' inn, aren't you?"

Her smile was a strange one, but the words were even, undistinguished. "Yes, I'm familiar with it."

"Would you take us there, please?" he asked.

"Are you certain you want to be seen with me?" she asked, perhaps a little bitterness in her voice now, though she managed to keep her smile.

"I have no objection," he said. "Eric?"

"So that's your name," Gwendalfa said to me.

"A lot of people know me by that one," I told her, "and I have no objection to being seen anywhere with a woman as attractive as you."

She smiled again, but there was no humor in it. "Even if she's one of the most notorious whores in the city?"

"Even then," I said.

"Would you show us the way?" Von Heinen asked.

Without speaking, Gwendalfa headed left down the street, in the direction away from the cinema.

The area we were in now separated—or joined, if you want to look at it that way—the city's two divisions, the older inner circle, the newer outer circle. It was a mixture of the two. Some of the buildings were of the older, medieval style, and others were of a more modern design. The cinema was a combination of the two: an older, blocky, rough-hewn building on to which had been placed a contemporary façade, glass and shiny metal over the worn stone.

There was a red-and-blue-clad policeman on every corner and two soldiers for every policeman and there was about the city an air of repression and something bordering on hostility, even some distance as we were from the heart of the rebellious Gregorian quarter. The people we met on the streets were mostly of a Nordic, Teutonic racial type, blond or brown hair, fair of skin, though there was a smattering of darker, southern Europeans and more than just a few who could have only been of Skralang blood, pure and half-breed. Most of them, clad in their drab and all-but-colorless clothing, looked at us suspiciously, save for a few of the better, more stylishly dressed types, Teutonics all, who chose to ignore us—excepting one or two who recognized Gwendalfa and had the boldness to raise a hand or yell a greeting to her.

Gwendalfa led us some three blocks in one direction, then angled off down a side street and led us another three dark blocks in toward the heart of the old city, where darker skins were more prevalent, and to a small building nestled between two larger ones and before which hung a sign painted with the image of a large-uddered cow, purple in color, and obscure lettering I couldn't read. Gwendalfa told us—or rather me, since I assumed Von Heinen could read the sign—that this place was called "The Sign of the Purple Cow" and it was the inn of Artos Alaricson, or Rudolph Genseric, the name he used here.

"Gentlemen," she said, pausing before the door.

Since I was closer I opened the door, and she preceded us into the inn.

It was dark and smoky, a place of candles and torches and open beams above and plastered walls around, concrete and sawdust below, a place of the odors of beer and wine and roasted meat and hot bread and human sweat, a place of men clad in an assortment of clothing from the rags of a beggar who knelt just inside the door and held out a metal cup to the colorful lace and frills of a drunken dandy who pounded on his table with a metal tankard and demanded another jug of "Rudolph's" best wine, a place where a half-clad girl whose parentage might have been partly Skralang danced on a low stage under two incandescent spotlights while a young, fair-skinned man played on a guitar in a style that could have been called "flamenco," a place where another woman, twice the age of Gwendalfa, with painted face and tight clothing, plied her trade in the semidarkness, hoping to find a night's trick among the more drunken.

As the doors closed behind us and our eyes began to adjust to the large room's dimness, half a dozen male voices called "Gwendalfa" or merely "Gwen."

Gwendalfa yelled back to them, her face broken by a wide, wild smile, a grin of flashing teeth, her long, dark hair swirling behind her turning head, while with one arm she clung to Von Heinen and with the other to me.

Carefully steering us with her arms, she led us across the room to the far end of the bar where there were fewer people, pounded on the bar with open hand and called, "Rudolph, Rudolph . . ."

A few moments later a heavy-set, bearded man in a stained leather apron came bustling out of the back of the tavern.

It took me a few long moments to believe that *he* was someone I knew, had met at Tapferkeitenhaven. It was more than merely a change of clothing, more like a total change of personality, that made the difference between the Anglianer officer Artos Alaricson and the tavernkeeper Rudolph Genseric.

"Ah, Gwennie," he cried, rushing up to her and kissing her across the bar as if it had been weeks, not hours, since he'd seen her last. He spoke a few words to her, she to him, and then she introduced us, Ferdinand Gottfried and Conrad Albertric, as I heard the names. I was Conrad, I think.

A few moments of unintelligible pleasantries went by and then "Rudolph" sat a tankard of ale before each of us, urging us to drink, drink, drink. At least I think that's what he was saying.

Then, while we were doing as he requested, he whispered to us in Anglisch, "Third room on the left, top of the stairs." This said, he took away our now empty tankards, refilled them to overflowing, made another, more open gesture toward the stairs at the end of the room and went to see about another customer who'd begun to pound on his table.

"We'd better do as he says," Gwendalfa whispered, took a deep drink of the dark, pungent ale and broke away from us, leading the way up the dark stairs, and an equally dark hallway to the third door on the left. She paused, knocked twice rapidly. We waited.

After a long pause we heard the shuffling of feet on the other side of the door, again a silence, then a voice speaking a single word of query, *"Voe?"*

"Glitterstraggin," Gwendalfa answered.

The door clicked from the inside, opened inward. The light of incandescent bulbs spilled out, bright and yellow in the darkness of the hall.

"Come in," Devoto Baugh said in Anglisch.

Inside, awaiting our arrival, were the Paratimer leader, Kjemi Stov, Geoffry Dunstanson, Wexstan, Herr Jurgen, and the Skralang, An Mona Steorra, dressed in the garb common to the lower classes of Sclavania.

"So we were assembled," the Paratimer leader said as he closed the door behind him.

"So we are," Von Heinen agreed. "I'm surprised you got here this far ahead of us."

"Those steamers of yours are hardly the fastest means of transportation available," Baugh replied, "even on *this* Line."

The manner in which he said those last four words did nothing to endear him to the others present in the room. The locals seemed to take an unvoiced offense at them, though I don't believe they'd had any particular love for the Paratimer even prior to this.

"No problems?" he asked Von Heinen.

"None."

"Very good. We seem to have gotten this far without difficulty. I hope we can do as well with the next stage." Von Heinen nodded.

"And exactly what is your next stage, if I may ask?" Herr Jurgen, apparently ill at ease in the presence of the Skralang, asked.

"A resumption of our journey west," Devoto Baugh said. "As soon as there is cover of darkness we shall continue on, planning to be in place outside Fort Lothairin by the last hour before midnight."

"What about the other elements?" Von Heinen asked.

"They are proceeding with relative smoothness," Baugh said, "although element number three has had some delay. Nothing serious."

We were element one, by Devoto Baugh's designation. The element proceeding from the west of Fort Lothairin was two and the one from the northwest was element three. It was three that was to create the diversion that would give elements one and two the opportunity to stage their attacks at separate points along the fort's perimeter. We needed number three very badly. Even I knew that.

"Then it would appear that my services are no longer needed," Herr Jurgen said, shifting nervously in his chair.

"For a while longer, sir," Baugh said. "At least I would like you to remain available in the city until we are all outside its limits. Then you may consider yourself free of any further obligation. I would suggest that you return to Tapferkeitenhaven at once."

"That is exactly my intention," the Sclavanian nobleman said. "Anyone caught outside his home this night will be under the gravest suspicion."

"Of that I have no doubt," the Paratimer said.

"And your means of escape?" Herr Jurgen asked.

"If we need them, these are provided for," Devoto Baugh said.

Early in our stay at Tapferkeitenhaven the Paratimer leader had told us that once Fort Lothairin was in our hands, New East Anglian forces poised only a few miles beyond the border that separated the two nations would sweep across the less-than-forty miles and complete seizure of the fort. I didn't believe it. I'd said as much to Gwendalfa earlier. From what little I knew of the situation I didn't believe New East Anglia to be in a position to do even that, nor did I believe that the Mootan or General Breccason or the Anglianer chiefs of staffs would be willing to commit so great a breach of the rules by which this border war had thus far been fought, not at this stage of the game, anyway. I believed the Anglianers involved in this mission to be sacrificial lambs to be yielded to the Sclavanians and the Imperials once the primary Paratimer goal had been achieved: the destruction of the Krithian HQ and the capture of its skudders and other Outtime equipment, and its Outtime personnel, if possible. Devoto Baugh and Kjemi Stov didn't really give a damn about what happened to Aelfric and

Freya and Gwendalfa and Artos and all the others once they'd gotten their hands on what they wanted.

But was I in any position to be critical of them?

Did I have any more noble intents in mind?

I didn't, though I thought that I could justify my means—weren't my ends worth it?

But surely they each, Baugh and Stov and Von Heinen, in each of their separate ways, must have felt the same way.

God, how relative is morality!

During the hour or so that followed, in the small room above The Sign of the Purple Cow, Devoto Baugh once more went over our plans. From time to time Artos would drop in on us and during one of his visits he brought us a huge platter of sandwiches, went back down and returned with two gigantic pitchers of ale. We ate well, we for whom this might be a last meal. Artos had also arranged for several street urchins whom he trusted to deliver hampers of sandwiches to the steamers prior to our departure from the steamer park later in the day.

Finally, satisfied with our food, though apprehensive of the next few hours, Devoto Baugh dismissed us, though only after a quiet, private talk with Von Heinen in a corner. I could hear nothing of what was said, though I noticed the senior Paratimer's eyes on me more than should have been usual and a very frequent shaking of Von Heinen's head. When the *tête-à-tête* was over, Baugh nodded as if grudgingly; Von Heinen smiled and patted him on the back. I was allowed to leave the room alive. Von Heinen must have talked well in my favor.

It was later than midafternoon when our steamers chugged to life, raised a head of steam, and slowly rolled out of the park and back onto the streets of Trier. We headed west out of the city.

Fort Lothairin lay some ten miles or so southwest of Trier, but we covered only about half that distance by steam-driven vehicle. Five miles beyond the last military check point the steamer's driver turned off onto a dirt road that led back into nearly virgin forest—lumbering hadn't yet hit hard on this side of the city, as it had to the north and east.

A mile or so south on the dirt road the steamers took another turn, this time into even denser forests, down a road that became a trail that became a path that vanished. The steamers ground to a halt; the engines were allowed to bleed their steam into the air while the petro-fueled boilers cooled. The vehicles would be left there to cool, to rust, for none of us ever expected to come back for them. They'd served their purpose.

"This area has been thoroughly mapped and scouted," Von Heinen told us as we knelt in the small clearing where the steamers had come to a halt. "We should encounter no obstacles for the next four miles. After that it's possible we'll run into one of the infrequent patrols sent outside the fort's fences. But if we stay away from the roads we should have no trouble avoiding them. And we need to cover most of that four miles before dark. There'll be few enough paths for us."

He looked at each of us as if asking for final questions or comments before moving on: Gwendalfa, Freya, Faeder Baldwin, Harold, Efor, the others who'd been in the other two steamers. No one said a word. Words enough had already been said.

Once guns and equipment had been distributed, Von Heinen checked his watch, ordered each of us to synchronize his own watch with his, and then ordered us to move out. Gwendalfa and I were to take the point at the beginning. He and Harold Winfredson would bring up the rear. Later he would trade places with Gwendalfa.

As before, Von Heinen wanted me with my augmentation in the lead, though I hoped that this time I wouldn't need it—not until we were inside the fences of Fort Lothairin.

And I didn't relish having to use it then, but I knew I would, to suit my own purposes if nothing else.

I had a long way to go before the sun rose, on this Earth or on any other across the Lines.

13
"Alarums in the Night"

The sky was clean and clear and the stars seemed impossibly bright, a painted sky or a piece of some black material pierced with holes through which lights from some grander world than ours shown, or like jewels embedded in black velvet. There was no moon. It had set early.

There was a display of meteors, bright pinpoints of light flashing out of the sky, seeming to come from the constellation Leo like a fleet of attacking starships or a sign from pagan gods of approaching disaster.

We sat on the cold ground, wrapped in warm clothing, though shivering from the cold and from something more. We glanced at our watches and then up at the sky and then ahead through the forest where we could see the lights of Fort Lothairin beyond the electrified barbed-wire fences. And we waited.

My arms were folded across my chest, my gloved hands tucked under my arms. A woolen cap was pulled down over my ears. My carbine was in my lap, my .441 Slean on my hip, six hand grenades dangled from my belt. I carried no additional equipment.

Gwendalfa sat beside me on my left and Faeder Baldwin on my right. We'd just sipped away the last of his sherry and wished for more.

The little priest had given us one last blessing as we'd neared this place and then requested that Von Heinen give him a weapon. This was his war too, for this *was* a war against the antipope who called himself Benedict XIV and it was his duty, as a Soldier of God, to wage His war on Earth however he could.

Von Heinen asked him whether he knew how to use a gun. When the priest displayed half a dozen marksmanship medals, Von Heinen ordered that he be given one of the extra carbines and an ammunition belt. The

143

priest thanked him, loaded and cocked the weapon after dry-firing it several times, then slung it across his shoulder as the last stretch of the march toward Fort Lothairin continued.

Now we were there, the last hour before midnight less than sixty minutes away.

And we waited.

"Eric," Gwendalfa whispered. "That is your name, isn't it?"

"Yes," I said, not wanting to waste time explaining my "names."

"Forgive me for being such a bitch. You've done nothing to cause me to take my bitterness out on you."

"That's okay."

"No, it isn't," she said, "but I don't guess there's much we can do about it now."

"I appreciate that, Gwendalfa."

"There'll be other—" she started to say, then bit off the words. "Who am I kidding? There may never be another chance. . . ."

We both looked at our watches in the starlight. Their luminous dials told us we had forty-three minutes before the diversion began.

"We have time enough," she said slowly, softly. "Come with me." She began to rise.

I thought I should protest, but . . . As she said, there was time.

Von Heinen looked at us as we started back into the forest, away from the line we had formed facing the fence.

"Thirty minutes," I whispered to him.

He nodded in reply, a ghost of a smile on his lips.

Faeder Baldwin said something in Latin, a blessing, I think.

A hundred yards, no more than that, Gwendalfa led me back into the forest, not far, but far enough.

"I wish we had more time, Eric," she said, stepping away from me and dropping her carbine to the leaves and pine needles that formed the forest's floor. "We'll use what time we have."

She didn't speak, nor did I, as she unclipped her web belt, dropped it, removed her jacket. I started to protest when she removed her blouse, to tell her it was too cold for that, but held my tongue. If this was the way she wanted it, then this was the way it would be. Her boots and then her trousers followed her blouse and she stood in the cold night air in only her undergarments.

"You know I'm a whore," she said as she unsnapped her bra. "I've done this with hundreds of men."

"I know."

"But this—well, it's different, Eric." She slipped her panties down her hips, her legs, kicked them aside.

"I know that too," I said, looking at her for long moments before I began to undress.

There was a strangeness in the air, something more than the chill of the night and the cold light of the stars, something beyond the rustling of the night wind in the upper limbs of the pines and the sounds that came, faint with distance, from the fort, something I couldn't identify, but would remember. A sense, perhaps, of enchantment.

In the darkness and starlight, Gwendalfa stood naked and beautiful waiting for me, her body a lighter shape against the trees and brush behind her, the darkness of her hair as it stirred in the cold breeze, soft curves of light across her breasts and waist and hips and thighs, shadows under those breasts, rounding into her stomach, the blackness of the triangle between her thighs, her eyes bright as if they too were stars. She was half human, half a strange forest nymph come to make love to me for some purpose unknowable to mortals. I shivered as I dropped my jacket to the earth, but from something more than the cold.

As my clothing joined the dark pile of hers, I felt the cold raise bumps along my arms and legs. Then I stepped toward her and forgot about the cold, as I think she had forgotten about it.

We stood together for a long while, our bodies pressing together, blending, melting, merging as were our lips, and then Gwendalfa slowly slipped from my grasp and lowered herself to the leaves of the forest floor.

"The time, Eric," she whispered.

"I know," I said. "I know."

* * *

We waited until the last possible moment and then dressed quickly, terribly aware of both the shortness of time and the cold breeze against our skin.

"I'm glad," she said to me, looking up at me, her eyes still as bright as they'd been before.

"So am I."

We slung our carbines across our shoulders, exchanged one last kiss, and headed back the hundred yards to Von Heinen's line.

We were halfway there when . . .

The quiet and darkness of the night were torn to shreds.

From somewhere some distance away, far beyond the nearer buildings we could see through the fence, came a great flash of light followed by a tremendous roar and a shaking of the earth. For a moment or two I thought I was going to be both blinded and deafened by it. I hurried forward.

"That's some diversion," I said, but I doubted Gwendalfa understood me.

Von Heinen was on his feet when I reached him and was yelling something. I could tell he was yelling because his mouth was open, but I could hardly hear what he was saying. I didn't really need to know. None of us did. We acted.

So did the others of our unit and the other two units of our element.

Several hundred feet to our right in the forest lay Devoto Baugh, Kjemi Stov, Geoffry Dunstanson, Artos Alaricson, and the other members of the largest unit, number one, whose goal was the power plant. Some distance to our left was Aelfric's unit three, the one designated to take the communications center.

Unit one moved out first, hit the fence in three places simultaneously with thermal grenades that burned and melted their way through the metal strands, creating a great deal of light and arcing of electricity, but little noise, but it would have taken a very great deal of noise to be heard over the sounds coming now from the far side of the fort: smaller explosions, the roar of a great fire coming into being, the burp! and chatter! of handguns, machine guns, the crump! of a mortar, the boom! of a hand grenade and even the yells and screams of men and women.

There was no question that element three had arrived on time and was doing its best—and a bit more!—to create the diversion required by our element and the other, some distance away, bent on some other errand.

A large selection of the electrified fence had fallen before the onslaught of unit one, collapsing into smoldering, sizzling piles of metal, some little more than slag. The men of unit one, led by Devoto Baugh, a submachine gun in his hand chattering, swarmed across the broken fence, headed toward the power plant and toward a guard post that sat beside the large, unlighted warehouse across a wide firebreak from the power plant.

The sentries had come staggering out of their hut, half-asleep during the dull duty near the fort's perimeter, raising their weapons and yelling incoherent words. Geoffry Dunstanson's submachine gun chattered as had Baugh's and the stunned guards staggered back in bloody surprise, some falling, grasping wounds, screaming. Other weapons joined Geoffry's and the perimeter guards died before having the opportunity of taking down even one of the Anglianer attackers.

Then Geoffry was joining the rest of his unit as they stormed the power plant, Devoto Baugh in the lead, screaming like a madman and cutting down anyone in his way with his blazing submachine gun. Hardly the quiet man we'd known at Tapferkeitenhaven, but I wasn't surprised.

Those of us in unit two stood on the edge of the forest, yards from the broken fence, waiting for the time to come when we'd move out. It wasn't long now. My palms had gone dry and my mouth felt as if it were filled with cotton. There was an angriness in my stomach that wasn't butterflies, though I couldn't have described what it was. I knew that in a very few minutes it would all be gone. When I began moving I'd forget it all, concentrate only on what had to be done, what I had to do to achieve my goals and to stay alive.

Gwendalfa stood beside me, a quietness in her now, her face bathed in the red and orange light of the distant fire. She was an avenging angel, a dark-haired

Valkyrie satisfied in seeing something done at last to destroy her enemies.

She watched the men who ran across the clear area toward the great doors of the power plant, then batter them down, watched the tan-and-olive-clad soldiers coming to protect the plant, dashing into the light to be cut down by the New East Anglianer marksmen Devoto Baugh had stationed just beside the fence, watched her friend Artos Alaricson take a Sclavanian bullet in his chest, spin on his feet, cursing and then falling, perhaps dying. She sobbed loudly when this happened. I put my arm around her shoulder. That was all I could do.

In moments, in hardly more time than it takes to tell it, Devoto Baugh's unit one was inside the power plant and from there we could now hear the chattering of submachine guns, the less rapid firing of semiautomatic carbines and pistols, then the roar of a well-placed grenade or explosive charge. A dynamo let out a great metallic scream of agony that rose above all the other cacophony that filled the night. Lights across the area flickered, dimmed, but didn't go out. Moments later the metallic screams had died away and the standing lights along the firebreak were again as bright as ever.

"Let's go!" Von Heinen yelled and from some distance away, to the left, I heard another voice that was probably Aelfric's yelling a similar thing.

We headed forward at a trot through the verge of the forest, to the fence, through it and onto the reservation.

Not far behind us, I could see as I glanced over my shoulder, was unit three, Aelfric, Wexstan, An Mona Steorra dressed now in his usual poncho and leather trousers, a carbine in one hand, a bright-bladed knife in the other. Some Sclavanians wouldn't die easily this night. The rest of unit three was on his heels.

The area of our concern consisted of nine buildings and the guard hut. To the left of the firebreak stood the guard post nestled under the bulk of a warehouse equally as large as the power plant opposite it. Beyond that warehouse was the skudder pool, surrounded by a high fence, though this one wasn't believed to be electrified. The skudder pool consisted of several closed sheds, the roofs of which joined to make them effectively a single, partitioned structure. Beyond the skudder pool was another warehouse.

To the right of the firebreak was the power, plant which was already being taken by Devoto Baugh's unit. Beyond that were four smaller structures set two by two. The nearer right, hidden behind the bulk of the power plant, was an electronics repair shop; the near left was a supply room. The far-right building of the four, also hidden from our view, was a small electronics warehouse. The building to the far left was the critical one of the cluster—it was believed to be the Krithian communications center for all Timeliner operations on this Line. That was Aelfric's goal. Beyond the cluster of buildings was another large building and an even larger parking area filled with various types of military vehicles. A motor pool. Our only concern with it was to see that the vehicles weren't used against us. A few of Aelfric's men would fill that place with explosive charges.

The layout of this area of Fort Lothairin was fresh in my mind from the maps and aerial photographs I'd seen so frequently during the last few days, and now were fleshed out into three dimensions as I saw the structures themselves, lighted by the mounted lamps that lined the firebreak and by the garish light of the blazing fire that now towered over the buildings it consumed.

My carbine was in my hand, safety off, cocked, when I caught up with Von Heinen who'd taken the lead. Now we were into the firebreak. There was hardly any opposition before us, only a few scattered Sclavanians and Imperials not taken by Devoto Baugh's men—Was it too easy? I was asking myself. Were they letting us in . . . ?

"When are you augmenting?" the German asked in gasps as we ran, pausing briefly to cut down a foolhardy Sclavanian who showed himself, both our weapons firing at once.

"Not until I have to."

Now, more quickly than we'd expected, we were within hand grenade range of the fence that surrounded the skudder pool, the locked gates, and of the men who'd come running out of the sheds, armed and ready to defend the Outtime vehicles in their care. I wondered how many of these men were locals, Sclavanians and Imperials, and how many of them were really Timeliners brought in by the Kriths, men whom I might know, might have worked with in the past. Then I had no more time to think of that.

In the hellscape of red-orange, flickering firelight, long and strangely illuminated shadows, of exploding bombs and firing handguns, the smell of burning oil and wood and plastic and flesh thick in the air, a cacaphony of noise composed of booms! and cracks! and sizzles! and screaming of wounded, dying men, Von Heinen and I both knelt, dropped our weapons and pulled grenades from our belts. Small-arms fire popped! into the dirt around us. Other weapons from behind covered our movements, defended us. As if from long practice, together we pulled the grenades' pins, drew back our arms, pitched the bombs into the air—and threw ourselves onto the earth of the firebreak.

The grenades went off almost simultaneously, two or three yards apart, caught in the mesh of the wire fence, ripping, tearing, bringing down a section of the fence wide enough for three or four men to enter abreast.

Then we were on our feet again, spitting dust and tasting oily sand, our weapons in our hands and firing again. The rest of unit one, Harold, Gwendalfa, Freya, Faeder Baldwin, Efor, and the others were on our heels as we leaped across the broken fence and stormed the skudder pool, all but stumbling and falling across the dead and dying bodies of men we'd killed to make our entry.

By the time we were inside the multistructure of the sheds our number had been reduced by a third, the mangled, broken, bloody bodies of Anglianers fallen across those of Sclavanians, Imperials, Timeliners.

Faeder Baldwin lay dying behind us, a ragged string of holes across his chest and abdomen. Harold limped and almost collapsed from a jagged wound in his left thigh. Von Heinen's right arm ran with blood, though the index finger of that hand kept pulling back the trigger of his submachine gun. There was a redness of her own blood in Freya's blond hair, a fragmentation wound across her scalp that hadn't slowed her.

Yet still I felt, *It shouldn't be this easy.*

I stood for a moment gasping for breath, Gwendalfa half a pace behind me, her carbine still firing through the wooden doorway before us. The Fiurer carbine in my hand had roared until its firing pin had clicked on an empty chamber and as I paused I threw in a fresh clip, while Von Heinen kicked open the last door, sprayed the interior of the shed with bullets. Gwendalfa did the same. Then she and I followed Von Heinen in.

And there in the shed, under the row of naked incandescent bulbs that ran in a line slung just below the ceiling, reflecting their light, was a huge, glasslike bubble mounted on a small, dark base, a squashed spheroid with a hatch and leatherlike seats inside and a control panel for the pilot—and a series of projections upon the base I'd never seen before, bright and shiny metal as if but recently installed.

We'd found the skudders.

We'd also found one of the Krithian masters, standing only inches from the device, shock and fear on his olive noseless face, his great pupilless eyes wide. His naked body shown under the lights like metal, the sweat of fear. He was unarmed and seemed too frightened to think of self-skudding, though that was a natural protective action of his race. Wasn't it?

I shot him three times, slowly, carefully, precisely. Once in the face, once in the middle of the left breast and once in the abdomen, just above the navel. He moaned once as he fell to the floor. Then he died.

I hadn't fully realized until that moment how much I'd come to hate his kind, an insane, irrational hatred that only later would I come to despise in myself, justified as I might think my hatred to be.

The others of our unit poured into the shed, stopped and gaped in awe of the dead being and of the machine.

It wasn't that the skudder was all that large or imposing, but it was obviously the work of a technology far in advance of that of this world, and the Anglianers could see that instantly. And they had some idea of the capabilities of the vehicle, of its ability to pass from this world into others, Earths different from this one, parallel worlds split off from the main branch of Time by *either/or*.

And if they'd doubted the Paratimers' stories of a race of non-humans behind the Timeliners and the war that now erupted across the borders of their nation, they could no longer doubt. The creature who lay dead on the floor before them had never been born from a woman's womb, had never come to life on *this* Earth.

"Mathers," Von Heinen said, speaking only my name and giving me a significant look. I knew what he meant. This one was *our* skudder.

"Okay, spread out," he yelled. "Let's find the others."

Just as the party was about to do as he orderd, the ground shook under our feet again, the air roared with sounds an order of magnitude louder than before, and the shed was plunged into darkness as the incandescent bulbs faded to a dim yellow and then out.

"They got the power plant, and damned good," someone said unnecessarily.

Then there was a brief respite from the sounds of war from outside, a moment of shocked silence as all of Fort Lothairin was plunged into the same darkness, a darkness unevenly lighted by the great fires outside.

"There are auxiliaries," Von Heinen said.

"Probably," I agreed, fingering the hot barrel of my carbine, wondering when I should go into augmentation. I'd held off for a long time. "And they should come on automatically."

With the power plant knocked out, though probably not seriously damaged, Baugh would have accomplished his primary goal. The time between the planting of the last bomb and his arrival where we stood could only be a matter of brief minutes. I'd hoped to be gone before he came.

In the darkness I took a few steps in the direction of the skudder. The time had almost come.

Then came sounds of more people entering the skudder pool's shelters, the yelling of voices in Anglisch, the cry of our code word *leoghin*. I recognized none of the voices.

"*Leoghin*," Von Heinen yelled back, something strange

in his voice. "Mathers," he called to me in Outtime English, "watch yourself."

"What do you mean?" I asked in the same language. I brought my carbine once more into firing position, took a few more steps toward the skudder, readying my augmentation.

Von Heinen didn't answer.

Since it was one of the models equipped for it, I shifted the Fiurer carbine from semiautomatic to full automatic. It held a nearly full magazine of ammunition. I had the sensation I was going to need every bit of it.

Somewhere not too far away an auxiliary generator, its system triggered by the power failure, came into operation with a loud coughing of a petro-powered engine and an unpleasant, grumbling electrical hum. The row of bulbs inside the shed flickered to glowing, though dim and yellow.

But that was light enough.

The interior of the shed was a tableau: I was nearest the skudder; Von Heinen only a few feet from me; Gwendalfa, Harold, Freya, half a dozen other Anglianers between Von Heinen and the shed's door. We'd all turned to see who it was entering, who yelled "Leoghin" again in an outlandish accent as bad as mine.

"Mathers!"

The word was a scream, a yell, a curse.

"Mathers!" it came again.

Two men stood in the doorway and neither of them had been born in this Timeline—and maybe neither of them were men.

One was Devoto Baugh, his clothing tattered and stained, his face blackened with soot and ash and spotted with tiny burns. But it wasn't him I saw.

The other, who also held an automatic pistol in his hand, was tall, thin, his skin a cadaverous white even under the yellow light in the shed. He'd never really looked quite human to me before. Now I was certain he wasn't.

I'd hoped that Mica was dead.

I could tell he wasn't.

"Good-by, Gwen," I yelled and would have liked to have said a great deal more, but there wasn't time. I cut in my augmentation and squeezed the carbine's trigger simultaneously. A stream of bullets burst from its muzzle, headed for Mica and Devoto Baugh.

They leaped out of the way, both of them going into augmentation only instants after I did.

Von Heinen must have expected this, or at least feared it. He must have known that Mica would be among the Paratimers involved in this venture; I should have guessed it days before. He'd really have been Von Heinen's superior. He'd have been on this Line.

And the German nobleman hadn't seen fit to tell me that. There was probably a hell of a lot more he hadn't seen fit to tell me, despite the confessions he'd made. And if I felt any loyalty, any obligation toward him that wasn't yet fulfilled, now I had ample excuse to forget it —as I'd planned to do anyway.

Von Heinen could worry about his own neck now.

My own was concern enough for me.

I ducked in the yellowish light that seemed to have gone reddish in X5 and heard the long, low sounds of augmentation as the pistols in each of the Paratimers' hands fired. I squeezed off a second automatic burst from the Fiurer, hoping to hit the Paratimers but miss the Anglianers who stood between us, who were now slowly throwing themselves to the floor, realizing something of what was happening. I only chipped paint from the wall and the doorway.

Firing again, I danced backward toward the skudder, hoping to pin the Paratimers against the wall until I could reach my destination. I wasn't very successful.

With a yelled word from Mica, the two Paratimers leaped toward me, both pistols firing. I felt a searing pain across my ribs, felt a fist knock me backward, but as I staggerd I let off still another carbine burst that cut across Devoto Baugh's upper chest, neck, and face. His head seemed to explode like a rotten melon.

Mica kept firing at me as I regained my balance, fell back against the glasslike dome of the skudder. Holding the carbine in my right hand, I fired two short bursts that narrowly missed him, but shook him so that his aim was bad. My left hand fumbled for the skudder's hatch.

I hadn't been watching Von Heinen. I'd hardly considered a non-augmented man a danger even though he was certain to understand now that I was betraying him. I was foolish. Even as slow as he was relative to my augmented speed, he could still bring his submachine gun up, aim it, pull the trigger.

I saw the bullets coming, cursed him, ducked, jumped aside, knew he was trying to kill me. I didn't want to kill him, but . . .

My carbine slugs cut his legs out from under him and he fell slowly, heavily to the floor.

At this moment Kjemi Stov stumbled into the open doorway with the slow movements of an unaugmented man, a smoking gun in his hands, incomprehension in his eyes.

Now the skudder's hatch yielded to my hand, popped open. I fired one final burst at Mica, hoping that this one found its target, but not taking time to see, turned and leaped through the open hatch as quickly as I could with the pain I had in my side.

Two slugs roared through the hatch before I was able to get it closed.

Mica was moving more slowly when I saw him next, and redness was beginning to blossom across the front of his New East Anglian army blouse, but he hadn't stopped. Stepping across the prone Von Heinen, he grabbed up the German's submachine gun and aimed it at the skudder's most vulnerable part—its base.

Freya, dazed, confused, bloodied, moved slowly in the smoke and dim light, crawled across the floor toward the bleeding form of Count Albert von Heinen. She'd left her weapon behind, but she didn't seem to care about anything but getting to her man. No one else seemed to notice her. I wondered why I did.

My hands danced across the skudder's controls, bringing the probability generator to slow life. Some of the contols were new, unfamiliar to me, but I'd worry about that later. Right now all I wanted was to get off this Line— and quickly.

The weapon Mica held now had begun to fire, waving back and forth across the base of the skudder, slugs ricocheting away, though I knew that before long one of them would find a seam in the black material that composed the base, make its savage way in, shattering delicate circuits, fragile components. I had to get out before that happened.

I wondered what would happen to the skudder—and to me—if I were to hit the actuating switch before full potential was reached. I didn't know. I didn't really want to find out.

Mica's submachine gun continued to fire, though there was total silence inside the skudder's dome.

The Paratimer would probably have been able to stop me, destroy my skudder, had he not made the same mistake I had—ignoring people without augmentation. They might be slow, but they weren't *that* slow.

Gwendalfa apparently comprehended what was going on, apparently knew that the blur of motion she saw as Mica was trying to kill me—and for some reason she didn't want that to happen.

While the indicators made their slow way to full power, while Mica sprayed the skudder with leaden shot, Gwendalfa, with what appeared to me to be agonizing slowness, raised her pistol, aimed at Mica, pulled back on the trigger—and sent a .441 slug into his back.

The Paratimer fell forward, a final burst of slugs slapping against the skudder's base. One of them penetrated. . . . The skudder screamed. . . .

The next events took place too quickly for me to fully comprehend them, even in X5, though I had some awareness, some shock, some horror. . . .

The skudder pool's lights surged back to full brilliance, illuminating the broken, bloody tableau. Kjemi Stov, now in augmentation, came from his frozen state, charged toward the skudder, a cry of half-insane rage on his lips, though the words he yelled could have only been a Timeliner's Shangalis!

And into the bright and bloody skudder pool charged the troop which had waited until this moment to spring their trap, a troop of blue-clad Timeliners with energy weapons, olive-clad Sclavanians firing slug-throwers, all led by a sable-skinned Krith with a look of fury and of triumph on his flat features, Tar-hortha!

He too was in X5 and he yelled above the roar and the screams in Shangalis, and I thought I could hear him even through the skudder's dome: "You have lost, Eric. You have lost again."

Still moving as only a man in augmentation can, though wounded twice, Mica turned as he fell, and fired his submachine gun once more before he hit the floor, not into the Anglianers so much as through them toward the Krith and his augmented Timeliners. Energy weapons replied to his slug-thrower—and Mica's mutilated body seemed to explode in their blaze.

Caught in the sudden and swiftly ending cross fire, Gwendalfa had taken two of Mica's slugs. She pitched backward as if struck a giant's blow, two bloody holes between her breasts. On her face was a shocked expression, then it went blank and her eyes stared emptily at the ceiling. I knew she was dead.

The other Anglianers had no more chance than she. The Timeliners' weapons caught them in blazes of coruscating energy. I watched my friends die so quickly that few of them even knew what was happening, dying as their bodies were torn apart by energy weapons.

Kjemi Stov, untouched by the lead and coherent energy that swept the shed, had almost reached the skudder. Now Tar-hortha was close behind him.

And as I screamed out my fury at Mica's dying retaliation, something happened in the circuits, the wiring, the generators of the skudder under me. A scream to match my own, a yell, a roar of mechanical pain came from it. Lights flickered erratically across the panel. My hands fell to the controls, but I didn't know what to do. Something was wrong, but . . .

Ignoring Kjemi Stov, Tar-hortha had come to a stop only a short distance from the skudder, looked at me through the glasslike dome, a strange expression on his alien features, a look of concentration and of something else, something more. For an instant a smoky, inhuman, unholy figure seemed to fill the space between us, a thing that brought to mind a mythological being I'd once heard of that would come back into the world only at the very end of Time itself, and then to announce the End of the World.

Then the world outside the skudder grayed again. It didn't exactly flicker, but it was gone, and for a few moments there was nothing, nothing at all but grayness.

I was moving across the Lines, but . . .

Then there was a true flicker, a ragged, uneven one, a sick and screaming one, but it was a flicker and then a world appeared outside and then it was gone, a world of darkness and distant lights, here no Krithian base at Fort Lothairin, yet there was something: not far from the skudder, silhouetted against the distant lights, barely illuminated by light that now spilled from automatic illumination that had come on inside the skudder, was the six-foot-plus, sable-skinned, naked figure of a Krith, and though I couldn't see it, I knew that there was a look of triumph upon Tar-hortha's face. I couldn't escape *him* by skudding.

The skudder's generators screamed again as it flickered, as lights died across the control panel, as smoke came from unseen places into the interior, as the smell of ozone and burning insulation grew stronger.

Grayness.

Then darkness and the dim figure outside, unmoving in relation to the skudder.

Then grayness again, a faltering flicker.

Darkness once more and the final agonized scream of mechanical pain as the skudder, damaged too much to go on, died and with it the power that moved it across the Lines.

Outside Tar-hortha yelled: "Give it up, Eric. I told you that you had lost again."

14
... and in Another Place

I came out of augmentation and for a few long moments sat unmoving in the dead skudder, nausea and pain filling me, blood trickling down my side from the wound I'd received.

Lost. It's all lost, I thought. Everything. The Anglianers had fallen into the Kriths' trap. The Paratimers had failed in their attempt to take the Krithian headquarters in Sclavania and were dead. And so were Gwendalfa and Freya and Faeder Baldwin and so many others. So was Von Heinen. So was . . .

I alone had escaped, if but momentarily. Outside was the Krith who'd sprung the trap. I'd lost just as had the Anglianers and the Paratimers. Now Tar-hortha would . . .

As a sense of utter futility filled me, and a depression and a self-disgust threatened to carry me to inaction, I remembered the side arm I still carried, the .441 Slean revolver in its holster on my hip. If Tar-hortha wanted me, he'd still have to fight me.

Painfully I rose from the control seat, moved to the skudder's hatch, manually opened it since it was no longer powered. Outside, in a dim shadowiness, the Krith awaited me.

"Come on out, Eric," he said as I stood in the open hatch, my eyes slowly adjusting to a faint illumination that came from unseen sources. "I wish you no physical harm."

I kept my hand away from the pistol. Maybe he hadn't noticed it, hadn't thought about my still being armed.

"Come down, Eric," he said slowly. "We still have a long way to go, you know."

"I know," I said, meaning things I didn't yet fully comprehend, as I leaped from the lip of the hatch to the hard pavement, the shock of my heels hitting it flashing up my weary legs.

Pavement! I thought suddenly, for the first time becoming aware of my surroundings.

We weren't in an open field as I'd thought, as I'd seen outside the skudder during the previous flicker. Oh, we were outside. I could see the sky above, hard pinpoints of lights, stars almost untwinkling. But the area in which we stood was enclosed on three sides by the high walls of buildings, hard, unyielding walls of buildings that might have been made of concrete, but which might have been of some substance unknown to the world of the Anglianers. And there was about them a strangeness of design, an alienness, perhaps, that brought into my mind remembrances of remote dreams, nightmares of other worlds, of death and destruction in unknown places.

Enclosed on three sides, the fourth side was open. Away stretched the pavement as if to the horizon, where the blackness of Earth met the lesser blackness of the nighttime sky. Perhaps there were tall, cylindrical shapes outlined distantly against that sky, but I wasn't certain.

And it was quiet, terribly quiet.

There seemed no sounds save my own labored breathing and creaking and popping that came from the damaged skudder as overheated components cooled.

"Come, Eric," Tar-hortha spoke softly, his voice sounding terribly loud in the silence. "We still have a long way to go," he repeated. "I will find you conveyance. We must go to where Sally is."

I turned to face the Krith again and let my right hand drop to the holster that carried the heavy revolver. "I'm not going anywhere with you, Tar-hortha," I said.

"But you must."

"I'll find my own way to Sally."

"I doubt that you can do that."

"I've already done a lot of things you didn't expect," I told him.

"Not as many as you might think, Eric."

"What do you mean by that?"

He laughed softly in the night, but only said, turning has back on me, "Come this way, if you please."

"It doesn't please me, Tar-hortha," I said and pulled the weapon from its holster.

The Krith paused in midstep as I cocked the pistol, slowly turned as he heard the click of its chamber turning into position, aligning a bullet with the barrel, with the firing pin.

He laughed again. "Please do not be foolish. Can you not realize that you have lost?"

"Maybe I haven't yet," I said, leveling the pistol at his chest, "but I'll follow you. Just remember I have a gun on you."

"I will remember," he said. "Now please come with me."

I knew that he was leading me into another trap, but I also figured that somewhere inside that trap would be another skudder. If he wanted to take me anywhere, to any other Line, he'd have to have a skudder. And I *did* have a gun on him. Maybe that would be enough to get me out of the trap. I hoped. . . .

The sable-skinned alien led me across the pavement at a slow walk, away from the openness that seemed to stretch to the horizon and toward the most remote of the three gray walls.

"Where are we?" I asked after we'd walked in silence a distance that must have been a hundred yards or better.

"Oh, you might call this a marshaling yard, Eric," he said without looking back at me, seemingly uncaring of the weapon only inches from his naked back, "or a material depot. No doubt you saw places like it during your service with the Timeliners."

"I'm not sure," I said. I'd seen places *something* like this before, of course, vast storage places of the Timeliners on uninhabited or sparsely inhabited worlds where supplies and equipment were kept for their endeavors across the Lines. Yet there was a silence and an alienness about this place that was like nothing I'd ever seen before. Whatever else they might be, Timeliners are human . . . and this wasn't a human place. What it was I didn't know.

We walked on.

"You are puzzled, Eric?" Tar-hortha asked. The wall was nearer now. We must have crossed half the distance to it. "This does not quite seem like a Timeliner depot to you, is that so?"

"That's so," I admitted.

"About that, you are correct. This is not a place built or manned by Timeliners. This is strictly *ours.*"

I didn't speak. I thought I knew what he meant by that.

"As you already suspect, there is a great deal about my race that you people do not know. There are a number of things we have chosen not to reveal. One of these things is the fact that we have a few selected Lines set aside for our own use. This is one of them, but newly established. You might say that the paint is hardly dry."

Was this an uninhabited Line? I wondered. One so near that of the Anglianers? If uninhabited, how had it become that way? Or if inhabited, what had the Kriths done with the inhabitants? I didn't think any of the answers would be very pleasant. I didn't have a very high opinion of the Kriths' tactics then.

We were quite near the wall now and Tar-hortha spoke a single, alien syllable. The wall before us broke open, a portion of it sliding away to reveal a long, brightly lighted corridor leading into the structure.

"If you will continue to follow me, I will lead you to the place where skudders are kept," the Krith said with a pause in his stride. "You will need one to continue to our destination."

"What makes you think I'll go wherever it is you want me to go?" I asked as we stepped across the threshold into the building, into the bright white light of the corridor.

"You have questions you want answered, do you not?" Tar-hortha asked, his simian tail swishing in the air behind him. "The only way you will find these answers— and the only way you will find your Sally—is to do as I say."

"I don't understand you, Tar-hortha," I said.

"I would be rather surprised if you did," the Krith replied, glancing over his shoulder and giving me a strange, though rather human smile.

Some feet into the corridor a panel slid open in one of the walls and a device of gray-metal, about four feet tall, not anthropoid but a machine with arms and hands and glittering lenses for eyes, rolled out into the passageway. Tar-hortha spoke to it in a language I'd never heard before. It fell in beside him rolling silently on hidden wheels, or perhaps on a cushion of air, two or three feet to his left.

"A mechanical companion," he said.

"A bodyguard?" I asked.

The Krith shrugged.

The corridor seemed endless, leading farther and farther into the building. There were a million questions I wanted to ask, but right then none of them seemed worth asking. The answers I really wanted wouldn't come easily.

There was a growing nervousness within me, a fear, a realization that I was doing exactly what the Krith wanted me to do, that somehow he'd planned for me to come to this Line in that damaged skudder, or had at least *known* I'd come there, and a realization that if this were a trap, I was doing absolutely nothing to avoid it.

Yet there was also within me a sensation of—what?—inevitability? Predestination? That what I was doing I had to do, I'd already done, and there was nothing I could do to alter the events that were to take place, that had already been charted in a past/future that was as fixed as the events of recorded history. If I were to fall into Tar-hortha's trap, that was because I *had* to, and if I were to avoid falling into his trap, that also was because I *had* to. It wasn't just fatalism, depression, fatigue, but something more, something deeper, something far more awesome and frightening, as if both the Krith and I were caught up in the workings of forces far greater than either of us, forces perhaps greater than even those of the vast Krithian machine that sprawled across the Timelines.

I shuddered with a chill though it was quite warm within the strange building, within the bright corridor.

More panels of the corridor's walls slid open as we passed, more machines of gray metal came out to join us, silent, anonymous, identical, all gliding silently beside us. At last there were six of them, one before Tar-hortha, one on each side of him, one on each side of me, and one behind. My revolver was still pointed at his back.

"We are almost there, Eric," the Krith said, speaking after a long silence.

By then I felt so weak I could hardly speak, the wound in my side, the period of augmentation during the battle at Fort Lothairin, the long, long hours without sleep had all combined their weight upon my shoulders, yet I knew that rest, the kind of rest I really wanted, wouldn't come for a long while. I spoke to the Krith, "Almost where?"

"To where the skudders are kept."

To my surprise the corridor before us branched and without being told the leading robot turned and headed down the leftward one. The Krith, the remaining robots, and I followed.

Some hundred feet more and the corridor ended before two large metal doors marked with characters as alien to me as were the robots. Whatever language was used in this place, it wasn't Shangalis.

The first machine paused for a moment before the doors which quietly opened, sliding away to the right and left. The robot moved forward. We followed.

Beyond the door was a huge chamber, high and wide and as brightly lighted as the corridor, and in it sat some half-dozen skudders, large ones, elongated ovals of metal and paraglas capable of carrying a dozen or more people and tons of equipment, and I noticed that they were equipped with the projections I'd seen on the skudder in the Sclavanian pool, part of the system that allowed them spatial movement as well as transtemporal.

"We are here now, Eric," Tar-hortha said, stopping and gesturing toward the skudders. "I suggest that you allow me to set the controls of one of them for you. It will carry you to our destination."

"I'll do my own control setting," I told him, stepping forward and pressing the pistol into his back. "I'll—"

"Eric, please do not be foolish," the Krith said calmly. "It would be very unwise for you to do anything other than what I suggest."

"Your robots?" I asked.

"They will see that no harm comes to me."

"Are you sure?"

"I am sure."

Three of the devices moved closer to me, raising their

metal arms in a manner that wasn't menacing, but could have been.

"Put the foolish pistol away and come with me," Tar-hortha said.

The robots moved closer.

"I'm going to have some answers," I said.

"Of course you are, but killing me will not give them to you."

"And if I do as you say . . . ?"

"You will be my prisoner, of course."

"I won't put myself in that position again, Tar-hortha."

"I believe you already have."

A metal hand shot out from one of the faceless machines, clamped down suddenly on my right wrist.

I tried to jerk away, to pull myself out of its grasp, but the second of the machines came up behind me, grasped both my arms above the elbows, pulled me backward.

"Tar-hortha!" I screamed in anger.

The thing that held on to my right wrist must have weighed a ton or better, but as I unconsciously switched into augmentation, as the world slowed, as electrobiological circuitry came into operation once more, I felt that I could move it, or at least the pseudohand that held my wrist, if only an inch or two.

Pain reddened my vision as I fought against the two machines that held me, as I willed my right hand to move against that pain, as I swung the pistol's barrel a few inches to the left, as I pulled back on the trigger. . . .

The roar of the pistol was sudden and loud in the room's near silence, unexpected and terrible.

I felt a bone snap in my wrist and I saw my fingers release their hold on the pistol; I saw it drop slowly toward the gray floor, but, dammit! I'd done something, I thought, as I came out of augmentation.

Tar-hortha was screaming shrilly, staggering away, clutching at a wounded arm, broken between the wrist and elbow, red, manlike blood gushing from an open wound. He slowly dropped to his knees and there was no anger in his eyes, no look of triumph now, only fear and horror, for he'd been hurt, hurt by a human being, and that was something that never, never happened to a Krith.

"You will die, Eric," he cried, resting now on his knees, blood pooling below him. "You will die!"

And with the words the four gray robots moved toward me to aid the two that held me, one by my upper arms, one by my broken wrist.

The pain was coming to me stronger now, and along with it vertigo and nausea. So now I'd never know. Now I'd . . ."

A grayness came over the room that I thought for a moment was caused by the pain, by a coming loss of consciousness. I thought I was going to go under and would probably never wake up again. Yet . . .

The Greeks had a phrase for it: *deus ex machina.*

Only this "god" wasn't from a machine, at least no metal and ceramic, silicon and germanium machine I knew about. This "god" was a hazy fog in a shape something like that of a man, though vaguely.

"This isn't the way it should be done, Eric," a strangely familiar voice said from nowhere and from everywhere, "but there's no other way now."

I wanted to ask what was happening, but the words wouldn't form in my mouth.

The robotic hands that held me relaxed their grip; the machines glided back a few paces.

"Quickly now," the voice said out of the air. "I can hold them only for moments. Act, dammit!"

Somehow I managed to get to my feet, looked at the limpness of my right hand dangling from a broken wrist, looked at the Krith who knelt in a pool of his own blood.

He had a way out, didn't he? Yet I knew that a Krith *couldn't* self-skud while in pain or fear, and Tar-hortha was feeling both now, yet . . . Yet if that were a natural action of self-protection as I'd been told, wouldn't evolutionary processes have made such moments as those of pain and fear the very ones during which self-skudding could be achieved? Why was it that . . . How rational was *I* then?

"The gun, Eric!" the shadowy voice out of the air said.

I remembered the pistol, bent to grasp it in my left hand, looked at the now immobile robots.

"Hurry!" the voice said. "We haven't long."

I stood up, holding the pistol awkwardly. "Into the

skudder," I told the Krith, shaking my head to clear it, moving toward him.

He shook his head too in a very human fashion.

I pointed the .441 revolver at his face, only inches away. He sighed deeply through wide, wet lips, his great, pupilless eyes wider than ever, but then slowly came to his feet, moaned, staggered before me toward the nearest of the transtemporal machines.

How long the robots would remain immobile I didn't know, but the voice had said not long. I didn't want to have to fight them again. I knew who'd win.

Prodding the wounded Krith on, we soon reached the skudder's hatch. It popped open at the touch of my pistol's barrel and we tumbled in.

I reversed the pistol in my hand and swung it toward the Krith's skull, hopefully not hard enough to crush it, but hard enough. Tar-hortha seemed more shocked than stunned, his great eyes accusing me as they opened wider, then closed as he fell forward to the deck, into the silence of unconsciousness.

Pulling the hatch closed behind me and dogging it, I turned toward the pilot's compartment at the forward end of the roughly egg-shaped craft, half transparent, half opaque, about the size of a Greyhound bus of Sally's native Line. The control panel I found was twice the size of that I was more familiar with, and filled with controls I didn't recognize, though there were enough I did to satisfy me. I could at least get it going, out of *this* Line. Later I'd worry about the strange knobs and dials and meters.

It all seemed familiar now, hitting the switches, adjusting the levers and dials that would bring up the probability potential, while outside robots of gray metal came out of their mechanical lethargy and glided across the large room's floor toward the shudder, their arms reaching out as if to grab my vehicle and keep it from slipping into Probability.

Oh, so damned familiar.

Green lights clicked on across the panel and I prayed to twice a dozen different gods that I could get away from this Line before the robots found some way to damage the skudder—I didn't want to have to start all over again. I didn't think I could have.

More green lights clicked on. Meters showed rising potentials.

Outside the gray machines came closer, their extended appendages all but reaching the skudder's metal base.

Inside, inside me was a great weakness, a dizziness, a desire to forget it all and lie down and sleep and never, never . . .

"Probability Potential Achieved," a green light told me, a meter repeated.

With my left hand I moved the destinatrol for several dozen Lines to the East, then shifted that hand toward the main actuating switch as metal clashed against metal, as the robots reached the skudder, struck it, rammed it, fought to hold it in. . . .

Flicker!

And the cavernous room was gone. I was in darkness, in a Line where there was no building, no lights, nothing at all that I could see outside the skudder.

Flicker! again.

And I thought I was going to pass out.

I held myself up in the seat and tried not to think about the throbbing in my broken wrist, my lacerated side.

Flicker! Flicker! Flicker!

Maybe I'd make it after all.

15
Tar-hortha's Answers

I had to reset the destination controls twice more, moving much farther to the T-East than I'd intended before I found a world sufficiently ruined.

Outside was a desolate, moonlike Earth similar to those Sally and I had seen in the far T-West in the so-called Albigensian Lines, a world without life or atmosphere and high in nuclear radiation. Here technology had advanced a little more quickly than it had on the world of the Anglianers and the Sclavanians, perhaps, and conflicts had arisen that hadn't been settled at negotiation tables or in brushfire guerrilla war. Here nuclear warfare had swept the world and its inhabitants had blasted themselves to radioactive ash. It was sad, but I didn't take time to ponder over it, nor to concern myself with the radiation. Inside the skudder I was safe, and I didn't intend to go outside. Not on this world.

After resting for a few moments in the pilot's seat, I took pills from the first-aid kit to help ease the pain, then crudely splinted my broken wrist and bandaged my other injuries, had a long, sweet drink of a high-energy liquid from a long, red bulb, took the .441 Slean into my left hand, rose, and went back to see about Tar-hortha.

The Krith had regained consciousness, was holding his wounded, shattered left arm in his right hand. There was great pain etched in the lines of his alien face, but a kind of bitter satisfaction as well.

"You are a fool, Eric Mathers," he said in a cold, crisp voice that betrayed none of his pain, "a damned fool. You have ruined everything now. You have lost again and in a way you cannot understand. Your beloved Anglianers are all dead now and you are . . ."

I stood above the alien, my hatred for him and his kind and all they had ever done rushing up at me in a maniacal rage. I could see Sally their captive and

Gwendalfa and Freya and Faeder Baldwin and all the others dead behind me; I could see world after world after world in ruin, desolation, submission. . . .

He laughed at me.

I shot him.

Later I realized what a stupid, savage, insane thing I'd done, firing that pistol at Tar-hortha then. But I don't believe that at that moment I was quite sane. I'm not certain that anyone could have expected me to be.

But I won't try to justify my actions. I did what I did, and whatever the guilt or blame might be, I will accept it, for that and for so much more.

Tar-hortha didn't die at once, though I'm sure a man would have with that kind of a hole in his chest oozing blood and body fluids. He was in terrible pain at first and I did what I could to stanch the flow of blood and ease the pain with drugs—the Krithian metabolism is surprisingly like ours. I didn't tell him I was sorry.

When he was able to talk, weakly, feebly, not altogether coherently, he said, "I fear that yours is something of a Pyrrhic victory, Eric. I take that as a comfort."

"I don't understand," I said, standing above him, holding myself erect by sheer will, looking down at the dying Krith.

"You are alone, Eric," Tar-hortha said. "Whatever you might be, whatever powers might sometimes be behind you, you are now very much alone. There is no one to aid you, to assist you in this thing you are setting out to do, this thing the real nature of which you do not yet know."

"Then tell me, dammit!"

"I will not. The power behind you has not told you, perhaps cannot tell you. You must learn for yourself if you are able. So the Tromas have said, even as they said you would come to me in the skudder pool, that we would travel to . . ." He smiled a weak and humorless though almost human smile. "They did not predict *this*, however."

"I still don't understand."

"I regret to say that I have no sympathy for you, Eric. You would destroy my people as I have destroyed your

Anglianers. I have no love for you. No desire that the power behind you—whatever it is"—there was true anguish in his voice—"destroy my people."

Puzzled, more confused than ever, I asked, "But will you answer me three questions?"

"Why should I?"

"I can make you suffer more," I said, though inside me was a sickness and I don't believe that even then I could have brought myself to torture him. I was sick of it, so damned sick of the pain and the killing and . . .

"I could hardly suffer more," the Krith said, bitter satisfaction again. "But what are your questions?"

"One, where's Sally? Two, what are the co-ordinates of your Homeline? Three, just what the hell *are you,* you and the whole damned Krithian race?"

Tar-hortha chose his words carefully, hoarding what little strength was left to him. "I will answer one of your questions," he said. "That may bring you to the answers to the others." He paused and breathed deeply, painfully. "You will find, among the references in the pilot's compartment, a book which lists the co-ordinates of the major Lines, among them you will find listed KHL-ooo."

"That's the Krithian Homeline?" I asked.

Tar-hortha didn't answer. He closed his eyes and willed himself to die.

So I'd avenged Jock Kouzenzas. Somehow it didn't seem to mean so much now.

As Tar-hortha had said, there was a book in the pilot's compartment that listed the probability indices of several hundred major Lines, each followed by a brief description. And I wondered why I'd never seen such a book before. Was it something new, recently introduced? Or, more likely, was it something reserved only for certain skudders stationed on Prime Lines? Or . . . The speculation was pointless, I opened the book. The first entry was:

"KHL-ooo, the Krithian Homeline . . ." It gave the probability index values, co-ordinates in paratime. "This is the home and major headquarters of the Krithian race. This is the Line upon which they evolved and from which they began their exploration of the Timelines." The book was lying, of course. "It is a sacred world to the Kriths and may be entered only with express authorization from the highest authority. WARNING: UNAUTHORIZED ENTRY OF KHL-OOO WILL NOT BE TOLERATED. UNAUTHORIZED SKUDDERS WILL BE DESTROYED ON SIGHT."

I looked at the probability indices again. It *was* a long way in the T-East. A hell of a long way.

But that's where I was going, to Sally perhaps, maybe to some answers, probably to my death.

But that's where I was going.

16
To Line KHL-ooo

It was winter across the Lines, January, maybe, but more likely February—I'd lost track of days and weeks—and the broadleaf trees of the forests of the North Temperate Zone had long since lost their leaves. There was a chill across the Earths, across so many of them, as if this winter were to be an unusually long and cold one. I felt it in the marrow of my bones, this long, cold winter, yet with it was a satisfaction, and a sadness.

Before this winter was out I would know something. Or I would be dead.

My stolen skudder was moving smoothly and silently across the Lines of Time, flickering from grayness to grayness as world after world, universe after universe fell behind me.

My injuries were healed—thanks to the skudder's automedic—and I'd made some modifications of the skudder's controls and some of its systems. I added missile bays and launching tubes that could project small, nuclear-tipped rockets. I'd added defensive force-field projectors and I'd found a means of coupling additional modules into the skudder's computer, increasing its capacity several fold. I thought these things might improve my chances of staying alive. Might.

I thought I was as nearly ready to meet the Kriths on their own ground as I would ever be, though exactly what I was going to do when I got there, when I got to KHL-ooo, I didn't really know. Chances were I'd be putting myself exactly where the Kriths had wanted me for so long.

But, dammit, I was coming in under my own power. I was coming in armed to the teeth. I was coming in with a skudder that could move through space as well as though paratime. Maybe I would have *some* bargaining power.

And maybe I just didn't care any longer.

I wanted some answers.

And I was going to get them if it cost me my life.

But they'd know I'd been there.

Damn the torpedoes and full speed ahead!

The counters clicked down the number of Lines. I'd checked and rechecked the co-ordinates of the Krithian Homeline against known locations in paratime, and each time I'd seen that the settings had been right.

I'd cleaned my personal weapons, rifle and pistol. I'd dressed in a survival suit, complete with battle armor, body shield, and life-support systems.

Now, with the last few Lines flickering by, ready for just about anything the Kriths might throw at me, I sat down in the pilot's seat, popped open my helmet, smoked a final cigarette, looked out at the black-white-black-white of the worlds snapping past.

Many thoughts went through my mind then, a chaotic jumble of thoughts, feelings, memories, impressions, hopes, dreams, people, places, things. . . .

Maybe it was all going to end there, a few Lines away. Maybe I'd have the answers and maybe I wouldn't. Maybe . . .

Maybe that's what Tar-hortha had meant by a Pyrrhic victory.

Maybe.

The last flicker was coming up.

I crushed the cigarette beneath my heel, said aloud to myself, "This is it," took a deep breath, prepared my augmentation circuits should I need them, prayed, waited. . . .

Flicker!

The probability generator went to stand-by. Some systems temporarily closed down. Others opened up. The skudder had ceased its flickering.

I looked out.

I had only moments.

And what I saw in that brief span wasn't all that impressive, not the sort of thing I'd imagined of KHL-ooo during those long, sleepless nights of preparation and waiting.

What was outside the skudder, a place that in another

space/time was an area of northern Georgia, was a scene bucolic, pastoral, a long vista of undulating landscape, carefully cropped grass, groves of fruit trees scattered here and there, a remote building that might have been a farmhouse or might have been the temple of some rustic god, two or three bipedal figures that at that distance could have been humans or Kriths; nearer the skudder, beside a stream that had, somehow, an artificial, not-quite-natural look about it, were half a dozen white, fluffy animals that could have been nothing but sheep, but were something else, guarded by a big, shaggy, bright-eyed dog upon whose back perched a winged creature that was not a bird, something like a giant butterfly with a body more mammalian than insect. Had I been able to hear sounds from outside the skudder, had I thought to turn on the external microphones, I felt that I would have heard the sounds of real birds singing and bees buzzing.

But all that lasted for only a moment, seconds or less than seconds.

A speaker in the panel before me, despite the fact that my communications systems were on stand-by and not fully activated, came to life and a harsh masculine voice —whether human or Krithian I couldn't tell—said in Shangalis:

"You are in violation of prime ordinances. Express your authorization to enter KHL-ooo at once, or you will be destroyed."

Outside the skudder there was no sign of the point of origin of the signal, no skudder nor aircraft nor ground car, only the sheep-things and their dog and the remoter bipedal figures whom I thought had now turned to look in my direction.

Without thinking it out, my hands fell to the controls of the radio-video transmitter, and I found myself speaking as lights across the panels told me they had come to life: "I am here under no authorization but my own," I said. "My name is Eric Mathers, né Thimbron Parnassos, former Timeliner agent, and I have come to ask some questions of the Tromas. I request permission to remain in KHL-ooo until I have accomplished that purpose."

I don't know what I was thinking at that moment, that long awaited moment when I was finally, at last, within the Krithian Homeline, but my hands were doing some of my thinking for me. Even as I spoke those hands were activating the firing systems of the missile launchers I'd mounted on the external hull.

"Permission denied," the voice said harshly. "You have five seconds to depart this Line."

I had no intention of leaving. My self-directed hands were now moving to the spatial positioning controls, the locomotive facilities of the skudder I'd learned to operate during the weeks since leaving the dead Tar-hortha on some unnamed, atom-blasted world in the T-West.

"You have three seconds to depart this Line," the voice said as the skudder, moving more quickly than conventionally propelled craft, rose vertically into the air, a quick, lurching sensation that should have left my stomach sitting on the ground below me, but didn't. Some sort of inertial compensating device?

The skudder rose several thousand yards straight up and I was preparing to move off in a horizontal direction —but which way? I had no idea of how this world was constituted politically, where might lie the centers of power, where I might find the mysterious authority that the Kriths called the Tromas.

I elected to head east, toward the coast; there, along the seaboard, in most worlds, would be the centers of population—and power.

Another set of controls was activated and the skudder leaped forward, eastward toward the coast, accelerating up to hundreds of miles an hour faster than I can tell it —but it was still too slow.

"You are judged to be in violation of prime directives and are hereby ordered destroyed," the harsh voice stabbed from the loudspeaker. . . .

. . . and from out of the sun, somehow undetected by the skudder's automatic sensing gear, came three swept-wing, teardrop-shaped craft, plummeting toward me at supersonic velocities, weapons already beginning to blaze.

What happened next was too rapid for human senses to deal with, to react to even in the X5 augmentation into which I had gone. I let this skudder's computer take over —and was damned glad it was a sophisticated one with some fine offense/defense programs.

The skudder began evasive action, darting in an arc toward the trees and the earth below, bringing from stand-by to full operational modes a set of inhibitor and deflector fields around the craft. The world outside took on a yellow-greenish hue as the fields broke apart the white sunlight, then turned the red-orange of flame as a laser beam from one of the attacking craft splattered against the fields.

Helpless and horrified, I sat and watched as the skudder leaped skyward again, its fields opening for split fractions of seconds so that the missile launchers on the outer hull could throw needles of steel and nuclear fire back at my attackers.

The skudder lurched again, an oncoming missile exploding only yards outside my paraglas dome, half-blinding me despite the defenses of the fields. I felt the heat and the shock wave, but not the awful acceleration as the skudder leaped and lunged again, spitting out more needles of death. Had it not been for the skudder's inertial compensation, I would have by then been nothing more than a red jelly spread across the inside of the pilot's compartment.

But one of my missiles had found its target, broken through the defensive fields of one of the delta-winged craft. For instants there was a new sun in the sky, only thousands of feet from the earth, yellow-white and blinding in intensity. Then it faded and became a climbing, boiling ball of superheated gas.

I had no more time for observation. The two remaining craft now began to co-ordinate their actions, directed themselves in a graceful dance across the sky until they were in a position to make simultaneous attacks upon me from widely separated directions. Their lasers blazed and they spit out their missiles as they converged on the skudder that could no longer outmaneuver them—but then no skudder had ever been designed for this sort of thing.

I gave the computer a brief command—my own defenses dropped for a moment and every missile I had left was launched as quickly as possible, two clouds composed of three-foot-long lances, propelled by small but powerful cores of solid fuel, carrying tiny, sophisticated thermonuclear warheads. I couldn't beat them, but I'd damned well . . .

Then the two aircraft bent from their trajectories toward me, swung in sharp arcs. And my computer was trying to tell me why. I saw why.

Help had arrived.

But not for me.

A behemoth skudder had appeared in the sky a few hundred feet above my own skudder, an egg-shaped monster the size of an ocean liner or a starship.

. . . and the power that drove my skudder through space and through paratime died within the bowels of the craft. Suddenly the machine was nothing more than a lifeless, powerless collection of metal and paraglas and ceramics, a heavy jumble of plates and panels and solid state circuits which happened to surround a very fragile organic creature—name of Eric Mathers.

The dead skudder began to describe a trajectory that would bring it to earth some few miles ahead, somewhere in the middle of a forest that had suddenly leaped across the horizon, accelerating as I fell at 32fps^2.

Again the communications loudspeaker came to life; some few, select circuits returned to power for a moment, and a new voice said, "Repeat your true name and give your former Timeliner identification number."

My voice worked, though I didn't expect it to, and I said, "Eric Mathers, born Thimbron Parnassos, former Timeliner identification number . . ."

Somewhere along in there, just as I was concluding rattling off that series of numbers that had been indelibly etched into my brain, I must have begun to black out. The ground was rushing up to meet me, the vague formlessness of the remote forest beginning to define itself into separate trees as the trajectory brought me ever nearer them, when a grayness began to creep over my vision, a remote kind of buzzing enter my ears.

But there was no time to think about that. I was going to be dead in seconds. There was only time to curse my foolishness at not having made some kind of preparations against this, some means of protecting my power sources and circuits—but then I'd had no way of knowing they could do something like this, no way of knowing how they were accomplishing it.

Dammit! My first step into the Krithian Homeline, and without batting an eye they'd canceled me out. They'd gotten me where they wanted me and now they were finishing me off.

Tar-hortha had been right. I hadn't known what the hell I was getting into.

Then the trees, turning gray in my vision, resolved themselves into leaves and branches and the egg shape of the skudder was crashing into them. . . .

I thought I was dying, and I was furious.

Mager was dead, and so was his look-alike, a fellow who'd called himself Kearns, but for a moment, as I opened my eyes and blinked them into focus, I could have sworn that they'd both been resurrected and sent to haunt me.

The two of them stood beside the bed upon which I lay, dressed in simple white clothing of an unusual cut and design. Their hair was short and they were beardless. They carried no weapons and something about them— maybe it was the way they smelled—suggested the medical profession.

They looked enough alike to be twins: slender, wiry, with sharp, angular faces lined with tiny white wrinkles that could have been scars. And neither one of them was a human being, not the way I would have then defined the term.

Once I'd gotten over the shock of seeing them, and after I realized that they weren't the ghosts of Kearns and Mager, only peas out of a very similar pod, I raised my head up enough to look around the room I was in, surprised to find that my injuries consisted of nothing more than a few bruises and abrasions.

The room was clean and antiseptic, walls and ceiling and floor of a pale green, with only a functional white cabinet and the bed on which I lay for furniture, with only one door leading out, and no windows. In addition to the antiseptic smell in the air, there was a faint, remote humming sound, like that of a distant generator, or maybe a giant air-conditioning unit.

My two companions didn't move, didn't speak, waiting for me to finish my inspection.

"Well, you didn't kill me," I said when I looked back at them.

"No, we did not," said Thing One. "I am not certain why."

We were speaking in Shangalis, of course. It came to me more naturally than the language I'd learned as a child.

"We have been instructed to keep you well," said Thing Two.

I looked at them questioningly, but didn't speak. What was there to say?

"You wonder why?" asked Thing One; Shangalis didn't come as easily to him as it did to me.

"Yeah," I said, raising myself on my elbows and feeling a surge of dizziness go through my head, but passing quickly. "But maybe I wouldn't like it if I knew."

A wooden smile came across Thing One's craggy face. "The orders are from the Tromas, Mathers," he said. "From the Tromas themselves."

"Oh, how nice," I said in as acid a tone as I could. "I'm very flattered that the Tromas show so much interest in me."

"I do not think I would feel that way if I were you," said Thing Two.

What could I say in reply to such sparkling wit? I gave him a dirty look.

I lay back on the bed, feeling more naked than dressed in the thin smock that was now my only garment, and wondered just what the hell was going to happen next.

At least I was still alive, and I hadn't much expected to be. Not that there was very much I could do right at the moment. Even if I hadn't felt as weak as a kitten, I didn't think I could accomplish very much against the two of them unarmed, not if they had the other characteristics of Mager and Kearns, and I was certain they did, augmentation and all.

And even if I could jump out of bed and overpower the two of them, where the hell could I go? Outside, no doubt, was a whole world filled with their kind and with Kriths.

I figured I'd better wait a bit and see what developed. As it turned out I didn't have to wait too long.

The two Mager types retreated to opposite walls and stood silently like turned-off machines, their hands behind their backs and their backs against the walls, both pairs of eyes remaining fixed on me.

Maybe thirty minutes went by—though at the time it seemed like hours—before the room's single door opened and in walked two individuals. I say "individuals," not people. One was a Krith, big, naked, hairless, and olive-green, and another Mager type, dressed in white and carrying a bundle under his right arm.

The Krith, a specimen even larger and uglier than the late Tar-hortha, raised a hand in greeting, smiled a toothy, wolfish smile, approached to within a few feet of my bed and stopped.

"So you are Eric Mathers," he said simply, in perfect Shangalis, yet with a kind of precision artificial even for Kriths, and I was certain for the first time in my life that Shangalis wasn't their native language, at least it wasn't his.

I raised myself on my elbows again—it's awkward as hell greeting someone from flat on your back, especially if you're not sick. "I am," I said.

"I am Cal-sarlin, a Minister to the Tromas," he said, bowing slightly, a gesture I still find ridiculous when performed by a naked monster. He glanced at the two characters who'd been keeping me company. "You may go now," he said. "He is in my charge."

The two Magers bowed in return, departed.

"Rise, Eric," Cal-sarlin said when the door had closed again. "The effects of your, shall we say, recent debacle should have worn off by now. You can rise, can you not?"

"I can."

As I slowly sat up on the bed the Mager type who'd come in with him stepped forward, presented his bundle to me. As he did I noticed a bulge under his left armpit that didn't look like a part of his anatomy. The butt of a pistol in a shoulder holster, no doubt.

"Clothing for you," Cal-sarlin explained as I sat the bundle in my lap. "I would like for you to dress."

"Why wasn't I killed?" I asked, looking up into those

deep brown eyes. "I thought unauthorized entry into KHL-ooo was supposed to bring about immediate destruction."

"It almost did for you," Cal-sarlin said, smiling a carnivorous smile again. "You were saved only in the last moments, and only because the Tromas have a special interest in you."

"How flattering," I said. "It's nice to know you're loved."

"I said 'interest,' Eric, not affection," the Krith said, still smiling the same smile. "It may be that you will find what awaits you to be less desirable than the death you might have had."

"Your words reassure me to no end."

The smile went away in annoyance. "Your flippancy will gain you nothing, Eric. I suggest you offer full and complete co-operation. Only in that way might you hope to gain anything at all."

"And what might 'anything' be?" I asked.

"Would you be so good as to dress?"

I got dressed. And what I got dressed in wasn't the antiseptic white garments I'd almost anticipated, but rather a double-breasted shirt of a design and colors you'd expect to see at a Hawaiian luau, trousers as gaudily decorated and that came to just below my knees, soft leather ankle-high boots, and a hat, the kind you're supposed to wear in the Tyrolean Alps. When I had them all on I wasn't certain I was any better dressed than I had been in the white smock, and wondered if maybe, among other things, I was the butt of a not-very funny practical joke. Did people around here really wear this sort of thing?

Cal-sarlin didn't seem to think it was funny, but then maybe he had no sense of humor. Kriths usually don't.

"Let me advise you of this again, Eric," the Krith said. "The only thing you can possibly do to improve your fortune in any respect is to co-operate fully with the Tromas and their ministers during the forthcoming interview. Lack of co-operation will be punished. Cooperation will be rewarded, in so far as it is possible to reward one under a sentence such as yours."

I wanted to give him another wise answer, something

to show him that I wasn't afraid of his threats, but some-how I'd run out of them at the moment.

All I said was, "Okay. I'm ready."

He nodded toward his white-clad companion who opened the door for us and held it open as Cal-sarlin led the way out of the room.

17
The Tromas

I had little opportunity to observe my surroundings, to determine whether I had been held in a hospital or a prison or something entirely different from either, for Cal-sarlin led me from the room where I'd awakened down a short, empty hallway directly to a closed conveyance that somewhat resembled an elevator: a cubicle some eight feet or so on a side that began to move as soon as the doors closed behind us. The initial sensation was that of vertical movement; later there was movement in a more lateral direction, through some underground tunnel, I thought at the time.

At the end of the trip that may have been forty-five minutes long, the "elevator" made a final upward lunge and came to a stop in a low building of unusual architectural design, little more than an earth-covered mound surmounted with a high peaked roof. It served as nothing more than a terminus for the cubicle.

The Krith led me out into a parklike area between clusters of buildings, no two of which seemed to have been designed by people of the same era, or even of the same Timeline; all in all a strange conglomeration of contrasting and often conflicting architecture, as if a miniature Taj Mahal had been placed beside an Inca temple, across a grassy avenue from Saint Sophia, a few hundred yards from a pagoda on the north and a Swiss chalet on the south. Equally odd was the admixture of trees and shrubs that dotted the park area: a cluster of half a dozen carefully tended poplars separated from another cluster of date palms by trellises and arbors covered with something that might have been related to grape vines; tropical plants grew alongside vegetation from far northern regions, and interspersed were plants of types I was certain I had never seen before, plants that might not have been native to *any* Earth.

Within the parklike area, which must have covered several acres, there were, walking in twos and threes, Kriths, unclothed as Kriths always are, and men in costumes of various places and times, costumes, for the most part, brightly colored and lavishly decorated, costumes Burmese and Peruvian, Elizabethan and Malayan, Tahitian and Roman.

I say "men" though I'm not at all certain that some other word from some other language might have been more appropriate; they were persons of the Mager type as I'd begun calling them in my mind, all of them slender and wiry, with lined angular faces, with expressions on their faces, looks in their eyes that I was certain I would never be able to read. Oddly enough, it seemed to me at the time in this bucolic, almost pastoral setting, a number of them appeared to be armed, for here and there under their clothing were bulges that had distinctive, gunlike shapes.

Few of them seemed to be aware of us as Cal-sarlin led me through the park and down a path, dark and shadowy under towering oaks, that led out of the park and toward a low, rambling white building that stood alone some distance away.

Finally Cal-sarlin volunteered some information: the place we were approaching, he told me in Shangalis, was something that could be roughly translated into English as "the palace of the Tromas," or could be translated as "the place wherein dwell the all-wise Mothers." This was the first time I'd heard the word "mother" used in connection with the Tromas, and I wondered exactly what that meant. I didn't ask Cal-sarlin. I didn't figure he'd answer.

As we crossed the last few hundred feet to the entrance of "the palace of the Tromas" and the armed, uniformed Mager guards who stood silently on either side of it, a flight of dartlike aircraft swept across the sky, half a dozen silvery shapes that had a very military look about them, revealing no sign of whatever propulsion systems they used. I was becoming convinced that KHL-ooo was not quite the idyllic place it might look upon first glance.

Then we were at the doors and Cal-sarlin was speaking to the guards in a language I didn't understand. The guards saluted with their weapons, doors opened and we entered.

Inside, "the palace of the Tromas" was plain and quite the sort of thing you might expect of those who supposedly are the wise and ancient givers of guidance to a race whose power spans uncounted hundreds of Earths. It wasn't the sort of thing I'd expected, anyway, though I'm not really certain of what sort of ostentatious show of power and wealth I'd expected. I don't suppose I'd given it much thought.

Cal-sarlin led me across a broad, empty entrance hall, undecorated save for a wall-size inscription in a language I couldn't read, and then down a long corridor to where we were met by two other Kriths, these two wearing what I at first thought to be some sort of jewelry: silvery disks maybe four inches in diameter and half an inch thick suspended around their necks by fine silvery chains. Later I found out what they were, after Cal-sardin had donned his and I had been given one to wear.

The Krith who brought me there bowed slightly toward the two, who bowed in return, and then introduced me to them: one was named Vor-kawin and the other Ces-karlet. They were also "Ministers to the Tromas."

Vor-kawin now seemed to become the spokesman for the Krithian trio, telling me that, "This is a very great honor for you, Eric Mathers, though I am not altogether certain why the Tromas have summoned you. I have some inkling, perhaps.

"Nevertheless, remember your place. The number of other humans"—there seemed to be a bad taste in his mouth when he said that last word—"who have been given audience with the Tromas could be counted on the fingers of one hand. It is an experience you will never forget."

He paused, seemed to ruminate for a moment, scratched himself as Kriths often do, then continued. "I doubt that there is very much I can say to prepare you for your first meeting with the Tromas. I could try to explain to you who and what the Tromas are, but then you will learn that for yourself very shortly. I could try to answer for you some of the questions your *people* have been asking about us for many decades, but again those answers will soon be obvious to you. I would warn you of the power and the wisdom and the insight possessed by the Tromas, but once again this will all soon be made known to you by the power of experience, which is far greater than mere words.

"So I will say only this to you, Eric Mathers: be fully aware now and henceforth, you are about to enter the presence of the most powerful and most wise beings in all the Timelines, the rulers of the Krithian race, the framers and the guardians of all the plans and hopes and dreams and aspirations of our people. Remember at all times that a single word from the Tromas is enough to bring about the destruction of an entire world.

"You will be expected to behave with the proper respect." There was a long pause which could only be described as pregnant. "Failure on your part to do so will bring about the most dire results. Do you understand?"

As much as I hate to admit it now, Vor-kawin had put into me exactly the fear and awe he'd hoped to. I nodded, said, "Yeah, I understand."

"Let us proceed," Vor-kawin said and led the way, with Cal-sarlin and Ces-karlet walking on either side of me. I wouldn't have been surprised if there'd been a pair of Mager types with big, heavy guns bringing up the rear, but there seemed to be none of *them* inside the building.

The plain, functional hallway down which we walked made two sharp turns, one right and the other left, and finally brought us up to a pair of doors, decorated with obscure carvings resembling the inscription I'd seen in the entrance hallway, and bracketed by two more Kriths wearing silvery medallions. They were not introduced, did not speak; they merely opened the doors and let us enter into the presence of the Tromas.

Whatever I'd expected, whatever I might have imagined the almost mythical Tromas to be, I wasn't prepared for what I saw when Vor-kawin led me through those doors and into their presence.

There were about a dozen of them; I never did count the exact number. But that number seemed to fill the large room they occupied, seemed to fill it both physically and in some other way, some psychological fashion, and though my initial sensation was one of revulsion, I was never totally unaware of that second kind of presence, that almost overpowering psychological aura, that sense of power that filled the air, and even though the Tromas themselves didn't always seem to be its source, I'm certain they were.

I'll try to give a physical description, though I feel a terrible inadequacy of words. Oh, but could I trade a thousand of them for just one photograph!

Imagine, if you will, a Krith: a naked male mammal, erect and biped, standing in excess of six feet tall, coloring ranging from sable-brown to olive, a big, egg-shaped head, enormous eyes like brown marbles, below the eyes a nostril row and below that a large, toothy mouth, along the sides of the head feathery membranes something like the gills of a fish, almost no neck, broad shoulders leading down humanlike arms to five-fingered hands, broad chest, flat stomach, manlike genitals, short legs, webbed feet, humanlike buttocks sprouting a prehensile tail like that of a monkey.

That's the sort of Krith I'd always known before, a male Krith.

Now I learned that there were females to the race, a few at least.

Now, with that Krithian image in your mind, remove the male sex organs, add vagina and breasts, keep it still naked, still hairless.

Now add five hundred pounds of flesh and a hundred years of age.

Got that in your mind? A gross, deformed series of mounds of flesh, wrinkled in places, but mostly bulging blubber, so heavy that it is unable to get around under its own power, but must be carried from place to place on wheeled, electrical carts; sable or olive sheen blotched here and there with liver spots; face almost obscured by folds of fat, holding in deep sockets eyes still bright and brown.

I couldn't help my feelings of revulsion; I don't think anyone could have. But I also felt a kind of unwilling respect; I still felt that aura in the air, that sense of power. I was awed, in several ways.

Foremost of the Tromas—the word is the same singular and plural—was the most ancient-looking one of all, one whose once-olive coloring had gone to gray and purple splotches. This one spoke in a high, twittering, almost girl-like voice, and in a language I'd heard only once before.

The medallion hanging from a chain around my neck began to speak as well, in Shangalis—some sort of translation device, probably hooked through a radio linkage to a computer which did all the work. Neat.

What the medallion said was this: "So you are Eric Mathers."

I nodded, bowed, said, "Yes, that was the name I used on my last Timeliner assignment. I've grown rather accustomed to it." As I spoke I heard alien words from the Tromas' own medallion in a voice that resembled my own.

"Then that is the name by which we shall call you." A pause, a wave of a gross hand. "Vor-kawin," the Tromas said, "you and your companions may depart. We wish to speak with this one alone."

"Is that wise?" he asked, and added some word that the translator was unable to convert into Shangalis, a word that carried respect and sounded something like "Kiotogivan," yet rolling and twittering. "You know this man's history. He is dangerous and is not to be trusted." Vor-kawin paused, then added the clencher, "And he has been responsible for *killing two of our people* and others of the *Kanombajil.*"

"*We* are aware of that, Vor-kawin." The translated voice sounded a bit peeved. "But we do not foresee danger at his hands. We are safe. Leave us."

"Yes, Kiotogivan," Vor-kawin said, bowed, and with Cal-sarlin and Ces-karlet, left the large room.

"You know who we are?" the old Tromas asked when the doors had closed and I was alone with the dozen or so *female* Kriths.

"I think so," I said. "You are females of the race."

"*The* females of the race," the Tromas said. "The only living females of our race."

I was stunned at that moment, shocked, but after another moment I found that I wasn't all that surprised. I was beginning to understand why I'd never seen a female Krith before, or ever met anyone who had.

"You find that surprising, do you not?" the translator on my chest asked.

"I do."

"We are all pregnant. We each give birth at least once a year. Yet still we are few, terribly few to maintain a race as widely spread as ours, is that your thought?"

"It is."

"There are other means of maintaining our race, of propagating our species, not always satisfactory, but available and used. It was not always so. Once our chances of survival were minimal. You might find it a wonder that there are Kriths in this universe at all."

"Other means?" I asked.

The ancient-looking female Krith nodded her great head, smiled through her folds of fat, seemed again to be speaking not only for herself but for the silent, motionless others in the room: "Laboratory methods, you might say. But all that is unimportant in our present conversation, Eric. There are other things of much greater significance."

"Yes, there are," I said quickly when she paused, wishing I could sit down, but I hadn't been offered a chair and was forced to remain standing. "I came here to ask some questions, to KHL-ooo, that is, and I would appreciate very much the opportunity of asking them." Politeness to the Tromas seemed to be in order; I'd been warned that I'd better be polite.

"We will answer some of those questions without your asking them, Eric," the speaker for the Tromas said, "and the others we will, perhaps, allow you to ask later, but there are some things we would like to know about you."

"About me?"

The gross head nodded again. "We have many questions about you, Eric Mathers. Many questions."

"I'll answer them if I can."

"Very well." There was a long, thoughtful pause. "Perhaps you are aware of the reputation we have among our own people of being able to see into the future. Is this so?"

"I've heard Kriths say things about the Tromas that sounded as if there were precognitive abilities involved."

"Carefully put! You tread this ground with caution."

She smiled. "And it is true that we do have certain, as you say, 'precognitive abilities,' among other, er, 'gifts.' In some place/times we might be called 'clairvoyant,' though that is an awkward and sloppy term, as are most others connected with psionic abilities. You humans know little about such things, but—alas!—*we* know but little more, though we sense the gifts when they are bestowed upon us, and use them."

There followed another long, thoughtful pause. Since I didn't know in which direction the Tromas was heading, I didn't speak, but waited.

"Our psionic abilities, it would seem," she went on at last, "are something to help offset other handicaps, some of which are now obvious to you, I am certain. We of the Tromas and our ancestors of the Tromas before us have made every effort to put these abilities to use for the benefit of our race. It has been said that these abilities have enabled our race to survive and to achieve the place in the Timelines it holds today. That may be an overstatement, but I feel that there is some truth in it. We are proud of what we have done for our people, and hope to continue to assist our race in the achievement of its goals."

In the pause that followed, I threw in one of the things I wanted to ask: "And just exactly what are the goals of your race?" Maybe my voice was a little harsher than I'd intended.

The Tromas smiled again. "In time, Eric. First, our questions. We know much about you: your birth name and the place of your birth, the history of your younger years before entering the service of the Timeliners, your training there, your operations as an agent of the Timeliners, and your final defection. Up until the time of your defection, up until the time of your captivity in that place called Staunton by the Paratimers, your record was a good one; you showed devotion and ability. You were an *almost* exemplary example of your profession. Then all that changed.

"We are not asking you to tell us why you defected, if 'defected' is the correct word. We know of your flirtation with the Paratimers, and of your subsequent disillusionment with them as well. We know *why* you have done many of the things you have done in the months since your rescue from Staunton, but we are not certain *how* you have done them."

"How?" I asked. "What do you mean?"

"You are not gifted with psionic powers yourself. We are certain of that. If you were, this would have been detected years ago, and if not then, we would have known it when you came into our presence just now. You are not psionic, yet sometimes you behave as if you were."

I started to ask what she meant by that, then began to have some inkling of what she was getting at, things about me—or things that happened to me—that had disturbed other Kriths. I let her go on.

"There are times when there is another force about you, something that connects itself with you and helps you alter the normal course of events." A pause. "You should have died in Staunton, you know. In reviewing the events, in immersing ourselves in the progression of time in that time/place, all things point to your death then and there. But you did not die. Why?"

Without giving me a chance to answer, she went on in a sterner, more anxious voice. "You should have believed the things Kar-hinter told you about the Cross-Line Worlds, you should have accepted the mental programming given you. But you did not. Why?

"Again you should have died in the so-called Albigensian Lines. You did not. Why?

"Closer in time: How is it, against all odds, when you escaped from Tar-hortha's moving skudder, you found yourself in a Line where there was another Outtimer known to you, who befriended you—when he should have been your enemy—and enabled you to gain access to another skudder? What got you *there,* Eric Mathers?

"Even among the Anglianers, there were times when you *should have died,* but you did not. Why?

"We want to know why!"

The eyes that looked at me now were not soft and warm, brown and friendly but cold and hard, a bitter, frozen fire.

"The Shadowy Man," I said, not knowing exactly what I meant or what I was trying to explain.

"The Shadowy Man!" the Tromas said. "What is the Shadowy Man?"

"I don't know," I said simply, honestly.

"You do not," the Tromas agreed. "We are aware of that. Yet you must have feelings about this thing, some theories, perhaps."

"Feelings, yes," I said. "But I don't have any theories. I don't know what he is or why he has—well—befriended me."

"Tell us about your feelings then."

"Well, my initial sensations, I suppose, were fear. It was like seeing a ghost or something. Yet, there was something familiar about it—him, I began calling it in my mind, for the Shadowy Man is male and more or less human."

"Familiar?" the Tromas asked. "In what way?"

"I don't know. There was just a sense of familiarity, friendliness, as if he were someone I'd known once, or—or might know in the future."

"Ah!" the Tromas cried. " '. . . in the future.' You had a sense of futurity about him then?"

I nodded. "Each time I encountered him I got a greater sense of, well, 'time,' as if time, the future and the past, were all wrapped up in him."

"Is there anything more?"

"Nothing I can put into words."

"Yet you have this feeling of *time*."

"I do."

"There is another falsehood that you and countless others have come to accept, a falsehood which has been 'proved' mathematically to a vast number of scientists."

"And what's that?" I asked.

"That travel through time is impossible, travel from one point in time to an earlier point in time."

I looked at her.

"Time travel *is* possible, Eric, travel from one location in *linear* time to another location, future and/or past. It is something we do not wish to become common knowledge. It is a secret *we* must keep at the peril of our racial lives."

I'm not certain that I believed her then, but I said, "Why tell me?"

"We do not believe that you will be in a position to reveal this to others."

"Oh," I said. The sword was still dangling precariously over my head.

"And the Shadowy Man, whatever he or *it* is, is aware of the possibility of time travel—is, in fact, a time traveler or something somehow akin to that. That is one of the reasons we fear him—and you."

For a moment I thought I had misunderstood her. They were afraid of me? The Kriths with all their power, all those vast worlds under their domination, were afraid of *me*? It was almost laughable. Almost.

"We can tell you that, Eric. We fear you—you and your Shadowy Man because you are a factor in muddying the waters of the future. Events that involve *you* and this—this Shadowy Man do not turn out as they should." Perhaps a bit petulantly: "What good is it to be precognitive if the futures you see do not work out as they are seen?"

What could I say to that?

"Eric Mathers, you are a danger to us." The words were spoken in a voice strong and harsh, a voice accustomed to exercising power and demanding respect. "You make it difficult for us to perceive the events that are to come, and that is one of our foremost functions. Yet"—the voice softened just a bit, a note of sadness entered, maybe—"we can still recognize some things about the future, some things involving you and this Shadowy Man that, shall we say, manipulates you?"

"I don't like that term, 'manipulates.' "

"Yet you are being manipulated by him."

"Okay, maybe I am, but that's not half so bad as being manipulated by Kriths."

"Are you certain?"

I didn't answer that one.

"What we see is some great power behind this Shadowy Man, some great power that may not yet have even come into existence, that is reaching back through time to alter events—perhaps it is altering events in order to bring itself into existence."

"What?" I asked involuntarily.

"This is a universe of probabilities, Eric, *Probabilities*.

Higher orders and lower orders of probability. It is a universe in which the *future* can reach back into the past in order to increase its *probability*. Lower orders of probability. That is so! Kriths know that.

"This power," she went on after a short pause to allow me to digest what she had just said, "is reaching back in time, we believe, in order to manipulate you and those you come in contact with toward some dark future end that is involved with, in some way we do not yet fathom, the *possible* destruction of the entire Krithian race!

"Your Shadowy Man is trying to kill us, Eric."

"That's what Tar-hortha said," I muttered almost to myself, the words of the dying Krith coming back to me.

The Tromas nodded. "Exactly how this Shadowy Man intends to accomplish this goal, if in fact this is his goal, we do not know. We are merely aware, in a vague and often insubstantial way, that this is so."

"And you blame me?" I asked.

She nodded, but with no great zest. "We know your feelings toward us, Eric Mathers. We know you have no love for us, that you would prefer that we did not 'meddle' in human affairs. You do not know our goals, but you suspect them to be sinister and you believe that we do not have the best interests of the human race in mind. Is this not so?"

"It's so."

"You believe we have lied to you and to thousands of others. You believe the future danger to mankind and Krith to be a falsehood. You believe we have told the 'Greatest Lie' and many, many lesser ones."

"That's also so."

"In some respects, you are correct. In some you are not." There was a long pause, and during it I felt something in the air, an electrical charge, perhaps, and yet not that. What it was I couldn't be certain, but I had the feeling that, below or beyond my senses of perception, a complex conversation—and a judgment—was going on between the members of the Tromas, the gross and ugly female members of the race of Kriths.

Finally their speaker addressed me again: "Well, Eric, we will tell you some things few humans have ever been privileged to know."

The way she said it had the sound of another nail being driven into my coffin.

"We will tell you a tale," she began. "There is a certain human Timeline, the designation and co-ordinates of which I will not tell you; that is very carefully guarded by the Kriths and their Companions. Even the highest ranking Timeliners are unaware of it. It is one world that we will allow no tampering with, no inrush of Outtimers, no alterations. The natives of that Line are unaware of alternative Earths and shall be kept that way for some time into the future—until *we* are ready. It is a very important world to us—exactly how important I will explain to you.

"This particular world is more technologically advanced than are most of the Lines. Though its inhabitants are unaware of other worlds in paratime, they are well aware of other worlds in space. They are already, in this year, planting colonies on the Moon and Mars and soon will go on to the stars. Within a few decades they will invent a means of circumventing the speed of light and the stellar universe will be open to them. They will, in a little over a hundred years, begin to establish colonies on worlds outside the Solar System.

"They will encounter many obstacles among the stars. There are few worlds as hospitable to humankind as is this Earth. Most of the planets they will find will be forever beyond the reach of human colonization, and many of the others will not be suitable, for one reason or another, for settlement by human stock of the kind evolved so tediously over the ages.

"Yet the technologies of these people are not limited to those of space flight alone. They have also made great advances in the life sciences. They are—or will be—masters of biology, of genetics. Genetic engineering—the manipulation of the chromosomes of newly fertilized human ova—will be one of their accomplishments. With radiation and with microscopic instruments, with transplantation of DNA, it will be possible for them to vastly alter the genetic patterns of the unborn, to create from offsprings of humankind other sentient beings who may not always look as you think humans should look, descendants of humankind adapted to environments far colder or far hotter, far dryer or far wetter than any in which *you* and people like you could survive.

"They will seed the star-worlds with *people* of this kind."

Nothing of what she was saying was new to me. I'd seen or heard of all these things before on other Lines, but there was something about the way she was stringing them together that made a chill run up and down my spine, that brought a flat, dry nervousness into my mouth. I had some idea of what she was getting at.

"You are familiar with the Breston Star Catalog?" she asked.

I nodded. "It's in use on a number of the more advanced worlds," I said, "though few of those people are aware of the Breston Survey, at least by that name."

"Just so," the Tromas said. "There is a K0 star some twelve light-years from Earth, a star orange in color, with an absolute magnitude of +0.8. A pleasant enough star. It is listed in the Breston Catalog as UR-427-51. On some Lines it is listed as Beta in the constellation of Gemini, the zodiacal sign of the Twins. It is the companion star of Castor and is often called Pollux. You may be familiar with that star, if you have ever been given to stargazing.

"Its fourth planet is of greater size than Earth and is largely covered by water. It is a very cloudy world, given to vast and terrible electrical storms. It would not be a pleasant place for the likes of you.

"Yet, it is a world rich in resources, rich in life, mostly aquatic—multitudes of swimming creatures abound in its vast seas. It is a world that some found—will find, I should say—most interesting, and one suitable for habitation by properly adapted, genetically modified colonists.

"Someday in the future the people of the Line we told you of will find it desirable, for reasons that are of no great interest to you or to us now, to plant a colony of properly modified human stock on that world.

"They will do so. It will have fateful consequences for the future, I assure you."

She paused for a long while as if thinking carefully over what she would say next.

"Eric, I will tell you another story before I conclude

this one, for the two stories must come together in the end, or we fear their meanings will not be clear to you.

"This universe, this universe of universes, of parallel worlds, of alternative Timelines is a more fragile thing than you might think, far more fragile than we have ever revealed. It appears that this universe of universes of ours is not as utterly vast as we might like to think, not as limitless in its resources. There is, in a way that you might have never imagined, a very real Law of Conservation of Matter/Energy. The universe is limited in its resources. That is, it cannot go on forever spawning Timeline after Timeline after Timeline. There are limits! And once those limits are past, there will be disaster."

I was trying not to form judgments, not to come to conclusions. On the one hand there was a sense of sincerity, of total and complete honesty exuded by the old female Krith, yet, on the other hand, over the years the Kriths had told so many lies, so many lies that had seemed to be totally convincing, I found it hard to credit truth to anything a Krith said without hard objective proof to back it up. And yet . . . this wasn't an ordinary Krith; this being before me represented the masters of wisdom of their race, the fountainhead of their plans, the guardians of their knowledge and maybe also their most accomplished liars?

I wasn't believing or disbelieving yet. I wasn't even certain I fully understood what I was being told.

"Try to imagine this, Eric," the speaker for the Tromas was going on. "In the beginning, when the universe first came into being, when there was only one master Timeline and it existed in and of itself, it contained in itself all the chronal or parachronal energy, all the temporal potential that would ever exist. Then as the Lines began branching, as the various alternative worlds came into being, that temporal potential began being divided among them."

"I understand that much," I said in the pause that followed. "The various probability potentials, East, West, positive, negative, are what make passage from Timeline to Timeline possible."

"That is correct," the Tromas said. "But have you ever considered that each succeeding Timeline, as history progresses, is lower in potential than those which had existed earlier?"

"Of course," I said, not yet realizing the full implications.

"And that the universe *is* limited?"

"Yes," I said. "We know that the universe isn't really infinite, but—"

"Something is either infinite or it is finite, Eric," the Tromas said with a voice like steel. "If something is infinite there is no end, *ever*. If it is finite there is a limit that, sooner or later, must be reached.

"The probability energy, one might say, of the universe is large, large beyond imagining, yet it is not infinite, and for billions of years it has been spreading itself thinner and thinner as more and more Timelines come into being to further subdivide that potential. The introduction of sentient life into the universe some tens of thousands of years ago greatly accelerated that process, a process that continues to accelerate as intelligent life spawns more and more alternatives, more and more probabilities."

It began to dawn on me what she—they?—were getting at. "You're trying to tell me that sooner or later the universe is going to—what?—run out of probability potential or something?"

"Not exactly that, Eric. There was so much parachronal energy available at the beginning of the universe and there is just as much available now—the laws of entropy, of increasing disorder, as they are normally understood, do not have full application regarding parachronal energy, since forces can, in a sense, reverse or reduce the amount of *parachronal entropy* in the universe. What I mean is that there is now no more nor no less probability potential available than there was, it is just spread more thinly."

"Are you saying then that there will come a time when that potential is spread between too many Timelines?"

"Exactly, Eric, and when that time comes, the laws of conservation of energy—or something very like them— will come into play to rearrange the probability indices of the Timelines."

"What?" I asked, getting lost with that one.

"In order to maintain itself—though not exactly in the

forms to which we have become accustomed—the universe will have to make major readjustments within itself.

"Timelines vary in their probability, Eric. Some are *more likely* than others, more *probable,* and possess, even now, greater values of parachronal energy than do Lines of lesser likelihood."

"I think I follow that," I said, finding that, despite myself, I *was* believing her.

"Those with lesser likelihood, with lower orders of probability will *cease to exist* and their parachronal energy will be redistributed among the Lines of higher orders of probability. That is to say that a vast number of Timelines will cease to exist in order that a smaller number, with greater likelihoods, will be able to continue to exist."

"I see," I said, not altogether certain that I saw it at all.

"All that I had been saying is a great simplification, Eric. Let me qualify it by saying this: there are *indications* that the universe has reached this sort of situation a number of times in the past, the *remote* past as humans and Kriths measure the passage of time, and has, in each case, reordered itself, achieving greater simplification and less entropy, reduced the number of existing Timelines, and increased their individual parachronal potentials."

"And this has something to do with the Kriths' master plan?" I asked.

"This has *everything* to do with our 'master plan,' Eric," the Tromas said. "Let me return to my original 'fable,' if I may."

I nodded. There didn't seem much to say at this point.

"Someday in the not-too-distant future, the inhabitants of a certain Line will establish a colony on the fourth planet of UR-427-51, a large, aquatic world given to vast electrical storms. Those who make up this colony will be of modified human stock, adapted to a very wet climate, a thick atmosphere, a higher gravitational field than Earth's and to a constant barrage of atmospherical electrical energy.

"Even for them, those genetically modified colonists, it will not be a pleasant world, and they will often dream of the Earth they left behind, the Earth to which they will never be allowed to return—even though, with minor adaptations, they could thrive in Earth's more benign climate. They are exiles, never really at home on the world they have been given, compelled to drag out their lives amid swamps, rain, and lightning in order to provide those on Earth with luxuries and delicacies they could well do without."

At this point her tense shifted from the future to the past. I didn't comment. I thought I understood.

"In a few more decades other things became apparent to these colonists, other even more unpleasant things. The genetic engineers on Earth had not done their job as well as they might have. There was a flaw, several flaws in the genetic patterns of the colonists. One was a sex-linked defect, carried by the males, but passed on to the females, one that caused a terribly high infant-mortality rate among the females of this new subspecies, and that left those who survived with glandular problems even the most sophisticated endocrinologists could not have remedied."

Of course I'd suspected who these modified-human colonists were. Now it was confirmed.

"Other genetic flaws showed up with the passage of time, even some that were, in the long run, beneficial. The females that survived the traumas of birth, that survived the effects of glands run wild, seemed to possess certain abilities not yet fully understood back on Earth, psionic abilities, limited powers of telepathy among themselves, the power to gain glimpses of the future—and to see that there was not a single, simple future, but a multitude of them, all existing simultaneously, real and valid.

"The colonists, in their rain-drenched huts in the swamps of UR-427-51-IV saw stretching to the parachronal East and West of them a multitude of alternative worlds, and dreamed of them, dreamed of escape, of flight to other Lines of Time where they were the masters and not the slaves of the *normal people* back on Earth.

"And they began questing about for a means of achieving those desires.

"You are following us, Eric?"

"I'm following you, but I'm wondering where you're going."

"You shall see.

"Decades went by, desolate, unhappy decades, until the colonists discovered that they had the power they sought right within themselves—the power to escape the world-frame that held them.

"You might consider this a coincidence too great to be countenanced, a wildly improbable coincidence not worth crediting if you did not have the living evidence before you of its truth.

"Yet, Eric, it is a coincidence only in one way of looking at it. There were a number of Timelines on which UR-427-51-IV was colonized in this fashion—Timelines branching from the very fact it was colonized—and on most of those Lines, on all of them but one, the colonists were doomed to a servile existence until Earth tired of them and forgot to send them essential supplies and the colonies died out.

"On one of these possible worlds, on one out of many, the right combination of factors existed, the right genetic *flaws* came together to produce what might be called a 'benign mutation' had normal evolutionary processes been in operation. In one of the UR-427-51-IV's these genetic flaws within the neural organs originally engineered to help the colonists cope with the vast electrical potentials within the atmosphere of the planet provided the means of escape—the ability to *skud* across the Timelines which the deformed, but psionic females had discovered.

"The Kriths were born."

The Tromas fell silent. I looked into her great brown eyes and, despite myself, I found myself believing every word she'd said. Somehow, despite all reason, everything she'd said made sense.

"We will try to keep the rest as brief as possible. Time is running short.

"In a nutshell, Eric: with this newly found ability, these abilities, our ancestors were able to psionically commandeer a supply ship from Earth and in it returned to their home planet. When there, as a collective group numbering only some several hundred, they began to skud across the Lines of Time in search of a suitable Timeline to call home.

"After some searching, this Line, this very world upon

which we are presently living, was found, far to the T-East and here, for a time, we settled. All would have been well for the descendants of those original Kriths, save for the precognitive abilities we females possess.

"In the long years that followed we peered into the future, we studied and researched our powers, and looked farther and farther into time to come, and at last we saw that, at some point in the future, exactly when is unknown, more than a few hundred, but less than a few thousand, years from now, the universe will be forced to 'reorder' itself along lines of fewer alternative worlds.

"*And* we saw that the Timeline that had given birth to the Kriths would be among those worlds, those Lines with too low a probability to remain in existence after the reordering. Timelines would wink out of existence as if they had never been, our Line of origin with them—and we ourselves as well.

"The race of Kriths had too low an order of probability to exist *after* the reordering."

"My God!" I said despite myself. Now I understood. If she wasn't lying. And I didn't believe she was.

"Perhaps you see now, Eric, why we have been doing what we have been doing. It is not so much to enslave mankind, as to save ourselves, to reorder as many of the Timelines as possible along lines that would not have existed without Kriths, to weave the Krithian race as firmly as possible into as many worlds as we can—in short, to create the highest possible probability for the Krithian race."

"This almost makes sense," I said, more to myself than to the Tromas.

"How it was we discovered the one Timeline that had achieved true time travel I will not go into, nor how it was that we, our entire race, migrated back in time hundreds of years in order to begin our 'remodeling' as early as possible. You must merely accept these things as so, as you have seen for yourself."

"But . . ." I stammered, a thousand other questions bursting into my mind.

"The time allowed for our interview grows short, Eric. Ask only your most important questions."

I fought to bring my jumbled thoughts into some sort of

order. There seemed no time to ask detailed questions, nor to form moral judgments. Later—if I had a later—I would take time to do that. Now . . .

"The Paratimers?" I asked. "What are they and—"

"We can tell you almost nothing about them, Eric. Our knowledge is nearly as limited as yours. Even our psionic abilities cannot reach far enough across the Lines of Time to locate their place/time of origin or to determine their real motives. We only know these things: they *are not* human nor are they likely to be of human stock; they are the sworn enemies of the Kriths and their plans, and perhaps of all mankind as well; and if they were to have their way and restructure the Lines to suit *their* purposes, *we* would lose much of the probability we have worked for so long to create. We cannot allow that to happen. We *will* find means of stopping the Paratimers."

There was finality in her voice, both in regard to the Paratimers and in regard to my questions about them, I thought.

"I came to KHL-ooo," I began in the silence she left me, "for two reasons. One was to ask—"

"We know the reasons, Eric," the Tromas said. "We have answered all the questions we may. When you leave here, you will be taken to the place where Sally Beall von Heinen awaits you."

"And then?" I asked, hoping for one more answer, hoping . . .

"We have not taken this time to speak to a man who will soon be dead, Eric Mathers. It is not *our* intention to have you taken from this place and be put to death."

"What is your intention?"

She smiled a long, languid smile that was somehow very out of place on that gross face, and I wondered what a female Krith would look like without those "genetic flaws" she'd spoken of.

"There are things about you *we* want to know, things you yourself cannot answer for us—and we want to meet this Shadowy Man of yours. We would like to talk with him —or it—or *them*. It may be that our goals are not as mutually irreconcilable as might first appear. There are perhaps mutual goals to which we can all aspire."

"Then I am to be kept as a prisoner?"

"A prisoner, yes. But we will make your captivity as pleasant as possible—and as pleasant as you will allow."

"I seemed to have heard that somewhere before."

"Among the Paratimers in Staunton?"

I nodded.

"Then there is nothing more we can say," the Tromas, in a collective voice, said.

The doors behind me opened and three Kriths, Cal-sarlin, Vor-kawin, and Ces-karlet entered.

"Come with us, Eric," Vor-kawin said.

I did.

What else could I do?

And hadn't the Tromas said that Sally was waiting?

18
Sally Again!

Cal-sarkin led me from the Palace of the Tromas. Vor-kawin and Ces-karlet, quiet and perhaps even respectful toward me after my interview with the Tromas—an interview during which they seemed to have expected me to be struck dead or something—gave us a terse good-by, remaining behind to minister to the Tromas, or whatever it was they did for a living.

"We have been informed that your execution has been stayed," Cal-sarlin told me as we walked down a long, narrow path through towering arbors that bore flowering plants that resembled roses, a little, leaving the palace on the side opposite the one we entered, "postponed indefinitely. The Tromas appear to have plans for you."

"So it would appear," I said, my voice as noncommittal as I could make it.

"Do you know what these plans are, Eric?"

Was he asking just to see if I knew? Or did he want to know himself?

"Well," I began, "it seems that the Tromas want me to help them get in touch with a friend of mine."

"And you are going to do it?"

I shrugged. "It would seem I have little choice but to co-operate but, to tell you the truth, I don't know how to get in touch with him any more than they do."

"A friend, you say?"

"In a manner of speaking."

The pseudoroses gave way to a large, circular grassy area dotted here and there with exotic, fragrant shrubs. The path led across the circle, through a cluster of willow-like trees to what at first appeared to be nothing more than a low mound of earth covered with grass and flowering plants. But it had a door in it.

In the sky above us birdlike creatures sang, and beyond

them, farther away, a delta-winged craft flashed in the sunlight, went on toward a distant horizon.

"Would this be the one called 'the Shadowy Man'?" my Krithian companion asked.

"It would."

Since leaving the presence of the Tromas I had been trying to avoid looking at the Krith, at any Krith. I didn't want to look at them, to see them in the new light cast by the revelations of "the guardians of Krithian wisdom."

But I couldn't help myself.

I *knew* the Tromas hadn't been lying, not this time.

The Kriths *were* human beings, or their ancestors had been. They were the descendants of *my kind*, modified almost beyond recognition by genetic manipulation. A new and different species, in some ways superior to *us*, in some ways with abilities far beyond those of mankind, yet in other ways so terribly handicapped I found it hard to believe they'd survived at all.

And when my eyes, despite themselves, strayed to the naked form of the Krith who walked beside me, I saw the resemblances, the evidence of their kinship to my people that had been there all along, which I had ignored all these years, which so many people had ignored.

They are bigger than us, and colored differently, with features and anatomical characteristics that varied from ours, yet on a moonlit night, from a distance of only a few yards, it would have been difficult to distinguish a large naked man from a large naked Krith, if you didn't happen to see the Krith's prehensile tail or his absence of ears or one of the other minor characteristics that would show up in silhouette.

Yet physically—and, I realized, maybe psychologically too—they had more in common with us than they didn't have.

Dammit! I should have known all along.

All the facts had been there. Except for this theory of "Universal Timeline Probability Potential Reordering" or whatever the hell you wanted to call it, everything the Tromas had told me had been out in plain sight for years. I'd known about Timelines that had starflight. I'd known Timelines that had mastered genetic engineering. I'd known about human adaptations to hostile environments. I'd known about . . . All of it!

Yet I'd never put all the separate pieces together to come up with the Kriths.

I wondered if anyone else had.

And if they had, what had become of them?

Squelched by the Kriths?

"This woman, this Sally," Cal-sarlin was asking me as these things were running through my mind, "is she really worth the danger you have put yourself in?"

"I think she is," I said, though Sally was but one of the two big reasons I'd come to KHL-ooo.

"I am no judge of your women, of course," the Krith said. I wondered what he meant by that.

We were nearing the mound at the end of the path. The one with the door in it.

"I am taking you to her now," he said. "That was my instruction."

"I was given to understand that," I said.

The mound's door opened automatically and we stepped into another of those elevatorlike cubicles. The door closed behind us and Cal-sarlin spoke a command in his alien language. The cubicle moved downward and then horizontally under the earth.

"I gather that you maintain that this Shadowy Man is as much a mystery to you as to us, is that so?" the Krith asked.

"That's so."

"Yet, this power has befriended you in the past?"

"That's so too."

"You are alive only through the agency of this Shadowy Man?"

I nodded. I didn't want to say "That's so" again.

"Yet you have no idea who or what he is?"

"I have ideas. Hundreds of them. But none that makes sense."

"And the Tromas expect the Shadowy Man to appear to you again, and they will then interrogate him?"

"Something like that, I suppose."

"You will go along with this?"

"Have I any choice?"

Maybe I should have been frightened. I'd been given a

sentence of death, and it hadn't yet been countermanded, just postponed, it appeared. And, probably, when the Tromas found out whatever they wanted to find out about the Shadowy Man, that death sentence would be reinstated and Eric Mathers would go to the block or the gas chamber or the firing squad.

But I wasn't frightened. Maybe I was numb. Or just stupid. Or maybe some part of my mind expected the Shadowy Man to come riding in like the U. S. Cavalry to rescue Sally and me just in the nick of time.

Or maybe I wasn't frightened because I was too excited about seeing Sally again.

The cubicle made a lurch and headed in an upward direction. In seconds it came to a stop and the door slid open.

"She is being kept here," Cal-sarlin said as he led me out and pointed toward a towering needle of a building that looked something like an Egyptian obelisk magnified a hundred times or more, set in the middle of a wide, grassy plain on the edge of which some bovine animals placidly grazed.

"A jail?" I asked.

The Krith smiled. "We do not call it that."

"What do you call it?"

"Oh, you might translate the term as 'restricted apartment complex' or even as 'minimal security detention facilities,' whichever is more pleasing to you."

"How about 'jail'?"

"If you insist." He was still smiling.

A flagstone path led from the cubicle's mound to the large glass door that led into the lobby of the "minimal security detention facilities" and a brace of Mager types with ugly automatic weapons that reminded me of characters I'd seen in a dream a long time ago. It had been a dream, hadn't it?

Cal-sarlin spoke briefly, in unintelligible terms, with one of them, who then turned and spoke into a communications device mounted in the wall. When equally unintelligible words came back in reply, we were allowed to proceed, entering another cubicle that was a real elevator that whisked us upward toward the top of the spire.

"You will be allowed to spend the night with this

woman," Cal-sarlin told me as the elevator climbed. I didn't care much for the way he pronounced the word "woman," but then Kriths are that way. "Tomorrow you are to be interviewed by certain members of the, er, government."

"Government?" I asked.

"Ruling council, chamber of elders, parliament, there is no exact term in Shangalis for their function."

"Okay."

"You did not think the Tromas exercised complete civil authority, did you?"

"I suppose I assumed it."

"An erroneous assumption, Eric. Their work is far too important for them to concern themselves with the day-to-day functioning of society. Such mundane work is in the hands of others."

"I see," I said, but wondered if I did, and wondered what kind of complexities there were in Krithian society. Were there in it, as in most human socieities, rival factions, contending bodies, divided opinions; was it possible that the great Krithian machine was not nearly so monolithic as it appeared from the outside? Maybe I'd never know, but it made interesting speculation.

Then we were there, somewhere high in the building. The elevator came to a stop, doors opened, and Cal-sarlin preceded me out of it into a short corridor that made a sharp "L" turn and led to two more Mager types, armed like the ones below, standing before a door marked with runic characters I couldn't read.

Cal-sarlin spoke to them, they replied, stepped aside and let the Krith knock on the door.

From a hidden loudspeaker—or something that served a similar function—a word I didn't understand was spoken by a voice I knew.

The door opened.

The Krith led me in.

Sally let out a gasp of surprise, astonishment.

She hadn't changed.

Sally Beall, once the wife of Albert von Heinen, once the mistress of Mica: blond hair, greenish eyes, five-five in unshod feet, built like a beautiful woman ought to be built.

212 RICHARD C. MEREDITH

Sally whom I loved. . . .

She was dressed in a short blue garment that had something of the look of Classical Greece to it, and her hair was done up in a kind of bun on the top of her head. There was a slender book in her hand. . . .

And in her eyes a look of surprised delight mixed with apprehension.

"Eric," she said slowly, mastering her astonishment.

I brushed around the Krith's big form, took her in my arms.

"Eric, what are you doing here?"

"I came to find you," I said, and then smothered her words with my mouth. I didn't give a damn if the Krith *was* watching. What did he know about such things?

Finally Cal-sarlin's voice interrupted us: "I will leave you to your pleasures."

I broke from Sally and turned to face him.

"Sally can explain the rules to you," he said. "There are but few of them. You will not find your confinement a hardship, I assure you, unless you are terribly foolish."

I nodded, grunted that I understood.

"Do not forget," he went on. "Tomorrow morning, as soon as you have completed breakfast, I will return for you."

"To see your government?" I asked.

The Krith nodded. "Until then, adieu." He actually said the word, "adieu." I wonder where in hell he picked that up. Then he was gone and Sally and I were alone. At last!

"You shouldn't have come here, Eric," Sally said when I turned away from the door that had closed behind the Krith. "You've done exactly what they wanted you to do."

"I know."

"Why did you do it?"

"Just don't have good sense, I suppose." But as I looked at her, I saw that I did have a very good reason for having come to KHL-ooo. Sally alone was reason enough. And I wondered how it was that I, that hard-bitten, free-booting old lecher, had ever gotten myself in this kind of an emotional relationship with a woman. Not *a* woman. With Sally. She was the reason. I actually did love her. . . .

"How have they treated you?"

"Not badly, actually," she said and made a sweeping

movement with her hands that took in the room we were in and the rest of the apartment I hadn't yet seen.

"They've questioned you?" I asked.

"Oh, yes. Under hypnosis and with drugs and once or twice I think they used telepathy on me. It was never actually painful. They haven't *really* hurt me, but I don't think I was able to keep anything from them as if I knew anything they didn't already know." There was a long pause. "But I was lonely, Eric. I missed you."

"I know. I came as soon as I could."

"You shouldn't have. They may kill you."

"I know," I repeated. "But I had to find you. And I had to ask the Kriths some questions. I just came from the Tromas."

"The Tromas!"

Briefly I told her of my interview with the females of the Krithian race and what they had told me about themselves, about their plans and goals, and about the future of the universe itself.

"And you really believe them now?" she asked when I'd concluded.

"I do. Damn me, but I believe that this time they're really telling the truth. I'm not sure why, but I do believe them."

"What kind of proof have they offered?"

"None. Maybe that's one of the reasons I believe. I mean, always before the Kriths have bent over backward to show proof of their tales, which turn out to be lies. Now they don't seem to care whether I believe them or not. I think that's the way they'd act if they were telling the truth."

"I'm not sure I understand."

"I'm not sure I do either."

"Are you hungry?"

"Famished. I can't remember the last time I ate."

"Let me get you something. And a drink."

"A drink. Yes. I can use one."

Thirty minutes later, sandwiches and the warmth of liquor inside me, my boots off and my shirt unbuttoned, more comfortable than I could recall having been since the days in Jock's diner near Daleville, Georgia, I sat back in a huge overstuffed chair in the living room of Sally's apartment/jail cell, my feet propped up and Sally sitting beside me on the arm of the chair.

"What are we going to do now, Eric?" Sally asked.

We were both drinking a delightful white wine and I was smoking a huge, mellow cigar she'd conjured up from somewhere. "Right now I don't plan on doing a damned thing."

"You know what I mean."

"I know. And I don't know what we're going to do." I looked around the room. "I suppose this place is bugged?"

"I suppose it is. I haven't tried to find out."

"With the technology they've got to call on, you'd never find evidence of it. But I'd be very surprised if they aren't watching every move we make, recording every word."

"I'm sure you're right."

I waved at invisible cameras, said "Hi!" to unseen eavesdroppers.

"Not that I've got any great big secret plans I don't want them to hear, I just like privacy when I'm with my woman." Unfortunately, I was telling the truth. I didn't have any plans. The plans I'd formulated had never gone beyond getting to the Krithian Homeline, finding Sally and some answers. What was going to happen after that I'd never worked out. Now that I was really there—had my Sally and some of my answers—maybe I'd better try to figure out what was next.

"We could turn out the lights," Sally said softly, her hand brushing my cheek.

"I doubt that would do much good. I'm sure they've got ways of seeing in the dark."

"I'd feel better if it were dark." The brush became a caress. She slid from the arm of the chair into my lap. My arms went around her, pulled her closer.

"God, I've missed you, Eric," she whispered.

"And I've missed you," I whispered back and drew her face to mine and kissed her longer and better than before.

"Let me show you where the bedroom is," she said softly when the kiss was over. "I think you'll like it."

"I know I'll like it."

I wanted to see my Sally again, see her body under the

gown she was wearing, see the curves and mounds of her as my hands touched and caressed and fondled, but she insisted on darkness, fooling herself that the Krithian spy devices couldn't see what we were doing in the darkness. I was sure they could, but . . .

So in the darkness, on a great bed that had been designed to hold more than one, I felt the warmth of her, the curves of soft flesh that my hands had felt so often before, and then the secret places of her that awaited me.

"I've missed you so much," she whispered to me in the darkness, yielding, opening to me. "I've wanted you so badly, but for your sake I'd hoped you'd never come."

"I had to," I whispered back.

The bed rocked under us, slowly at first, then with increasing tempo.

"I'm glad."

"So am I."

A gasp, a deeply drawn breath, a sigh. "Now, Eric. I can't wait any longer."

Now, I agreed silently. For neither could I wait longer. Oh, my Sally! My Sally. My Sally. . . .

19
The Shadowy Man

"What do you think they're going to do to you?"

Outside the world was in darkness, creeping toward a dawn but a few hours away. We'd slept and then awakened, like newlyweds on honeymoon, to make love again, and now we lay side by side on the bed, a dim lamp our only illumination, looking up at a mosaic ceiling, a half-smoked cigarette between my fingers.

"I don't know," I told her. "I suppose it'll depend on what happens."

"The Shadowy Man?"

"Uh-huh," I grunted.

"Do you think he'll come?"

"I don't know. I never know."

"What is he, Eric?"

"I wish I knew."

I snuffed out my cigarette and rolled over to kiss her again.

"Already?" she asked.

"Not yet." I said, smiling down at her. "But I wish . . ." She smiled back, didn't speak.

Another kiss and I rolled onto my back again, looking up at the dim and distant ceiling.

"If there were any way I could contact him—if I knew how—I'd tell him not to come here."

"Do you think they could capture a ghost?"

"I don't know. But he's been my friend and I wouldn't want to put him in that danger."

"Are you certain he's your friend?"

"He's helped me. He's kept me alive."

"I wonder . . ." she began, then let her voice trail off as she became aware of something that was also coming to my attention. There was in the air of the room something akin to a chill, a tension that also reminded me of the feel

217

of the atmosphere before the beginning of an electrical storm, and I thought I could almost smell ozone.

"What is it, Eric?" Sally whispered, sitting up in the bed, clutching the sheet at her breast and throat.

"Wait," I whispered back.

The sense of tension grew. I half-expected to see St. Elmo's fire dancing across the furniture, to see a bolt of lightning leap from the ceiling's light fixture to one of the bedposts.

Then there was a *presence* in the room, a vagueness with a manlike shape in the darkness of the far corner, a thing only half-visible in the gloom, yet there was in me no doubt that the room was occupied by *something* in addition to Sally and myself.

The Shadowy Man spoke: "It was very difficult this time," the strangely familiar voice said, "getting here. I didn't think it would be this hard."

"Eric!" Sally cried, dropped the sheet, drew herself against me.

"It's okay," I said. "I know who it is."

"That's your voice, Eric," Sally stammered out in a whispering voice.

"There is little time," the Shadowy Man said, now as solid and concrete as I'd ever seen the form, still little more than a column of smoke with a manlike shape standing in the gloom. "And the forces involved in this are beyond your present comprehension. In moments, if not already, the Tromas will know I'm here and then—Well, you've got to get out of here, the two of you."

"Out of here?" I asked stupidly.

"That's why I came, dammit!, to rescue you two." Somehow the voice, the words it spoke weren't as vague and alien as the shape that spoke them, but solid and real, the kind of words a human being would have spoken, that I would have spoken.

"There's a way to escape," the Shadowy Man said, "and if you'll listen to me I'll tell you how to do it."

"We're listening," I said.

"Very well," the Shadowy Man said, and in a terse, strained voice he told us how to get from Sally's apartment to the roof of the towering spire of a building, a half-secret stairway that would take us up to where there would be "a means of escape" waiting us. There would be guards and obstacles before us, though the Shadowy Man would do everything he could to help pave the way for us.

"And then what?" I asked, my voice coming out around an awkward lumpiness in my throat.

"You escape," the substantial voice from the insubstantial form said. "What you do after that is up to you, Eric, and you, Sally. I can't tell you what to do once you escape this Line. I've already done far more than I should. I'm not yet certain just where in the orders of probability —or improbability"—there was a half-chuckle in the voice—"all this lies anyway. We may one day find out that none of it has happened anyway."

"What do you mean?" I asked.

"Nothing," answered the Shadowy Man.

I thought I detected a second form of tension in the air, again something like the rapid approach of a thunderstorm, an electrical charge growing in the air, yet somehow different from what had gone before, in a way alien and full of menace, and in a fashion that brought into my mind the image of a gross form that could have been feminine in some other context.

"Now you must work out some simple ruse to distract the guards outside the doors of the apartment," the ghostly figure said. "Sally, you can help in this. Draw them into the room. Get their attention. Then perhaps Eric can do something. And remember, they have no women of their own. They're drawn to human women, some of them."

Sally might have asked him to explain that, but she too seemed to be growing aware of the new element of tension in the air, seemed to be caught and held by it like a fly in amber.

"They know!" the Shadowy Man said suddenly, his voice grown thin.

I knew exactly what he meant. For the briefest of instants I seemed to occupy the same place and time as the Shadowy Man, and if I did not see through his eyes and feel through his senses, I was aware of the same things as he, shared his memories and sensations, saw the danger that lay some miles away in space, yet which was exerting some powerful and rapidly growing force against him, a psionic force that in moments could sweep over him and destroy him.

I gasped aloud in shared pain.

"Eric!" Sally cried.

Another universe of memories, thoughts, feelings, impressions swept over me, shared with me in that fraction of a second by the being I'd been calling the Shadowy Man.

"You're me," I said aloud in a strangled voice.

"In a sense," he answered. "You might be me. You might become me, given time."

And I knew that the Tromas hadn't been lying to me. What they had said was true. But—but it wasn't the whole story. Not all of it. And there was much yet to be done. Oh, so damned much!

And the odds against my living were enormous.

Yet here was some future version of myself, some projection of a future version(s), somehow come back in time to aid me—the temporal paradoxes of it all were almost overwhelming.

The universe was a can of worms, and each worm was bending back upon itself to eat its own tail. . . .

Lightning flashed in the apartment's bedroom, leaping from some point near the ceiling toward the form of the Shadowy Man. And this time it wasn't imaginary lightning.

The Shadowy Man blazed with a halo of light.

"I will fight them as long as I can, but I don't know how long that will be. I'm a long way from home. . . ." Lightning crackled again, briefly illuminating the room, filling the air with the scent of ozone. "Hurry!" he cried.

By now I'd gotten myself out of bed and was drawing Sally with me. Among the things half-registered in my mind was the awareness that the Shadowy Man was fighting an unequal battle, was pitting *his* already strained psionic powers against those of the Tromas, fresh and strong and close. How far from us the Shadowy Man really was I had only the vaguest of concepts.

"Come on," I said to Sally and half-dragged her, the both of us naked, from the bedroom and toward the luxurious apartment's living room and entrance hallway. Behind us lightning, and other forces less apparent to the eye, flickered and flashed through the bedroom. It was a wonder that everything there wasn't already ablaze.

"What're we going to do?" Sally asked as we neared the door that led into the apartment—and out of it.

"Start screaming," I said, coming to a stop. "Just stand there and scream your head off."

"What're . . ."

"Just do it."

"Now?"

"When I say so. Stand right there."

At the end of the short entrance hallway Sally stood, naked and lovely. At the other end was the doorway beyond which stood the two Mager types who guarded us. At least I thought there were two and assumed they were still there.

I threw myself flat against the wall at the end of the hallway, around the corner, just out of eyeshot of someone entering the door. I triggered the preparatory circuits of my augmentation, those that I hadn't already triggered unconsciously.

"Now," I said.

Sally looked at me for a moment, a puzzled, frightened expression on her face. In the now-distant bedroom a caged beast growled savagely. Sally screamed. I don't think she had to fake it.

I shifted into augmentation and felt the world slow around me, heard the sounds of Sally's scream slide from shrill to a bassness like some terribly low, sad brass instrument, saw a redness enter the world that hadn't been there before.

An eternity slowly dragged itself along, limping like the world was whimpering to an end.

I heard a rumbling from the far end of the short hallway. The door was opening.

Then deep thuds, slow and menacing, and a booming bass drum of a voice asking Sally questions I probably couldn't have understood even if I hadn't been in augmentation.

Sally just kept screaming.

"Come on, come on, come on," I said to myself.

Thud. Thud. Thud.

With a slowness I didn't think I could endure much

longer, one of the Mager guards advanced into the room. His buddy must still be waiting outside, probably with one of those ugly automatic weapons aimed down the hallway. So be it.

Then he came into sight, the tall, slender form in an outlandish uniform, weapon in hand, yet with a puzzled bemused expression on the rugged planes of his face. What was it the Shadowy Man had said about their having no women of their own?

For a moment my attention was drawn away from the approaching guard, for from out of the bedroom behind us came a figure even more startling in its appearance, startling even to me who had seen him but moments before.

The Shadowy Man came into the apartment's living room, his smoky, ghostly form now clothed in glimmering lightnings and halos of incandescence; sheets of auroral flame surrounded him, flickering in neon colors across the spectrum from the edges of infrared to the margins of ultraviolet. The air around him was ionizing; carpeting and woodwork smoldered as he brushed across them, moving even more slowly and ponderously than could be accounted for by my augmentation.

For instants I was again a part of the Shadowy Man and "saw" what he "saw," "felt" what he "felt," fought with him against the Tromas who had wished him to come and now that he was here wished only to destroy him forever, him and all the menace he had brought to the Kriths and their plans to alter the altering of the universe.

The Shadowy Man was locked in combat—mortal or perhaps immortal combat—with the minds that guided the destiny of the Krithian race. Blindly he—and I with him—stumbled forward, hardly aware of the shadowy form that was all he had of a body in this space/time. His mind—his ultramind, his supermind, his composite mind—ranged beyond the spatial locus where plays of light and shadow, focuses of scattered matter and energy formed the figure which I had seen, the voice which had spoken to us.

And then, as quickly, I was myself again, and was

aware of the Mager type advancing slowly toward Sally.

Then I leaped.

Maybe the guard was ready to go Augie himself. He should have been. But I never gave him a chance. I was on him before he had an opportunity to wonder where I was, on him and carrying him down to the floor, one hand around his throat, the other doubled into a fist and battering at the cartilage of his nose, one knee in his groin. "Get down!" I yelled to Sally, knowing she couldn't understand me.

Then we were on the floor, the Mager type and I, his eyes bulging out, his tongue swelling, his face turning red around a shattered nose.

Sally was throwing herself down, and out of the way, a graceful slow-motion dance of escape as a splatter of bullets burst from an automatic weapon at the far end of the hall. The other guard was going into augmentation, but there was nothing I could do about that now.

It couldn't have been more than seconds, but it seemed like ages, that we rolled across the floor, bullets cutting the air around us, gouging through the carpeting into the floor—the second guard didn't seem to care whether he killed his companion, as long as he got me. But I killed his buddy first—I think—I felt the cartilage of his windpipe crush beneath my savage fingers; he gagged, spit blood, then his eyes rolled back and I tore his weapon from his weakening fingers, pushing him away from me.

If I hadn't been certain of killing him—for Magers, like Kriths, are unusually hard to kill—that doubt was settled for me when a random spray of bullets, meant for me, ruptured through his body, stitching a line down his side and hips. Nothing inside him could have withstood that!

But that second guard—Augie that he was—didn't give himself a fair chance. He was standing right there in the open doorway, light from the outside corridor behind him. He couldn't have set himself up any better if he'd been doing it at my suggestion. He was cut almost in half when he went down and I released my grip on the automatic's trigger. I was certain I'd gotten both the primary and the secondary brain.

I let my augmentation run down. As much as I wanted

to keep it on, I knew Sally couldn't keep up with me if I did, and I couldn't very well talk with her either.

"Let's go," I cried as the world came back into focus. "We need clothing and . . ."

I was coming to my feet, the blood of the dead man— or whatever he was—who lay on the floor splattered on my shoulders, face, chest.

"No time," I said, grabbed Sally's wrist and propelled her toward the door.

I grabbed the second Mager's automatic and threw it to Sally. It *might* help if we were both armed.

Waving good-by to the Shadowy Man, who I'm certain didn't see *me*, I said to Sally, "That way," and pointed in the direction where the Shadowy Man had said lay the half-hidden stairway that would take us up to the roof and our "means of escape."

And as we moved away from the apartment, I could feel, could sense the awful battle that was being waged there, the terrible energies that were flashing, flickering back and forth across time and space and coming together in that luxurious living room. The Tromas, ancient and wise in the use of their abilities, were bending all their available energies on the crushing of the insubstantial form I called the Shadowy Man. And I didn't think it would be long before they did. Maybe we could get away in time. Maybe.

But that was a chancy thing.

Though I couldn't hear it as Sally and I ran down the hallway and found the door that led to a small and dimly lit stairwell, I could feel the alarm that was already screaming through the building, an alarm that would have raised my hackles if I'd known what they were, and that sent a note of distress through the both of us. They knew —the Mager types and the Kriths—that Sally and I were trying to escape and they didn't plan on letting us do that.

We didn't take breath to talk, though we did clasp hands, and together leaped every other step on our way up. And now, when a spasm of weakness and vertigo went through me, the aftermath of augmentation, it was Sally's strength that carried us on.

How far? I wondered. Our shadowy friend—even now

that I had some inkling of what *he* was, I still thought of him much as I had before—the Shadowy Man hadn't told us how far it was to the roof.

From below, from far away, but soon growing nearer, were the sounds of our pursuit.

Half a dozen more flights of stairs, I thought, my breath coming raggedly and burning in my throat, and they'll catch us.

We went on. Step after step after step.

Hoarse voices called in an alien tongue. Other voices answered. Doors slammed. Feet sounded on the steps below. Dim lights flickered far below us. Then a gun fired. The bullet lodged in a wall or a step somewhere behind, below.

How much farther?

The alarm siren throbbed through me. A psychological thing? I wondered. Something to throw fear into the quarry?

Guns fired again. Nearer. But the maze of alternating staircases was too complex for a simple-minded bullet to find its way through unless aimed more expertly than those had been.

Is there anyone waiting for us above? I asked myself, a lance jabbing into my side every time I lifted my right leg, several times a second. Maybe not . . . Was that too much to hope for?

"Eric!" Sally gasped, loosed my hand, pointed ahead.

Above a dim red light blinked on and off, after one more turn, one more flight of stairs. The exit?

As we darted across the small landing and mounted still another flight of steps, I suddenly became aware of something else. For a moment I didn't know what it was, this loss, this absence. Something had been there, in my mind, only moments before and now it was gone. A tooth that I'd taken for granted had suddenly been removed and my tongue sought for it, found an empty socket— that's what it was like.

"He's gone!" I cried, almost coming to a stop. "They've beaten him."

Sally grabbed my hand, pulled me on. "Hurry," she said. "We're almost there."

The Shadowy Man was gone. I knew that. In the room far below, in the bedroom Sally and I occupied, where we'd made love, and in the living room where I'd eaten and sat and talked with her before going into the bedroom, there was no longer that vague shape of smoke with a manlike form. It was as if I could see those rooms: bedroom walls, floor, ceiling scorched and smoldering, bed turned on one side, sheets torn and flickering with dying embers, a mirror in a thousand bright fragments across the tattered carpeting; in the living room much the same scene of ruined furniture and pieces of art that had decorated the brightly colored walls, smoke and flickering tongues of flame, fragments of wood and plastic and pottery, a vase of flowers turned brown by the brief passage of intense heat. And all of it empty of life save for a gloating *presence* that had won, that had cast the Shadowy Man out of its world, that had broken him and the power that had propelled him across time and space to that strange battlefield.

We were alone again, Sally and I. . . .

She dragged me up the last few steps, to the door above which the red light flashed on and off, on and off. She dropped her weapon and with both hands jerked open the manual door and revealed to us a flat, moonlit pavement, dark like tarmac and as empty and desolate as the surface of the Moon.

My heart sank again. I'd expected a skudder waiting for us there, a skudder or *something,* but what I saw now was nothing, the empty pavement. Had the passing of the Shadowy Man left us without our means of escape? God . . .

Guns fired behind us. Close. Too damned close.

I broke out of the trance I was in, turned, fired back down the stairs toward our pursuers. Then we turned and ran on across the pavement toward—what?

There was a spot ahead of us, in about the middle of the paved rooftop, where the moonlight did not dimly illuminate the dark, flat surface. It was as if there were a spot there that drank the moonlight, greedily swallowed it, and left an area in space darker than the rest of the night.

"There's *something* there, Eric," Sally said between gasps for air.

"I hope so."

I let her run on ahead of me so that I could cover her lovely rear, then stopped for a moment and fired into the doorway we'd just left.

We must have been halfway to the inky blackness when it hit me.

It had all the strength of a physical blow, a poleax to the head couldn't have dropped me any quicker. Waves of pain shot from some point deep in my brain. My vision faded and most of my other senses failed me. My body went limp and I hardly felt it when the pavement came up and slapped me in the face, a sharp blow that opened my cheek to the bone.

"Eric!" I heard Sally's voice cry from a long way off, and then felt her hands touching a body that seemed only halfway mine. "Eric, what is it?"

Someone else, a wrecking crew, was inside my head, slashing out with sharp, heavy instruments, tearing through the fragile stuff of my consciousness, ripping to shreds my sanity. There was a force in my mind that wasn't a part of me, an angry, alien force that now desired only to see me dead. No words, no thoughts, no visual images came to me, no attempt at communication, only the awareness that something that now hated me was trying to destroy my mind and was doing it in the quickest, most brutal way it knew how.

"Eric, get up," Sally's remote voice yelled at me, angry now. "They'll catch us."

And then I thought I heard the rattle of distant guns, and moments later, closer at hand, louder and more savage still, Sally's gun replied.

"Dammit! Get up!" she yelled, and in my nose I could smell the sharp fumes of cordite or whatever they used here for gunpowder.

Sally's hands went under my armpits and she was dragging me across the pavement, not gently; my buttocks, thighs, calves, heels scraped across the rough surface. A still rational part of my mind realized she couldn't drag me all the way there—wherever *there* was.

But only a part of my mind was rational, only a small part. The rest of it was being battered to pieces by pain, by fire, by mental blows for which there are no words in any language I know.

I forced my mouth open, took deep breaths, willed augmentation circuitry into operation. Maybe it would only make it worse, but . . .

The pain seemed to become only more intense as the world wound down to one fifth its normal speed, as sounds dopplered toward the lower registers, and the moon and stars in the sky above took on a more reddish hue.

The blows came less frequently, came with a slower impact that I could more nearly deal with, could mentally duck away from, could hide from back in the deep recesses of the bony cavern of my skull. Maybe I could get far enough away from them, something in my mind said, maybe I could creep back down deep enough that they couldn't get to me. There was some remote recess in the more primitive parts of my brain stem that the Tromas couldn't reach. Maybe there I'd be safe.

Maybe that's exactly what they wanted me to do: give up the fight and hide away in some catatonic refuge.

Sally released me, let my head and shoulders fall to the pavement. I forced my eyes open and looked up to see her drawing her semirifle up again, level it and fire. I thought I could see the slugs as they erupted in flame from the weapon's barrel.

Now there were pauses between the psionic blows hammered at me by the Tromas and during the next pause I summoned together all the strength left in my body, drew it into my arms and legs, rolled over onto my stomach and forced myself to my hands and knees. Then I was standing erect, staggering forward in a half run.

Sally must have had some understanding of what was happening to me, had sense enough to take up the defense of our escape, and did her best to cover me as I stumbled toward the remote spot of total lightlessness that was our destination, fire her gun until its magazine was empty, and then grab up the one I'd dropped and fire again.

A few feet forward I'd staggered when the next blow came. I put my legs on automatic pilot and withdrew into what sanctuary there was for me, feeling the psionic blows smashing outward from some central point in my brain that the Krithian females had selected as their attack point. For a few moments there was painful darkness, filled with flickering reds and yellows and oranges like some great, world-consuming fire. Then I think I blacked out.

When consciousness came to me again I was on the pavement once more, another gash in my face, more blood on my shoulders and chest. Sally was beside me, speaking words I couldn't understand in their bassness, but felt she was telling me to get up again and go on, we weren't as far as we had been. I did like I thought she was telling me.

How many times I rose and stumbled forward and then fell when the war-ax blows split my skull open, only to rise again during the interval before the next blow, I could never say. Far too many times.

But I did keep getting up again, and I did keep stumbling forward a few feet, a few yards. And Sally kept firing, holding back the ones who'd come up the stairwell to capture us, to kill us.

I don't suppose there was time for them to get air support in. If there had been they'd have wiped us out with no great bother. One missile. One fire bomb. One strafing run. That's all it would have taken. I guess we were lucky.

Or did luck have any part in it at all?

Fire licked at what remained of my consciousness, my sanity. My body was a mass of bruises and cuts. Sally's gun, the one that had been mine, must have been nearly empty.

"We're almost there, Eric," Sally was crying—or at least I thought that's what she was crying—and through eyes that would only halfway focus, I could see before me a spheroid of total blackness, seeming to hang a few inches from the pavement like some ancient star collapsed down to a black hole whose gravitation was so great that not even light could escape.

Whatever it was and I couldn't even guess then—it was our escape route, and this was no time to question it. The Shadowy Man *must* have known what he was doing.

I grabbed Sally by the arm and threw the both of us into . . .

20
Vestiges of Time

I came out of unconsciousness, and out of augmentation, lying flat on my back on dry, dusty soil under a bright yellow-white sun that had the look of midmorning about it. The sky that contained the sun was a rich, pale, clean-washed blue with a few wisps of cloud near the horizon. The air was warm and dry, stirred by a breeze I probably would have found pleasant under other circumstances.

After a few moments of deep breathing I forced myself up on my elbows so that I could look around. A few feet from me, covered with dust and sweat, showing a few bruises and minor cuts, standing naked beside something that looked strangely like an overgrown mushroom, semirifle still in her hands, was Sally. Her back was to me, but she must have heard my movements, for she turned to face me, yet with a wariness that made my eyes search farther to where I saw the three dead Mager types a few yards beyond her, their uniforms ripped and bloody where the slugs from Sally's gun had torn into them.

Her smile was weak and sad. "I guess we made it," she said in a trembling voice.

"Yeah, I guess we did," I said.

Then she dropped her weapon, fell to her knees beside me, wrapped her arms around me, and said between sobs, "God, Eric, is it over now?"

Later when a little strength had come back to me and my hands had stopped their palsied shaking, when Sally had found water in a stream that flowed through a grove of willowlike trees not far from where she found the skudder that waited for us, when I felt not only that I would live, but that I wanted to live as well, she told me what had happened.

"When we leaped into that 'black hole,' " she said, sitting beside me in the shade of the giant mushroom, "some sort of, well, 'force' took hold of us, something that seemed to sort of turn us inside out and that carried us across space and time and—I guess—paratime. I guess this is another *Line,* isn't it?

"It was as if we were 'flickering' in a skudder, and yet not exactly that. I felt I could see, or sense in some fashion that wasn't quite seeing, each world click by, one after the other.

"I had a sensation of 'timelessness,' I guess I'd say, as if the universe had stopped in its tracks and then, maybe, began moving in the opposite temporal direction. It's hard to explain. It's something you're just as well without, Eric. I wouldn't have minded being unconscious then.

"Anyway, and I can't say how long—I have no idea of elapsed time, or even whether time can be measured in that context—I felt that we were falling. Then there was suddenly bright sunlight and we both plunged a few feet more until we hit the ground here.

"The first thing I did was check your pulse and after I found it and it seemed normal, I went to see if I could find the gun I'd had when we entered the 'hole.' I was afraid I might need it."

"And you found it," I said.

She nodded, said, "And I needed it. It couldn't have been more than a minute or two after we got here that *those three,* looking like they'd already been through a battle, fell out of the air. I mean that literally! Right out of the air! Well, I—I shot them. I didn't have any choice."

"I know."

"So then I just waited."

"And . . . ?"

"Nothing," she said, shrugged. "I just waited for you to wake up. There wasn't much else I could do."

No more Mager types came.

None ever came.

Sally told me that she'd seen the skudder even before I'd awakened, but she didn't want to leave me. So she waited until I woke up, until she'd gotten me water in her cupped hands.

"You feel like walking now?" she asked.

"I guess." I hurt inside and out, but figured I could walk as far as that skudder. I wanted to see it. "Help me up."

She did, and with a painful limp, I walked with her across the dry soil, through clustering clumps of grass, past "groves" of ten-foot-tall mushrooms toward the small stream and the skudder that lay beyond it. Among the bending branches of the willowlike trees, birds—or something very like birds—sang. From farther away, nibbling at grasses that grew within a great circle formed by gigantic red puffballs, the wary eyes of a four-hoofed, single-horned animal followed us. It could have been a unicorn had it not been so much overweight.

As we waded in the cool water of the stream I saw that the skudder was a beautiful one, of a design I'd never seen before, looking to be just off the assembly line, bright and untarnished, and ready to move as far across the Lines of Time as anyone might wish to go. I wondered whether it was armed.

Sally looked at the machine as we came out of the water, apprehension written on her face, then turned to me and said, "What do you think?"

"Another present from the Shadowy Man," I said, a sensation of sadness coming to me. Was he dead? Or . . .

"You're sure?"

"What else could it be?"

With slow, aching movements, I opened the skudder's hatch and looked inside. It was as beautiful inside as out, brightly decorated and luxuriously appointed. And there was a note taped to the main control panel, written in a handwriting that was painfully, shockingly familiar.

"That's your handwriting, Eric," Sally said, confirming what I already knew.

"But I never wrote it. I guess I will, one day."

I climbed inside and got the note, climbed back out as quickly as I could I wasn't ready yet for *that* skudder. It was haunted. By my own ghost?

I held the note so that we could both read it.

"Dear Eric and Sally," it began.

"If you read this note you will have escaped from the Tromas and have found the refuge I selected for you. You're safe here as long as you wish to stay.

"I know you're curious about your means of transportation from KHL-ooo to here and I would explain it to you if I could, but none of us has the proper mathematical background to really understand it. I could tell you it's a 'parachronal convolution,' but what would that explain? Labeling something doesn't necessarily define it.

"This skudder, from some decades into the future, as you two have been reckoning time, is yours. It's fully provisioned and ready to take you wherever you might wish to go, spatially or paratemporally. You may use it when you will.

"Some miles to the west of here you will find a village. It is an outpost of a kingdom barely out of the Bronze Age, though its inhabitants are friendly and pleasant people. You will find yourselves welcome there, though don't be too surprised if you're treated as something a bit more special than a pair of naked wanderers. They're expecting a couple of exiled godlings. Try to act the part.

"In time you're a few weeks 'downtime' from our conflict with the Tromas. In the past as you see it.

"In space you're still in North America, the Florida peninsula.

"In paratime, well, you're one hell of a long way to the T-East, far beyond the Lines the Kriths call KHL-ooo. It's as safe a place as any you could hope for, but try not to be disturbed by the oddness of some of the things you find here. There are some aspects of the evolutionary process that have worked out differently here."

When I read this line I looked up and saw the clusters of gigantic mushroom-things growing not far away and the brown, one-horned beast that grazed among them. Yes, the course that evolution had taken on this world so far distant across the Lines of Time was somehow slightly different from that on the Lines to the T-West of us, the Lines of Man. Were the *people* here the same as *us?* I wondered.

"The Kriths and their Companions can't find you here, except by hunting down that transmitter that's still buried deep in your flesh, Eric. But you *can* do something about that, if you must. You can find a Line not too far away where a good surgeon can go in and get it out and do away with it. That's really no problem.

"As for advice, I can give you none, as much as I would like to.

"The future is yours to do with as you wish.

"I think.

"Yours, Eric Mathers."

I read the note over again and then handed it to Sally. She carefully folded it up and put it inside the skudder's open hatch. I closed the hatch and then we bathed in the stream.

"Feel like taking a walk?" I asked Sally after we'd bathed and rested and eaten a meal from provisions we'd found near the haunted skudder.

"If you do."

"Which way's west?"

The world out there is pleasant enough. It's a world a long way from any I've known before, but somehow familiar. It's kind of like ancient Greece was supposed to have been, the Classical world. A world of small city-states, island kingdoms here and there, a few larger kingdoms, and maybe an empire or two on the continental mainlands. Maybe someone had discovered how to work iron, but nobody locally knows yet.

Oh, there are bad things about this world. Ignorance and cruelty, slavery and superstition. They're all here in more than ample measure—Sally and I *are* given a reverence beyond that deserved by mere mortals. But the bad things weren't as pronounced as on some Lines I've seen.

Sally and I are learning the language and I don't think it will take us long to establish ourselves rather comfortably, as if we weren't comfortable now, by local standards.

And the people—well, as far as I can tell they're humans exactly like us. If there are differences, I haven't found them yet, though Sally had put a limit to my, well, "anatomical studies."

Our skudder is still hidden away, sheltered in a remote spot where no one's likely to find it. It's safe until we want it. And I'm sure we will.

I've got Sally now and a lot of the answers I wanted, but . . .

There's still a lot left unanswered.

And a lot left undone.

I don't exactly see myself in the role that's been cast for me, but on the other hand I'm not certain that I can avoid the role even if I try.

I wouldn't be alive today, nor would Sally, if the Shadowy Man hadn't come *back through time* to help us, whatever his is/was/will be; however it is, I'm part of him and he a part of me.

So, there are things I have to do, things I don't suppose I can avoid doing.

Soon I'll have to leave here. I want Sally to stay until I can come back for her. I don't know whether she will, but I don't want her risking her life again.

Maybe one of these dark nights, when I'm certain that her place has been firmly established in this world and she won't suffer any want if I leave, I just may creep away and go to the skudder and quietly slip away across the Lines in search of the Shadowy Man. . . .

Anybody know where I can pick up a good time machine cheap?